Ac

Thank you to **Robyn**, for reading and being such an amazing friend, road buddy, roommate and partner in crime.

Thank you **Jim**, my friend and colleague for over twenty years. Your talent never ceases to amaze me.

Thank you **Molly** and **Mary,** my editors and grammar ninjas.

Thank you to my **KIW** writing crew in Kentucky. I feel beyond blessed to be a part of such a talented and special group.

Finally, thank you to my amazing family, **Rob**, **Luke** and **Haley.** We may not have it all together, but together we have it all.

SEX, LIES & LIPSTICK

A Moonlight and Magnolias Novel
Book 2

Kris Calvert

For my grandmother, Deb Calvert

Forget the lady called luck. She does not abide. I see her face framed in brown curls, the sun shining through her auburn light. What color I wonder and how straight it will turn when plastered back in her sweat and blood? Her lips, wet and bursting like a pulse of red from her throat. My pretty captive butterfly. My hand smears her wings filled with color until there's nothing left but crushed dreams. When time to time shall set us free. No forgetting me. Remember me.

1

MAC

I waited for her at the end of the petal-strewn aisle inside the flower-covered gazebo. The minister at my side, I gave a nod to my best man, Dan. I wasn't nervous. I was excited.

I felt my shoulders rise and fall as I took a deep breath. I closed my eyes and wished my father were alive to witness the day. I could hear the string quartet over my shoulder and I knew what was coming next.

I looked to my feet, twisted the Callahan crest ring on my right hand and told myself to hold it together. I wasn't a man who cried. I was an FBI agent for God's sake. But after witnessing the birth of my daughter three months ago and signing Dax's adoption papers just yesterday, I found the emotional lump in my throat reassuring. I'd led a disconnected life in the past and I was beyond thankful to now have moments that moved me beyond words or sentiment.

Bach's *Air* played and suddenly, there she was – my beautiful, blue-eyed wife to be, Samantha Peterson.

She whisked herself into place at the end of the path, the long white gown swooshing in the wake of her fluid movement. Her best friend and maid of honor Polly arranged the veil behind her as I bit my lip to keep it from quivering. I took her in fully and found it hard to breathe as I lay my hand on my chest – my heart pounding.

Polly walked the path first, giving me a sly wink. Tall, blonde and beautiful in the soft purple dress Sam had picked for her, I knew my FBI buddies would be asking about her later.

The music began to crescendo and everyone stood without a cue in Sam's presence as I blinked back the initial flood of emotion.

Sam's mother stood with the rest of the crowd and helped her ninety-nine year old grandmother Mimi to her feet. Mimi gave me a wink as our eyes met and I immediately felt more at ease.

Momma sat with my *other* mother, Miss Celia. Celia and her father Timms, Momma's long time driver, served as *my* family and support today. My mother had been on a downhill journey with her Alzheimer's as of late but was still here and was present in the moment as evidenced by her tears as she watched Sam make her way to me.

I swallowed hard as she approached me. Samantha Peterson was the most radiant woman I'd ever seen. The flowing white dress was simple, elegant and one of a kind. Just like her. In her hands she carried a bouquet of white roses and purple lilacs – her favorite flower.

I burst with pride as I watched her nod, graciously smiling and acknowledging the group of family and friends who'd gathered to witness our first moments as husband and wife. This amazing woman would soon be mine – until death do us part.

"She's amazing, Mac," whispered Dan as he watched her approach us. He'd been my friend and colleague through thick and thin. Never was there a finer FBI agent. He was my boss in Washington D.C., but today he was my best man.

The occasion seemed to overcome Sam's father. Although they weren't close, I knew he loved Sam and it showed on his face. He was proud of his daughter as he walked her slowly to meet me.

Looking to her, I leaned down to Dax without taking my eyes from hers. "Mommy is beautiful, Dax."

He smiled as he saw her come close and gave her a quick wave causing the crowd to react with an *aw*.

Dr. Peterson gave me a firm handshake as I met him and Samantha at the bottom of the stairs. I blindly took her hand and wrapped it around my arm, never breaking our gaze. Together we took the last three steps up and into the gazebo. They were my last as a single man.

I watched her with intent as her eyes sparkled with tears and I felt my own well up as I swallowed the lump in my throat. Her beauty overcame me. It was an amazing moment and I wanted to remember it forever. I gave her a reassuring nod and smiled.

A beautiful March afternoon, there was a light wind that sent the fragrance of the lilacs and roses entwined through the gazebo wafting with each gentle breeze. The sun was beginning to set and God had painted a beautiful backdrop of orange and purple in the sky. Everything was perfect on the grounds of my two hundred year old home, Lone Oak.

I watched as Sam gave Polly a wink when she adjusted the understated veil to pool at the bottom of the stairs. Samantha was as cool as a cucumber. I was a bundle of nerves.

"You may be seated," the minister instructed.

I couldn't take my eyes off of my beautiful bride. Her

5

long chestnut hair had been pinned up and away and the small ringlets that framed her face brushed her shoulder at every move.

I held Sam's hands in mine and the world became a small, quiet place where only we existed. I heard only the shallow breaths she took every few moments and the beat of my own heart.

It wasn't until the minister begged for my attention as he asked us to recite our vows that I realized how entranced I'd become.

I'd practiced long and hard to memorize them. Still, a copy was in my jacket pocket just in case. Sam on the other hand, didn't stumble once last night during rehearsal.

"McKay Waverly Callahan," Sam began as she pulled me close to her and smiled. "I promise to be your lover, your confidant, your companion and best friend. Your partner in parenthood, your ally in conflict, your biggest fan and your toughest adversary. I promise to be your student and your teacher. I will be your comfort in disappointment, your collaborator in mischief and I promise not to keep score, even if I'm totally winning."

The crowd chuckled, as everyone around us knew Samantha well enough to understand she was a true Southern girl – beautiful on the outside, and a Sherman tank underneath.

"I promise to put your happiness before mine and to always be worthy of your love. I thank God every day for allowing me to stumble into your life and fall into your arms. God has shown me that I *can* live happily ever after."

She paused and took a deep breath as her voice began to crack with emotion. "I promise to be your one and only until my dying day. Mac, this is my sacred vow to you. My equal in all things."

Her words washed over me like warm sunshine. I wanted desperately to kiss her when she finished, but knew from last night that I'd have to wait. Instead I lifted her delicate hands to my face and brushed my lips over the four-carat diamond ring she wore that proclaimed to the world that she was mine.

The minister nodded to me. I took a deep breath and began.

"Samantha Anne Peterson, I promise to be your lover, your confidant, your best friend and everything you need me to be. I will love you with all my heart and worship you with my body."

I smiled at her as I paused to allow the crowd to chuckle.

"I promise to be your partner in parenthood, your fiercest ally, and your *not* so tough adversary. I will be your co-conspirator in all our adventures. I will teach you everything I know and will always be your willing student. I will be your shoulder to cry on, your collaborator in mischief, and your one and only until my dying day."

Sam didn't know it, but I had more to say. I'd held back during rehearsal, saving part of my parent's vows to each other for today.

"On this day, my hand is yours to hold. My heart is yours to keep for all time. To tell you I will love you forever would never be enough. But with everything I am, I love you and I am yours, now and forever. This is my sacred vow to you, Samantha. My equal in all things."

I swallowed hard as Sam's baby blues glistened with tears. She gave my hand a squeeze and turned her face into me as I brushed a single drop from her cheek.

Taking a deep breath as I tried to compose myself, I turned to Dax and untied the two wedding bands with shaking hands. Dax smiled at me as if to say, *calm down*. He'd been amazingly patient during the ceremony.

The minister said a quick prayer over the rings as they lay in the Bible cradled in his hands and immediately looked to us to continue.

"Samantha." I paused to smile at her as I began to slip the diamond wedding band on her finger. I wanted to remember this moment for the rest of my life. "My darling Samantha. With this ring, I give you my heart. I promise from this day forward you will never be alone. My heart will be your shelter and my arms your home."

She gripped my hand tightly and I knew she was anxious to put her ring on my hand.

"Mac, with this ring, I give you my heart and promise from this day forward that you will never be alone. My heart will be your shelter and my arms will be your home."

I shook my head in disbelief. It was done. In one agonizingly long year, I'd finally made my dreams come true.

"By the powers vested in me by the state of Alabama, I now pronounce you to be husband and wife. Mac, you may kiss your bride."

I took her in my arms and cradled her bare back in my hand. I brushed a tiny curl from her cheek and looked into her eyes. "You are my everything," I whispered.

Before she could even begin to smile, I pressed my mouth to her beautiful red lips and kissed her deeply. She was mine and I longed to possess every part of her, every inch of her being. I pulled her hips to meet mine and squeezed her body against me. We were one. We were husband and wife and something inside me longed like never before to be as close to her as I could be. The crowd began to cheer at my over-exuberant display of love. It was done. Samantha was my wife.

She pulled away and gave me a wicked smile. I laughed and couldn't contain the excitement and happiness that poured out of me.

"Ladies and gentlemen," announced the minister. "May I present to you Mr. and Mrs. McKay Waverly Callahan III."

2

MAC

The reception was abuzz with friends and family sipping on sweet tea and mint juleps. It was simply the best day ever. I couldn't seem to let Samantha's hand go to save my life. Family had come out of the woodwork. I didn't know if it was the distant Callahan side that was so happy to see me wed or Sam's family, but we seemed to be receiving a lot of *I'm so happy for you* and *we never thought it would happen* comments from both sides.

"Samantha Ann," I heard over Sam's shoulder as we met our guests on the back lawn.

"Mac, I should introduce you to my cousin," she smiled as she gave my hand a squeeze.

"Richard," she sang sweetly as the portly man approached. His skin looked like skillfully tanned Italian leather, and I thought back to all the times in the past year Samantha slathered me in sunscreen.

"This is my husband, Mac Callahan. Mac, this is my cousin – my *only* cousin, Richard Peterson."

"Nice to meet you," I replied, giving him a firm handshake.

"The pleasure is mine, I assure you." Richard smiled through his thick Southern drawl and cigar-stained teeth. He was the kind of man who gave Southern boys a bad name. He was portly, wealthy, and full of himself. More than likely he was just full of shit.

"Samantha, it was a beautiful ceremony. The grounds here are just lovely," Richard drawled as he looked around and past us. "It would make a fantastic development."

"I forgot to mention," Sam interjected. "Richard is an attorney, but is really more of a real estate man."

"I see," I replied. "Well, thank you for the compliment, but Lone Oak has been in my family for years."

"How old is the plantation?" Richard asked as he looked around, eyeing the grounds like a dog on the hunt. "Shadeland, Alabama has had its share of breathtaking properties, but none as spectacular as this."

"Two hundred years."

"Yes, yes," he drawled. "I did notice the oak tree out front, but the back is just beautiful. With the pool, tennis courts and stables on the grounds already, you could easily develop some luxury condos and use the main house as a clubhouse or hotel. Have you always lived in Shadeland, Mac?"

I remarked at his ability to ask a multitude of questions on different subjects without taking a breath. "Much like Sam's home, Lone Oak is just as much a family treasure as it is a tradition. I can't imagine it will ever be sold off. And no, I was away at school for a good portion of my early years."

"Harvard man?"

"Cornell. Harvard Law. Then the FBI Academy."

"I'm a Harvard man myself," Richard smiled, the cigar smoke escaping between his teeth.

I nodded and he continued, although I found myself

looking past him and wanting the conversation to be over.

"Not all of the Peterson grandchildren have been as fortunate as Sam," he continued. "Sam got the house, which is a little bit of a shame considering she's not even going to live in it anymore."

"I know," Sam apologized as she adjusted the halter dress that showed off her lean and muscular back.

I'd been mentally undressing her since the ceremony ended. I stroked her bare back as she spoke and gazed at the small covered buttons above her perfect bottom. The silk Christian Dior gown was the only thing separating me from my wife and the suspense was killing me.

"It's just I've not discussed with Mimi yet what we should do," Sam continued.

"I'd be happy to take it off your hands, Samantha. I mean, if you ever need another family member to love it the way you have," he replied sincerely.

"Humph."

I turned to see Mimi standing behind me shaking her head as she held tightly to her walker. I had a special place in my heart for Sam's grandmother, Marilyn. Mimi, as she was known to most, was a good friend to my momma as well as a fellow resident at Autumn Valley. Never one to filter her comments, Mimi had a way of turning a phrase that was beyond compare. She was nearly one hundred years old and still sharp as a tack.

"What did you think of the ceremony, Mimi?" I asked, giving her a kiss on the hand.

"Honey, you know I loved every minute of it. Samantha?" she asked, turning her attention. "I didn't realize you'd invited so *many* of our family members to share in your day."

"Aw, Mimi," hacked Richard through his smoker's cough. "You know I love my family. I wouldn't have missed this for anything. With Momma and Daddy gone now, someone from my side needed to share in Samantha's joy."

"I know what you want a share of," Mimi hissed.

"Mimi," I began, hoping to change the subject. "Will you do me the pleasure of having your photograph taken with me?"

"Yes, of course, Mac," she sang sweetly.

Taking her by the arm and giving Sam a wink I turned Mimi toward the photographer. "You know I'll want one with all my favorite girls. You, Sam, Momma and Katy."

"Alright then." Mimi squinted her eyes and gave Richard a suspicious nod.

"Richard, if you'll excuse us, please."

"Of course," he grinned.

I gave Richard an understanding smile and took Sam and Mimi on each arm to guide them to the gazebo.

"You wanna tell me what that was all about, Mimi?" Sam protested, keeping her smile.

"I don't like him. I've *never* liked him. He's just like his mother. A two-faced, conniving little gold-digger."

"Richard's a gold-digger?" I asked, trying to conceal my grin at Mimi's remarks. "His teeth were fairly gold. I don't know about the rest of him."

"Hell yes he's a gold-digger. The worst kind."

"Can we keep the profanity to a minimum, please?" Sam asked.

"What's the worst kind?" I laughed.

"The kind that *has* money. He's greedy. *And* he's a dick. Why do you think his parents named him Richard? That's no coincidence."

"Mimi," Sam objected.

"Go on then, shake his hand," she chuckled with sarcasm. "But you'd better count your fingers when you're done."

"You girls never cease to amaze me. And I love you both."

"I love you too, honey," Mimi grinned as I gave her a kiss on the cheek and sat her down beside Momma and Miss Celia. "You might just be the most handsome man I've ever seen."

"Don't make me blush, Mimi," I teased.

"Sam, you picked a good one. Those green eyes and sandy hair," Mimi drawled. "Mmm, mmm, mmm. There's nothing like a handsome Southern gentleman. Mac honey, I know you are a tough man's man. But you're *all* man to a Southern woman."

"Well, I love all my Peterson girls," I said, feeling the heat in my usually unflinching face. "My amazing Peterson girls."

"Peterson girls are *amazing* at a lot of things Mac. And don't you forget it. We can shoot it, skin it and cook it without getting a hair out of place."

"Mimi, please," Sam pleaded.

I glanced at the women all sitting together, waiting for the picture taking to be over. Mimi, Mom, and Miss Celia, who was keeping an eye on Katy. I rubbed my hands through my hair and took a deep breath. It was over. And yet it was just beginning. I smiled at all of them. There they were, the most important women in my life together in one place.

"Mind you now, Mac was pretty when he was born, but I have to say little Miss Katy is prettier still," Celia gushed to Sam as they fussed over the baby.

"That's because all the good parts of Katy came from her mother," I offered as I took Sam back into my arms and kissed her again. "Will you ladies excuse us? I'd like a private moment with my wife."

They nodded, and I smiled at Momma. I knew she was here in spirit, even if I no longer saw a light in her eyes.

Sam and I took a few steps away from the ever-growing crowd. "You," I whispered as I pulled her cheek to cheek and nibbled on her ear, "are the most beautiful thing I've ever seen. I've never been happier or more proud than I am right now. And I can't wait to take you away and have you all to myself in Paris, Mrs. Callahan."

"Baby?" Miss Celia called.

Rarely referring to me as Mac, Miss Celia had called me Baby for as long as I could remember. It was either baby or McKay if I happened to be in trouble. Even at my age, she had no problem telling me when she'd had enough of my behavior.

"Baby, your momma's not feeling well so I'm gonna take her to a guest room to rest a spell."

"I'll take her up, Miss Celia," I nodded.

"Well…" Celia paused as she smiled at Samantha. "I can do it. You need to take photos."

"I want to," I protested. "The photographer can wait."

"Okay. We'll go together," Celia agreed. "Miss Mimi, it was so nice to see you again."

"You too, Celia," Mimi replied as she settled in her chair, closing her walker. "And thank you for taking such good care of my great-grandbabies."

I gave Sam a quick peck on the lips. "Don't go anywhere, Mrs. Callahan. I'll be right back."

"Okay, sweetie. But hurry. We need to finish taking photos at the gazebo and I'm sure the caterer would like to get dinner served."

"I won't be long."

I helped Momma to her feet and put her delicate hand

around my arm. Miss Celia took my free hand and gave it a loving squeeze. She knew how it pained me to see my mother this way.

"What happened?" I asked Celia as we distanced ourselves from the crowd.

"Miss Nancy got a little upset after the ceremony. I think maybe being here brings up memories of your daddy. She motioned to the house and began to weep a little. I think it's just all the excitement."

"I knew it might upset her routine to take her out of Autumn Valley for the day, but I didn't want her to miss the wedding."

"You did the right thing, baby. The Alzheimer's makes her more fragile than she used to be. That's all. We'll get her in a guest room and let her have a rest. She'll be fine."

We walked past the plain-clothed FBI agents who were watching the house during the wedding. With the unsettling notes still coming, I didn't want to take any chances on today of all days.

The extra security measures at Lone Oak were deemed a necessity now that we had children. I'd been an FBI agent for almost ten years and incarcerated plenty of scumbags, not to mention their questionable families who'd watched me put them in jail. I told Sam we couldn't take a chance. Now that we had not only one but two small children to think of, I would always be looking over my shoulder.

We entered the guest room on the first floor. The big window that overlooked the backside of Lone Oak would provide my mother with a great view of the reception even if she wasn't up to attending. I sat her on an oversized fainting couch and settled her in, bringing her feet off the floor.

"Momma?" I took her hands in mine, begging her to

look at me. "Momma, Miss Celia thinks maybe you should take a rest."

She nodded and then shook her head. She looked to me and then past me as if she wanted to be with me in the here and now but something was pulling her away. Her body had always been willing, but she disappeared a little more each day like melting ice on a summer day.

"Miss Nancy?"

She gazed out the window, oblivious to Celia's attempts to reach her. She talked less and less each day and her good days were few and far between. Still, she looked as lovely as ever in the dark purple dress Sam had picked for her. She was beautiful although her tiny frame seemed to be shrinking.

Around her neck she wore the pearls my father gave her, and I watched her stroke them with her open hand as she looked out the large window draped in white. It was a beautiful view of Lone Oak. I hoped she would be able to enjoy the party at least from afar.

"Miss Celia…" I began with a sigh.

"Don't worry, baby, I'll come in and check on her in just a bit. But the nurse from the Autumn Valley home is here too. I think she's gonna take a little catnap and then she'll be ready for the last part of the evening."

I nodded, not as convinced.

"If you let her rest now, you'll have a better chance of spending time with her tonight."

"You're right," I sighed. "I know you're right."

"This is your day. She wouldn't want to keep you from it."

"I know."

"Momma?" I asked, pulling her attention away from the window. "I'll be right outside if you need me, okay?"

She nodded, looking over my shoulder at the face of her nurse.

As I turned to leave I gave Celia a nod.

"Mac?" Momma uttered.

"Yes?" I turned, so happy to hear her speak.

"Help."

"Help with what, Mama?"

"I don't think she knows what she's saying," Celia smiled, trying to make the situation less uncomfortable than it already was.

Celia came to my side and took my shoulders in her hands. It was her usual way when she wanted to make sure I was listening.

"I don't want you to be all upset today over your momma. She loves you more than anything and there's no way she'd ever want to be a burden on your wedding day. Remember that. I'll sit with her a spell and then I'll leave the nurse to her duty."

"Okay, but I don't want you to miss anything either. You're my *other* mother."

"Baby, I'm not gonna miss one second of your big day. Now get."

"Yes, ma'am."

I stopped at the door and watched the two women who raised me holding hands. It was a bittersweet moment when I realized that the torch had officially been passed to my little family. We were the new generation of Callahans.

"Mr. Callahan," the photographer panted from the doorway. I was certain he'd been sent to find me. "Sir, are you ready to take some photos?"

"Yes. Wait. Come in and take a photo of my mother and me."

"Absolutely, sir."

I put my arm around Momma and pulled her close to me, kissing her on the cheek.

She turned to me and grinned. "What am I going to do with you?"

"Love me?"

"You know I do."

"Right here, folks," bellowed the photographer.

We faced the camera together and smiled for our photo.

"Get back to the party, baby. There're lots of folks waitin' to give you their best wishes. Not to mention your bride," Celia continued.

I gave Momma's hand a squeeze, thankful that we'd shared something special on my wedding day.

"Oh, hey," Dan remarked as he joined us. I could tell by the look on his face he worried he'd interrupted something.

"I'm doing my best man duties. We're waiting on you for pictures, Mac."

I gave him a grin. Dan Kelley looked better than I'd ever seem him. The Armani tuxedo that matched mine was a far cry from the usual bad brown suits and ugly ties he wore at the Bureau office.

"How you holding up?" he asked as we made our way back through the house.

"Great."

"I, ah…" he hesitated. "I overheard someone make a remark that you and Sam ate dinner before saying grace? What the hell does that even mean, dude?"

"We had the baby before we got married."

"And people care?" he asked.

"Look, I loved Samantha long before we knew she was pregnant. Hell, Dan. It was a one in a million chance I'd ever *be* a father. Katy is a miracle and I couldn't care less what anyone thinks."

"Yeah, I know," he sighed. I knew he felt guilty for saying anything. Dan of all people knew what family meant to me and having a family of my own was more than I ever thought possible.

"Fuck 'em all. Believe me, if a consummate bachelor like you can go from making it with every hot, available chick in D.C. to family man – well, there's hope for all of us."

"Thanks for taking me back *there* on my wedding day," I smirked.

"Yeah. Well, sorry."

I hurried back to Sam as she was taking photos with Mimi and Dax.

"Is everything okay?" Sam asked as she fluffed her veil, readying herself for yet another picture.

"She's just tired. The other photographer took our photo by the window in the guestroom."

Sam reached for me to join her in the gazebo. "Let's get these going so we can greet our guests and eat."

"And get on the plane to Paris, my love," I added as I climbed the stairs to her. "I've already told the crew we want absolute privacy," I whispered in her ear. "I'm not waiting seven hours to reach France before I consummate our marriage."

"Mac," she gasped.

"Surely you knew I had plans for you," I murmured as I kissed her sweet and beautiful lips. "We didn't take chances while you were pregnant. And *you* wanted to wait until after the wedding. So yes, my love. I have lots and lots of plans."

"I know it's been almost a year, Mac," she smiled wickedly. "But seven hours longer won't kill you."

"This way, Mr. and Mrs. Callahan," shouted the photographer.

"Get one of me kissing her," I shouted back. "It'll be

my favorite photo of the day."

"All the photos I've taken apart from the ceremony are of you kissing," he replied flatly.

"See Mac? Everyone knows you can't keep your hands off of me."

I laughed as I brought her in for another kiss. "I'm pretty sure everyone knows I couldn't keep my hands to myself as evidenced by Katy."

"Don't be a cad."

"I love you so much, I don't care who knows it or how much they know –"

"Or how much they hear or see?" Samantha finished with an edge to her voice.

"It's you and me forever. Understand?"

"I understand Mac. And I love you too. But I *do* care who sees or hears."

"Well, because you care," I smiled as I twisted her hips back and forth in my hands. "I will be more discreet."

Samantha gave me a forgiving smile and all was right in my world.

"Let's get this over with—we've got a party going on that we're not even attending."

"Alright, we're ready to take the formal shots. I promise not to kiss her anymore," I shouted to the photographer.

I looked back to Sam and whispered as she smiled for the camera, "For now."

3

POLY

"**D**r. King Giles, I presume."

I knew who he was. How could I not? The most handsome and eligible bachelor in the town of Shadeland, Alabama was Dr. King Giles. Problem was I was pretty sure he still had a thing for my best friend.

"Yes?" he looked up from his Kentucky bourbon and set his big blue eyes on me. "I'm sorry. Have we met?"

"I'm Polly. Polly Benson."

I held out my hand and was quickly startled when he opted to kiss it.

"I'm King. But I believe you already know that."

His voice was deep, and the low hum of each word he spoke reverberated in my body. With his tall, muscular body and the dark hair he chose to comb straight back, he was without a doubt suave in every sense of the word.

"I was privy to the seating chart," I confessed with a smile.

"So this is no accident?" He pulled the chair out for me and with a sweeping hand motioned for me to sit.

"If you're asking if I requested to sit next to you, the answer is no. But Sam and Mac must have their reasons. However dorky they might be."

"Lucky break for me," he quickly retorted. "I'm sitting next to the most beautiful girl at the wedding. Dare I even say more beautiful than the bride herself?"

The fluidity of his rugged voice and smooth phrases were hypnotic. I could easily see how a girl could get lost in every part of King Giles.

I snapped out of the dream and back to reality. "Look," I began firmly yet politely. "I'm not trying to be rude or anything, but I'm not going to fall for your whole Southern gentleman routine. I'm not from the South. I met Sam at Princeton, not charm school."

"Jersey girl?" he asked with a smile.

"No. Montana."

"Rancher's daughter?"

"Banker's daughter."

"Are you a financier as well?"

"I have a degree in psychology."

"You have a degree in psychology from Princeton?"

"You're quick."

I couldn't tell if he was impressed with my brain or my sarcasm, so I decided to keep the conversation going until I found out. "Sam told me you had a deep, sultry voice," I sighed as I leaned under the table to slip my shoes from my feet. Two could play this game.

"Did she?" he paused. "So what do you think?"

"I think you're handsome. You have nice blue eyes. And yes," I smiled, looking into my lap – suddenly embarrassed I'd been so honest.

"Yes?"

"Your voice is... sexy," I confessed. "And Sam was

right."

King moved his chair closer and leaned into me, refusing to lose eye contact. "Right about what, Miss Benson?"

"You're a nice piece of ...work."

He laughed deep and with honesty.

I was the kind of girl who said what she meant and meant what she said. I wasn't going to temper or censor myself for a man – even a Southern gentleman.

"Sam told me you were from here. Shadeland, I mean. Grew up with Mac?"

"Yes. Mac and I also went to school together – Cornell. We went our separate ways after graduation. He went to Harvard Law, I went to Johns Hopkins. How about you? How'd you meet the bride?"

"I couldn't get a job right out of Princeton. Neither could Sam. She finally took a position recruiting executives and I began to help her. We were a great team. I dug through the candidate's personal history and weird quirks and she handled the business end. Together we matched the best candidates with the right companies."

"Sounds interesting. That's why she had the position at Autumn Valley recruiting doctors?"

"Yes. Well, until Mac and the FBI raided the place and her boss put a bullet through his head trying to cover up the money he'd been giving to his hag of a secretary, hence screwing his gay affair with the Mexican janitor." I took a breath. "No pun intended."

King laughed and nodded. "I was there."

"Anyway, that's how Sam and I became a team. After Daniel died, Sam was a mess."

"How did her husband die?" he asked.

"A driver fell asleep at the wheel. His semi crossed the lane and hit Daniel head on. He never had a chance."

"Terrible," King sighed, shaking his head.

"I stayed with her. By that time she was pregnant and the doctors didn't know how well the baby would handle the stress."

"Yeah, that's tough."

"After Dax was born, I just…stayed. We were like a little family. Sam didn't want to be alone, and I certainly didn't want to be alone, or leave her for that matter."

"You're a good friend."

"I don't know about that. I only know I care about them. They're *my* family."

"What about your parents in Montana?" he asked, taking another sip of his bourbon.

"Dead."

"I'm sorry. But I understand. Really I do. My parents are gone as well."

"What happened to yours?" I asked. "Because it doesn't seem fair, you know? Sam barely even speaks to her parents and yet they're still here. Well, *here* is a relative term. I mean they spend all their time on every kid *but* their own. When Sam was growing up she hardly knew them. I talked with mine every day and then suddenly they're gone."

"I was practicing in Baltimore when my mother got sick," King began. "I came back to Shadeland to take care of her. By the time she passed, my dad was dying of cancer – I'd taken a year off to just spend time with him at our home near New Orleans. His family was from there and it's where he wanted to spend his last days."

"So we're both orphans?" I asked.

"We're a little old to be orphans, aren't we?" he replied with a grin, clearly trying to lift the mood of the dark conversation.

"And you live here now?" I asked.

"By here, you mean Shadeland and not Lone Oak."

"Yes, silly," I smirked as I flirt-punched him in the arm.

"I live in Shadeland. But my home is Rose Hill."

"You mean you have a place like this? Only it's called Rose Hill?"

"I live in my mother's family home and yes, it is similar. Less land than Lone Oak, but comparable."

"Interesting,"

"How so?"

"I was just saying to Mac earlier today…" I trailed off.

"Yes?"

"Nothing," I replied, remembering I'd told Mac I wished he had an available brother so I could live happily ever after like Samantha.

"Miss Benson?" he asked as he stood. "The band has begun to play. Would you care to dance?"

"I just took my shoes off."

"Do you need them?"

"Not if you're planning on sweeping me off my feet," I smirked.

"I'll surely do my best."

I stood and shook out my long lavender gown and gazed up at him as I brushed a blonde curl from my eyes. "Please call me Polly. That is, unless you're asking me to refer to you as Dr. Giles. In which case I'd rather not take you up on the dance."

He reached for me and brushed his lips lightly over the top of my hand. "Polly, I'd rather you *not* call me Dr. Giles and I'd be heartbroken if you decided not to take the dance floor with me."

"King," I said as he presented his arm to me. "You can save the bullshit, darlin'. I'm from Montana. I've been to the rodeo. I've seen the clowns."

"I assure you, Polly, I'm a lot of things, but a clown isn't one of them. Now, I think you're a smart, beautiful woman and I'd like to get to know you better."

"Hmmm…" I sighed. "I think I like you, King."

"The feeling is mutual, darlin'."

4

SAMANTHA

"Thank you, Mr. and Mrs. Callahan," chimed the photographer. "I'll be around taking candid shots until you cut the cake and then we'll stage some more."

"Thank *you*," I replied as I walked to Mimi who'd been holding a fussy Katy.

"This one's a fireball," Mimi smiled. "She's like her momma."

"I think she's probably more like her great-grandmother if she's a so-called ball of fire."

"Augusta Lily Kay Callahan. Why'd they have to torture you with such a long name?" Mimi smiled as she passed her to me.

"Mimi, we're calling her Katy."

"*Dax* named her Katy, so don't be telling tales."

"I know, but we wanted to use your mother's name and Mac's grandmother's name."

"And Kay for McKay?"

"Yes."

"I like it. I just think it's a enormous name for such a

little person."

"She's gonna need a big name as wonderful and accomplished as she's going to be. Aren't you, sweetness?" Mac baby-talked as he took Katy from my arms and kissed her, holding her tightly.

They'd been inseparable since she was born. Mac was adorable with Dax and Katy both. He was so excited to be a daddy and he spent every waking moment with them, reserving the evenings for just the two of us.

"Give that child to me," Miss Celia barked. "Now you two get into your own party. People are gonna start wonderin' what's happened to you."

Mac took my hand as we walked away. "I wish we'd spent all that time doing something else instead of taking all those photos. I could give him something to photograph, but I think it would be considered pornographic," Mac confessed.

"Mac," I scolded. "You're gonna have to keep your mind out of my panties for a few more hours. We have a reception, guests to greet, a cake to cut, a special dance…"

Mac stopped me in my tracks and pulled me to him. "Listen to me, sweetheart. This family – you, Dax, Katy – *you* all are the most important things in my life. My mind might be in your panties, but it's not in the gutter. I just want to celebrate our love. That's all."

I put my hands on his face and smiled. "Mac Callahan, you are the best person I've ever known. And I'm going to spend the rest of my life making you the happiest man alive."

"I'm already the happiest man alive, Sam."

I kissed him, pulling him deep into my mouth. I grabbed his bottom and pulled him closer, moving my hips into his body. Mac breathed in, moaning softly and I knew he was aching to have me. I paused only to take a nibble of his bottom lip before releasing him from my eager mouth.

"Sweet Jesus, Sam," he muttered. "You can't do that to me and expect me to walk."

I felt down the front of his pants and as promised, he was rock hard.

"What do you want me to do with *this*?" he asked as he stepped away from me and adjusted his crotch. "I'm pretty sure people will notice when we walk into the tent."

I giggled. "Please welcome Mrs. Callahan and Mr. Callahan's raging–."

"Not funny," he interrupted with a laugh of his own. "Seriously, Sam. Help me."

"I don't know what to tell you sweetheart. I don't know what to do with...that."

"Yes, you do," he whispered as he nuzzled into my neck for a kiss and pressed himself into my thigh.

"Forget it, Mac. Not now. No way."

"Fine," he huffed, clearly exasperated. "Let's just stand here a minute until it goes down."

"Okay. What should we talk about?"

"Anything. Just don't talk about it in your sexy kitten voice."

"I don't have a sexy kitten voice, baby," I whispered, trying my best to purr into his chest.

"Dammit it, Sam," he whined. "You're not helping."

"I'm sorry," I whispered as I began to unbutton his shirt.

"What are you doing?" he growled.

I put my hand through his shirt and onto his bare chest, giving him a sexy wink.

"Seriously. Not helping," he sighed, closing his eyes and dropping his head back.

Without hesitation or regret, I grabbed a small handful of chest hair and gave it a yank.

"Aw shit!" he yelled, pulling away from me and jumping into the air. "Jesus, Sam. That hurt like a son of a bitch."

"But is your erection gone?"

"Holy shit," he gasped, rubbing the front of his chest as if it would relive the pain I'd induced. "Yeah, it's gone."

"Then button up and let's get into the reception."

"You are a wicked, wicked woman, Samantha Callahan."

"I love the sound of that."

"Me too – even if you did just almost kill me. You're gonna pay for that later, darlin'. Mark my words."

"Promise?" I asked as I took Mac's arm and stroked his tight muscles under his tuxedo.

"Now don't start again. I won't fall for the hand in the shirt routine twice."

He truly was the most handsome man I'd ever seen. And he was all mine. I couldn't help but stare at him as we walked from the gardens onto the expansive back lawn of Lone Oak. Our guests were waiting and it was time to be introduced.

The large white silk tent expanded with the light spring breeze as if it was breathing in the fresh Alabama air. The sun had made its descent into the Southern horizon and as the weatherman promised, we had clear skies.

I could hear the band playing as I leaned into Mac's shoulder with my head, the long veil now off and lying safely in Mac's bedroom for safekeeping.

As we approached the tent, the wedding coordinator stopped us with her outstretched hand and silently asked us to wait.

"We're letting the band know you've arrived," she explained in an over exaggerated whisper.

I nodded as Mac leaned down to my ear. "Why is she yelling at us?" he joked.

I giggled, shrugging my shoulders.

As the band finished a song, I lifted Mac's left hand to my lips and kissed the shiny new wedding band on his finger.

"I didn't think you could get any hotter, babe. But you're even sexier in this ring," I purred.

"*That's* the sexy kitten voice," he growled as he lifted my chin to kiss me. "Unless you want my manhood to make a grand entrance before we do, you'd be wise to stop."

"Sorry."

"Don't be sorry. Just save it for later. I have plans for you, Sam. Plans," he murmured in a deep and graveled voice that turned me on in an instant. I felt the heat rise in my face and cover my entire body. Mac Callahan did things to me like no other.

He wasn't the only one who'd been waiting patiently to make love. I was just as ready to go as he was.

I fought back my urge to grab the front of his trousers and give him a quick stroke before we walked into the tent, but I knew I couldn't tease him anymore tonight. Even if the feel of his manhood was for my own enjoyment and not his.

"Ladies and gentlemen. It is with great pleasure that I present to you Mr. and Mrs. Mac Callahan."

"We're on, baby," Mac smiled.

We walked into the tent as a spotlight lit our faces and the band began to play a ballad version of Sam Cooke's *You Send Me*.

Mac picked our first dance as Sam Cooke had played in the car the night we first met.

Everyone came to their feet and applauded. I looked out

into the crowd and saw all the people I loved and cared about the most. The women were blowing us kisses and the men were slapping Mac on the back as we made our way to the dance floor.

A parquet masterpiece had been installed in the tent and the Callahan crest was projected onto the center of the floor from a spotlight high above.

The lights dimmed as Mac whisked me to the middle of the floor to dance, just as the bandleader began to sing. *Darling you send... I know you, send me... darling you send me...honest you do.*

"I'm the luckiest man on earth."

I smiled and gave him a quick kiss on the lips, much to the liking of Mac's FBI, college and law school friends. They began to clap and catcall as the rest of the crowd cheered again.

I looked over Mac's shoulder as we swayed to the music and saw Polly smiling through her teary eyes. I knew how happy she was for me. It was the beginning of a new life and an ending of an old one.

Behind her, King Giles lifted his glass to me in congratulations and I returned the favor with a small wave.

I saw Mimi, Miss Celia and my mother walk into the tent together sans Katy. The nurse we'd hired for the day from Autumn Valley was watching over her *and* Mac's mother.

As the song came to a close, Mac pulled me in tighter and whispered in my ear, "Thank you for loving me."

"Ditto."

Mac spun me out of our embrace and presented me to the crowd and we both took a little bow as the wedding coordinator whisked us to a table with champagne.

He popped the cork on a bottle of 1990 Cristal Brut

he'd flown in for our wedding. *Methuselah* as it was known in the world of champagne – it had a golden label and a twenty thousand dollar price tag. Mac wanted everything about today to be special.

We stood hand in hand as the crowd settled and Mac smiled, looking through me as he raised the crystal flute.

"Samantha and I just want to thank everyone for sharing in our wedding. You are all very special to us and we would never want this day to pass without telling you so. I just want to also say something about my beautiful bride, if I might."

I didn't know where he was going with this, but I couldn't handle even one more emotional moment today.

"If my father were here, he'd be the one giving this opening toast to welcome Samantha to the Callahan family and everyone else here today to Lone Oak."

I watched him, as well as many of our friends in the crowd drop their heads, remembering the great man who was Mac's father.

"He was a man of few words, but when he did speak it always meant something. About a year ago, I found a note he'd left for me letting me know that his job was to help me discover what it meant to be a real man. And I can honestly say that because of my love for this amazing woman and the way she loves me in return, I've finally made it. So please raise your glass and join me in toasting my beautiful bride. Samantha, I think my father...actually – I *know* my father would say thank you. Thank you for finishing what he started."

The tent fell silent as he captivated everyone with his tribute. Only the birds could be heard singing in the gardens as I took my hand from his to brush a tear from my cheek.

"So here's to warm words on a cold evening, a full

moon on the darkest nights and a smooth road," he sighed. "All the way to our door. To Samantha!" he announced with a smile.

"To Samantha!" the crowd replied and applauded yet again.

The wedding coordinator took the microphone from the bandleader and let everyone know to take their seats as dinner was about to be served.

Mac led me through the crowd as we stopped to hug and say hello to our guests. I thanked God we'd decided to have a small family and friends affair. Even with the hundred plus guests, it would be difficult to make it to each and every person to thank them. And leaving without doing so would be unacceptable and impolite.

As we shook hands and smiled, I felt a tug on my dress and looked down to find Dax holding tightly to Polly's hand.

"Mommy, it's time to eat."

"Yes, baby, I know. You are eating with Grandmother and Granddad. Polly is going to take you right over to their table. You may eat dessert with Mac and me."

"Mommy, is Mac my daddy now?"

Polly looked at me and shrugged with a grin. "I told him to discuss that with you."

"Why don't you ask him, Dax? Mac?"

"Yes," he replied as he turned to find Dax at his feet. "Hey, Chief. Are you ready to eat?"

"Are you my daddy? I mean, are you my daddy *now*?"

A smile spread across Mac's face and he dropped to one knee to look Dax in the eye and pulled him in for a tight hug. "You bet. I'm so proud to be your daddy."

"Okay," Dax chimed as Mac turned loose of him. He looked up to Polly. "I'll eat with Grandmother and

Granddad, but I'm eating cake with Mommy and Daddy."

"I'll let them know," Polly smiled and rolled her eyes as she pulled me aside. "I met the hunky King Giles."

"Really…" I droned. "And what did you think?"

"Is he for real? I mean, I know Mac is *all that* with the Southern charm and perfect manners, but really? I mean, *really*?"

I laughed, knowing the exact feeling she was getting. Having a true Southern man make over you as if you were the only woman in the world was a feeling that could never be duplicated. And when you did grow accustomed to it, it was hard not to hold every other man to that standard.

"I'm pretty sure he's for real, Polly. You should get to know him."

"I know – and that deep voice? I feel like Barry White or God is talking to me."

"So what are you waiting for?"

"What if *God* invites me into his bed? I don't think I could turn *God* down."

"Burn that bridge when you come to it, Polly."

"Right," she nodded. "See you in a bit. You're still gorgeous by the way. Happy and gorgeous."

"I love you, Polly," I said with a wink.

"I love you too."

Mac escorted me to our private table set for two. I gazed up at the ceiling of the tent as Mac held my chair and helped me to adjust my gown. Above, the night sky twinkled with stars that shone visible through the thin white silk. The space was aglow with candlelight and as I looked around, I couldn't believe my fairytale had come true.

"Everything okay, sweetheart?" Mac asked as he sat.

"Everything is perfect."

5

MAC

The camera flashed as I placed my hand over Sam's. We cut through the bottom layer of the wedding cake where instructed by our frisky wedding coordinator. The cake was almond on the bottom, and moist with a kick of bourbon. We quickly fed each other and I gave Sam a quick kiss and whispered in her ear, "Baby, it's almost time to get out of here and head to our plane. Let's eat cake and begin to say our goodbyes."

She nodded inconspicuously as I whispered, lightly grazing my ass as she pulled away from me. It sent me through the roof and I wanted to finish the required wedding rituals and move on to the honeymoon.

I gave her a knowing look and she winked back at me. If I didn't get out of here soon, I was ready to let the wedding party watch.

"I want a photo with the whole family," Sam shouted to the photographer who quickly followed orders, gathering up both sides.

"Yes, ma'am."

"Wait, where's Polly?"

As we all looked around the tent, no one could spot Polly in the small crowd. Sam, not one to be deterred, walked to the bandleader and asked for him to announce Polly's name.

"Polly Benson, your presence is requested in the tent. Miss Polly?"

"Maybe she's in the house," I explained to Sam, hoping we could take the photo and get to the honeymoon activities.

"There she is!" shouted Dax as he pointed to Polly coming in through the back of the tent with King.

"Well, son of a bitch," I mumbled. I arched my brow as Polly's eyes met mine and she knew she'd been caught.

"Bring King!" Sam shouted. "King, you need to be in the photo too."

I watched as King's face heated with embarrassment. I knew what he'd been up to, and by the guilty look on his face, he was very aware that his rendezvous with Polly behind the tent was no longer a secret.

Polly gave Sam an embarrassed nod and came into the growing crowd for the photo.

"Okay, folks. On three," said the photographer.

I put my arm around Sam tightly as I held Katy in my arms and she held Dax's hand. I knew in that moment my dad was watching.

In two flashes it was over, and as Mimi, my mother, Miss Celia, Timms and Sam's parents walked away from my new family, I kissed Katy, Sam and Dax. With the declining health of Momma and Miss Mimi, who knew if we'd ever have another opportunity like that?

"Did you have to rat me out?" Polly confessed as she glanced over her shoulder to King.

"How were we supposed to know you were out behind

the tent with Dr. Tall, Dark and Handsome?" Sam asked.

"He's not *that* tall," I added.

"Whatever," Polly snapped. "Are you getting ready to leave?"

"Yes," I answered before Sam could speak. I pulled her from the waist to meet my back and placed my head on her shoulder, quickly stealing a kiss from her long and sexy neck.

"Yes," Sam agreed, giving me *the* look all men get when they're about to cross the invisible line between acceptable and unacceptable. "We're going to say goodbye to Dax and Katy and change to catch the plane."

"What are you and Dr. Love going to do after the reception, Polly?" I asked with a grin.

"I'm not that kind of girl, Mac," Polly sang as she walked straight to King waiting by the bar.

"Yes, you are," I uttered under my breath.

"Mac," Sam scolded.

"Mommy? Are you leaving?" Dax asked as he looked up to Sam with sad eyes.

"Dax, you're the Callahan man in charge. You and Miss Celia will be taking care of everything while we're gone."

"The mail?" Dax asked.

"Sure. The mail."

"The secrets?"

I lowered my voice to him. "No playing around, Dax. Understand? But the horses, the garden – Miss Celia will need you to help her make important decisions while we're away for a few days."

"Okay."

I looked up to Sam who rocked the baby in her arms and gave her a kiss before handing her to Celia with a heavy sigh.

I leaned in to give Katy a final goodbye. As I kissed her

delicate cheek, she grabbed onto my little finger with a mighty grip that tore through my heart and turned me to mush.

"Somebody doesn't want her daddy to go just yet," Celia smiled.

"What did I ever do to deserve all of this, Celia? Really? It keeps me up at night sometimes."

"Baby, the Lord is good."

There were no words to describe the rush of feeling I had knowing the wedding was over and Sam and I could finally begin our life. As I watched my family scatter I said the only thing that seemed appropriate. "Amen."

As Sam and I walked through the back entrance off the veranda, we turned to see the tent lit up in the distance, music still flowing through the silk walls that moved with the evening breeze.

"It's been a perfect day," I remarked.

"That's because I married the perfect man."

I nuzzled her neck, turning to lead her into Lone Oak. "You drive me wild. Do you know that?"

We walked through the house and passed the nurse who was escorting Momma to the guestroom.

"Momma, Sam and I are leaving for a couple of weeks for our honeymoon. But I'll be back soon. You take care while I'm gone. Okay?"

She looked into my eyes with a blank stare as if she was trying to place me in her mixed-up world. "Okay."

I took a deep breath at her words, happy in the small instant of clarity.

"I love you, Momma."

Sam leaned in to hug her as I pulled away. I couldn't help but overhear Sam whisper in her ear, "I promise to take good care of him, Nancy."

Momma nodded as she took an extra moment to take us both in and smiled. When she looked back to the hired nurse, she became confused and the fleeting expression of awareness was gone.

I swallowed the lump in my throat and pulled it together. "Let's do this."

"Okay," she smiled as she took my hand to climb the imperial staircase that was one of the centerpieces of Lone Oak.

"I hope the wedding photos turn out," I said as we made the turn. "I can't wait until our portrait hangs here with the rest of the family. Since I was a kid, I wondered what my own family would look like right here on this wall."

Sam only nodded as she looked up and down the staircase at the generations of Callahans who'd lived in the house. I thought it astonishing how two hundred year old bricks and mortar could have such a profound impact on the lives of so many.

As we turned to enter my bedroom, I whisked Samantha off her feet and held her tightly in my arms. I was determined to carry her over every threshold for the next seventy-two hours. It was my duty. More than that, it was my privilege.

"Whoa!" she laughed as I tossed her in my arms to get a better grip before opening the door.

"Mrs. Callahan?"

"Yes?"

"Let's get this wedding day started."

"Started?" she giggled. "Don't you mean finished?"

"Baby, this is just the beginning."

6

SAMANTHA

As Mac carried me through the door of his bedroom, I thought of our first night together at Lone Oak. Our rain soaked bodies entwined as lightning flashed and the power went out. It was a defining moment in my life to learn I could love again.

I nuzzled my face into his neck and breathed in his smell. As tough and rugged as Mac was, to me he always smelled like a perfect mix of clean laundry and sugar cookies.

He sat my feet down on the floor inside the threshold and took my face in his hands as he'd done so many times before. "I've waited my whole life for you, Sam."

"I don't know if I've ever been this happy," I smiled.

He slid his hands over the smooth silk of my wedding gown from my bottom up to my shoulder blades and sighed as he pushed his hips into mine. "I don't want to wait for the plane ride to make love to you."

"I told you," I giggled as I pulled away. "I have no intention of making love to you on the plane to Paris. No matter what you've told the flight crew. *Especially* after what you've told the flight crew."

"Baby," he rasped. "I've waited almost an entire year to have you. Please don't make me wait another moment."

The desperation in his voice made me feel almost ashamed I'd put him off after Katy's birth. After a pregnancy scare early in my first trimester, Mac refused to lay a hand on me, afraid something would happen to the baby. He knew I was in no shape the first six weeks *after* Katy was born to handle what he'd described in detail he planned to do to me, but the past few weeks I knew had been torture. Because I wanted our wedding night to be special, he'd agreed to wait.

"What did you have in mind?" I whispered as I kissed his neck and slid my tongue up his Adam's apple while pulling the bowtie from its perfect knot.

"Sweet Jesus, baby. Don't do things like that to me unless you're prepared to back it up."

Mac dipped his knees and pushed himself between my legs forcing the thin layers of silk against my thighs. As he began to kiss me, I could feel how desperate he was. I was longing for him, but didn't quite picture my wedding consummation as a quickie before we said goodbye to our friends and family under a veil of fireworks.

Nevertheless, I stepped away from him, keeping his hands in mine. I wanted to take him in – all of him. My husband was the most beautiful man I'd ever known and I wanted to see him completely. I began to slowly unbutton the gleaming gold shirt studs down his chest without saying a word.

"Sam," he whispered.

"Shhhhhhh…" I placed one finger on his lips to stop whatever thought he was about to verbalize and shook my head. "I'm in charge, okay?"

He nodded and gave me a wicked grin.

"We have thirty minutes," I whispered. "Any longer and someone will come looking for us."

Mac dropped his head back with a deep breath as I pulled the shirt from his black tuxedo pants.

"Wait," he muttered.

"You can undress me when I'm finished."

I could tell by the timbre of his voice he didn't care who took their off clothes first – he was going to have his way with me. He caressed my shoulders as if he was afraid to touch the delicate pearls and stones on my dress. I pushed his tuxedo jacket off his muscular frame and felt him quiver at my touch. Slipping my hands around his torso, I pushed the heavily starched shirt up and over his arms.

"My cufflinks," he whispered as the shirt hung from his wrists displaying his biceps and tightly strung body.

I giggled, leaning down to put his cufflink to my mouth. I gazed up at him as I pursed my lips around the shiny Callahan crest and pushed the stem open with my tongue, pulling the gold face from the shirt with my teeth. I'd left a red lipstick stain on the cuff as a reminder of our love.

"You're killing me," he moaned.

I pulled the second cuff toward my face and he willing obliged me, turning his wrist to allow a better angle. I took the cufflink from my teeth and rose to meet his face with a lingering kiss and placed the links in the palm of his hand.

His shirt dropped to the floor and he tossed the cufflinks on the valet by the bed. I began to make quick work of the top button and zipper on his pants. I couldn't wait to get to what was underneath. Mac kicked off his shoes and tugged at his socks clumsily as I watched him fumble with a smile.

"I'll let you do the rest," he smoldered.

The bulge in his usual black boxer briefs was tight, waiting impatiently to be released. I ran my hands around the waistband and slid my hands over him, giving his perfect bottom a slight squeeze. I pulled him close and kissed him hard. My lips pressed so firmly against his mouth, he flinched with controlled desperation. I'd been thirsty for what seemed like forever and he was my first drop of water.

He let out a gasp as I slid my hands deeper into his boxers, pulling the elastic down just enough to rest on his manhood as his rapidly growing erection strained against the waistband.

"Please, God," he begged. "Don't stop."

In one lingering and liquid motion, I relieved his body of his clothes. Chilled molasses would've moved faster, and I relished each protracted second.

"Wow." It was all I could say as I stepped away to admire him in all his glory.

My husband was beautiful. Tall, sandy-haired and green-eyed, his body was perfect. The corrugated leanness and flat stomach that vee lined to his manhood was sexy beyond the norm. He stood in his nakedness with merely a smile and I nodded as if I'd won first prize at the county fair.

"My turn," he murmured, raising his chin with a smirk.

He walked to me and just as he moved in for a kiss, he turned me on a dime and began to unbutton the halter of my dress.

"I love your body," he growled.

I could feel his fingers trace a line down my bare back, meeting his other hand at the zipper resting on my waist. Matching the agonizing speed at which I'd disrobed him, Mac unzipped my wedding gown and opened the silk covered buttons at the nape of my neck. Not quite as complicated as his tuxedo, the white silk dropped to the floor, catching air and ballooning as it fell to expose the pale blue panties I wore for the day.

"My God you're beautiful, Samantha."

"So are you."

"I love the blue."

"Something blue," I whispered as I pulled him to me.

"What were the others?" he mumbled. "Something old, something new, something borrowed..."

"Mac Callahan," I teased as I gave his manhood a fleeting stroke. "I didn't know you cared about such things."

"Baby," he moaned as he slid his hands on either side of my hips and initiated the slow descent of his body and my silk panties to the floor. "I'm nothing if not traditional."

I pushed my hips into him as he kissed my stomach, and pulled away naturally when he stood to meet my lips. "Old is the emerald ring that belonged to your mother. New was my wedding dress."

"Mmmhmm," he replied as he began to kiss my neck.

"Borrowed was the silver nosegay holder that my bouquet was in. It belonged to Mimi."

"And blue," he murmured, taking my face into his hands.

"And blue."

He pulled my body close, grinding his hips into me. He was so ready to go I doubted that we'd even need the thirty minutes I'd told him we could steal from the party. As he dipped to pick me up and carry me to the bed, I wanted to pinch myself. How could I be so lucky? In one year alone, I'd gone from being a widowed mother of one to a wife and mother of two. It was almost too much happiness.

7

MAC

S am was naked and in my arms. We were finally married, and for the next two weeks she would be mine and mine alone.

I placed her perfect body on my bed and without hesitation pulled myself over top of her. As I ran my hand from her hipbone to her shoulder I watched in awe as she closed her eyes and took a deep breath, letting the past few months of babies and wedding plans fade into the background.

"This is just a preview of our next two weeks, my love," I mumbled, pressing my face into her breasts. I wanted to go slow, but knew that the lazy days of lying around naked in our hotel suite in Paris were still ahead of us. Right now, I just wanted to be inside of Sam. It was more than a want. It was a deep-seated need.

"Yes," she whispered as I moved carefully between her legs. The word only revved me more until I couldn't be without her body enveloping itself around me.

"Jesus, baby." I graveled, my throat dry from adrenaline pumping through my veins as I guided myself slowly, inch by incredible inch, deep inside. "You have such power over me – such a beautiful and mysterious power. When God made you, he was showing off."

She ran her hands through my hair, giving it a sexy tug. She was sending me to the edge without moving her body or kissing my lips.

She smiled as she closed her eyes, deep in the moment.

"We may be back at the party sooner than I'd hoped," I admitted as I delved deeper with each rhythmic thrust.

"Oh yessss…" she groaned.

"Oh baby," I said as my ragged gasps quickened.

Sam continued to caress my neck and kiss my ear. She grazed my throat with her teeth and sent me into a blissful agony where I barely held on.

"I love the way you love me, Sam," I said as I stopped to gain control and admire her beauty.

She drove her hips into me, taking us deeper into the impending ecstasy. "Yes," she moaned.

I pulled her down and lifted her knee to my chest, obeying the instinct deep inside.

Sam gasped with pleasure, and I couldn't hold out any longer.

"Oh God," I whimpered, pouring myself into her. Letting go, I felt pure ecstasy. Not until I felt her tremble under my body did I feel Samantha burst beneath me. I circled my hips inside her as she purred with satisfaction. I never wanted it to end. This was perfection. And it was only the beginning.

I rolled onto my back taking a deep breath. I pulled Samantha into my chest as she sighed heavily. "That was fast," I admitted. "But *that* was amazing."

"Yes it was," she said with conviction. "That *was* amazing."

"There's more where that came from, pretty lady. I want

you gleefully satisfied at all times."

"And I'll bet you're just the man for the job."

"Oooo yeah," I growled into her neck as I kissed her collarbone.

"I'm exhausted," Sam confessed.

"I know. I'd love just to lie here, but there are about a hundred people downstairs waiting to send us off. Let's say goodbye," I said. "And we'll catch our plane and do this again on the way to Paris. I promise it will be much more satisfying – on your end."

"On my end?" she asked with a smile as I took her hands and helped her to sit up in bed. "What does that mean?"

"It means that was fanfuckingtastic for me," I proclaimed as I stood above her. "Sorry to be crass. There was no other way to describe it. But I didn't give my wife enough time and attention."

"I'm very happy in this moment. But I'll take all the attention you want to give," Sam teased as she padded like the sexy little creature she was to the bathroom. My new wife had given birth three months ago and looked like a rock star. I was altogether turned on and proud in the same instant.

"Wanna take a quick shower?" she said over her shoulder. "It's gonna be a long flight."

"Yes. I'll clean up in here while you get started."

I gathered the evidence of our whirlwind consummation, throwing my tux onto the valet in the corner and laying Sam's wedding dress across the bed.

I was spent. I wanted to wish everyone well and get the hell out of town with Sam.

I saw the bathroom light click on in the corner and waited for the sound of the shower.

"Mac!"

I hurried through the bedroom, slipping on the marble floor of the master bath as I made my way to her.

Her hands were shaking as she pointed to the mirror. Scrawled in red lipstick were the words: *Remember me?*

"What *is* this?" Sam pleaded.

My heart raced at the sight of the words. I knew whose they were and exactly what it meant.

I grabbed some sweats and a t-shirt from the back of my bathroom door without answering and walked to the nightstand to get my gun.

As I loaded the magazine from the bottom, I turned to find Samantha behind me in my robe. Fear covered her face like a mask. "Tell me what's going on."

"Where are Dax and the baby?" I asked without answering her question as I picked up my cell phone.

"With Celia and Polly. Tell me what is going on!" she bellowed.

"Dan, find my kids and family. Bring them to the study. Hector's somewhere on the grounds."

"What?" Sam shouted as she grabbed my arm and I pulled her to me.

"He's been in the bedroom," I explained to Dan. "Seal the entrance to Lone Oak. No one gets out of here without being checked off the guest list!"

I slammed my phone onto the table and searched for shoes in my closet. "Stay here, Sam," I growled.

"Like hell I'm staying in here. My family is out there. And – Hector?" she gasped as she backed away from me.

"Hector's here? How do you know that's from him?" she asked as she pointed to the bathroom, hands trembling.

"Because it's not the first time he's sent a message," I confessed. "Now do as I say. The other agents are bringing Dax and Katy to the study downstairs. I'll come get you when everyone is safe."

"No. I'm coming with you," she protested as the tears streamed down her face and she frantically searched for something to wear.

After pulling an old shirt and sweatpants from my closet, Sam dressed quickly and walked to the door without me.

"Yes!" I shouted into the phone, barely allowing it to ring.

"We've got the kids, Mimi, Polly and Celia in the study. Sam's parents have already left," Dan reported.

"Where's my mom?" I yelled.

"Shit, Mac, I don't know."

"The downstairs guestroom," I shouted. "I'm bringing Sam to you. I'll go check on her."

I grabbed Sam by the arm and gripped my gun tightly. "Let's go."

"This isn't happening. This isn't happening," Sam mumbled as she trailed behind me. "What about all the people at the party?"

"The agents are clearing them out. They've got a guest list to check them against."

"What?" she yelped. "What else haven't you told me?"

"Sam, just let me get you to the kids and secure the house and then we'll talk."

We raced down the stairs and I rushed Sam into my dad's old study on the first floor. It had become my office since moving home from Washington D.C. I knew the room well, and the hidden walk-ins could prove to be a hiding place for Sam and the kids if needed.

"Mac!" shouted Dan. "I've got four officers at the gate, four at the tent. They're ushering everyone out. They're just asking for their names and explaining that we think there might be a gas leak on the property."

When I escorted Sam into the study, Mimi, Celia, Polly and the children were all safe and accounted for. The only face I was surprised to see was King Giles.

"Is everyone okay?" I asked.

They nodded as I escorted Sam to the couch to sit. "Stay here."

"Mac, you better tell me what's going on and you better tell me now," Sam said, quickly losing her patience.

I turned and wiped the sweat from my brow as I stared at the blank faces. "Miss Celia? Where's Timms?"

"He was tired and went home, baby," she replied. "I think your wife is right. You better start tellin' us what's goin' on around here."

"Everyone stay here. I need to get Momma from the guest room."

As the words escaped my mouth I heard a scream. I knew it was her.

Rushing down the hall I called to another agent to back me up. I opened the door to the bedroom and found my mother in her chair covering her eyes and rocking back and forth like a scared child.

"Momma, what is it? What?"

She sobbed and shook her head and pointed in front of her without looking.

"Mom, no one is there. We're alone. Where's the nurse?" I shouted as the hired nurse from Autumn Valley walked into the room.

"I'm sorry, sir. I needed to use the restroom. I heard all

the commotion in the hallway and went to make sure everything was okay."

"It's fine. Gather your things and head home. There are a couple of men who are checking names off the guest list on the way out."

"But what about Miss Nancy, sir? I'm supposed to bring her back to Autumn Valley with me."

"Miss Nancy is staying. She may be back a little later but I'll bring her myself."

"What's going on?" shouted Sam as she came to the door. "Is she okay, Mac?"

"Help me get her to the study!" I shouted at the agent who'd followed me. "And find Agent Kelley!"

"Yes, sir."

"Mac?" Sam insisted.

"Samantha, please get back to the study. Now!" It was becoming harder and harder as each second passed to hold back the rage that flooded my mind.

As tears streamed down her face, she turned without reply and walked out of the room, passing the agents combing the hallways.

From the front window I could see the line of cars waiting to leave. If Hector came by car, he'd be accounted for. My fear was he'd found my mother and when she screamed, he'd left on foot.

As I brought her into the study with the others I sat her down and quickly noticed Sam sobbing in Polly's arms.

"What is going on, Mac?" Mimi asked calmly. "And don't say 'nothing'. I think you've put enough perfume on this pig already."

"Hector. The man who tried to kill me and tried to kill Sam. He's alive. And he's been in the house today."

"What?" Polly gasped.

"He may still be here. That's why you all are in this room. Dan's gonna stay with you and I'm going out with the other agents to sweep the house."

"Dammit, Mac," Dan pleaded. "*You* stay here. I'll check the house."

"You don't know Lone Oak. There are plenty of places he could be hiding. Places you'd miss."

"Amen to that," Miss Celia said softly.

"Someone better start explaining *exactly* what's going on," Sam cried as she stood defiantly. "I mean the *real* truth. Not just another lie to appease me for the moment."

She shot a hateful look across the room at me as Polly stoically stood with her.

"We've been getting messages on and off for the past six months, Sam. I didn't tell you because you were pregnant. I didn't want to upset you. You were under enough pressure as it was. I was going to tell you, but after the preterm labor scare I didn't want to take any chances."

She walked to me. I thought she would want a reassuring hug or kiss, but she kept her distance and it broke my heart. "Please don't go out there looking for him. I can't lose you."

"You're not going to lose me. He couldn't kill me the first time. He's certainly not going to kill me in my own damn house."

"He almost did," Mimi chimed from the corner. "He almost killed you both."

"Miss Mimi speaks the truth, Mac," said Celia as she rocked a crying Katy in her arms. "You've got a wife and family to put first. And that means givin' up your old gun totin', crazy actin', criminal chasin' ways."

"It's not that simple and you know it," I pleaded.

"She's right, Mac," Mimi added.

"Mac," Sam whimpered. "I'm begging you."

I turned to Dan with disgust. "Sweep the house. I'll stay here."

Dan nodded to me and left.

"I can't fight all of you," I confessed, walking toward Sam to explain.

"Start talking," Sam demanded.

"Fine," I sighed as I led her to one of the many couches in the round room. I wanted to speak with her away from the family. "After I got out of the hospital we thought Hector might be dead – until he paid a visit to Momma at Autumn Valley. He was seen on the surveillance footage around the nursing home. Remember how we found my dad's book with her the day we came to tell her we were getting married?"

"Yes."

"Hector put it there. He'd stolen the book from this study. He wanted me to know he could get to me. To my family."

"Why didn't you say anything then?" Sam pleaded.

"I thought about it. I did. But when Dan ran a check on Hector, we came up with a hell of a lot more than just your average scorned lover. He wasn't just pissed because we busted up his boyfriend's crime ring – he was here to set up a drug route through the South from Mexico. We screwed up a couple of years' worth of groundwork for him."

"What?" Sam gasped.

"It's deeper than we'd ever thought."

"And all this was going on and you didn't think it was important for me to know about it?" Sam demanded. "Mac, we've started a family. Now what are we going to do? Be on the run for the rest of our lives from some drug cartel?"

"Hector went into hiding for a while for things to blow

over, but the people he works for don't take too kindly to their plans getting fucked with. Especially by the FBI."

"Mac Callahan," Miss Celia scolded. "I can hear you all the way over here. You watch that dirty mouth of yours."

"My apologies," I said. "To everyone."

"Mac," Dan shouted as he came into the room. "Everyone's out. House is clean. We think he left off the back of the property. There're tire tracks leading out of the field and onto a remote side road. We've got the state troopers on the lookout. What do you want to do?"

"Why are you asking him?" Sam interrupted. "He doesn't work for the FBI anymore."

I watched the look on Sam's face as Dan dropped his head, not wanting to respond to her.

"Mac?" Sam cried. "Is there something else you need to tell me?"

"Sweetheart," I pleaded.

"No!" she shouted. "Just no!"

"I'm not a full time agent."

"What does that even mean?" Sam cried, crazily pacing around the room.

"I help the Bureau with specific cases."

"Samantha," Dan continued. "No one cares more about this case than Mac. No one *knows* more about this case than he does. That's why he's stayed with it."

"I'm not letting Hector harm anyone in my family. By the time I'm finished with him –" I insisted, stopping short of what I really wanted to do.

"Mac?" Dan asked again. He was seemingly oblivious to Sam's concerns and I knew it was making her angry. "What do you want to do?"

"We're going to act as if nothing's wrong."

"What?" Polly objected.

"I want Momma and Mimi taken back to Autumn Valley. We will leave on our honeymoon tonight as planned."

"I'm not leaving my babies," Sam objected.

"We're not going to Paris. And we're taking them with us."

"Who?" Polly asked.

"All of you."

8

SAMANTHA

I paced the room, full of anxious anger and fear. He'd lied to me –again. Mac had lied to me again. I shuddered at the thought of how many times I drove around Shadeland thinking I was safe. All the times I was out running errands with Dax and Katy. Anything could've happened. Anything.

"Did someone see him? How do you know he's here?" Polly asked. "One moment we're all dancing and waiting for you to make your official departure with the fireworks, and the next the wedding lady is telling us there's a gas leak and everyone needs to move as quickly as possible to their cars."

"Hector," I whispered, still unable to process what was happening.

"I don't understand why you think he's been here," Polly blurted sarcastically.

"We know," Mac offered. "Because he made it a point to leave a note in red lipstick on the mirror in the bathroom."

"What?" Miss Celia gasped.

"What did it say?" Polly asked.

"It said *Remember me?*" I whispered.

"It's the E.E. Cummings poem," Mac hissed with frustration. *"And in a mystery to be, when time from time shall set us free, forgetting me, remember me."*

"Edward," Nancy mumbled.

I watched Mac's heart sink, knowing his mother knew the poem from his dad.

"We're going to act as if we're leaving as scheduled for our honeymoon. But we're taking everyone in this room…" Mac hesitated in thought. "Somewhere. Just give me a minute to think."

"New Orleans."

Everyone in the room turned and watched King step forward. "New Orleans," he repeated.

"No offense, King, but I wasn't including you in the family," Mac spouted. "You don't need to be involved and frankly, you're not at risk."

"Maybe not," King replied, walking to Mac without reservation. "And you're right. I didn't make this mess, but I can help fix it."

"Mess?" Mac snapped. "What in the hell are you talking about? Mess? This is real world, real life bad shit, Giles. I don't think they trained you for this in medical school."

"And you won't know how to care for anyone including your own mother and children if something happens. I don't think you learned *that* at the FBI academy."

"Mac, I love you," interjected Miss Celia. "But if one more foul word comes out of that mouth, I'm taking you down, son."

"Ladies, my apologies," Mac whispered as he backed his attitude down.

He was acting like a petulant child, and it was making me angrier at each tick of the old clock in the room.

"I want to hear about New Orleans," I blurted.

"Me too," Polly agreed.

I watched as Mac threw up his hands in surrender. "What's in New Orleans?"

"My family's vacation home. It's off the beaten path, hard to find and already set up with a makeshift hospital room."

"What?" Polly questioned.

"My dad and I spent his last year there. It's where he wanted to be. Where he died. I had the whole place equipped for him."

"What makes you think we'll need a hospital bed, King?" Mac asked.

"I know you're not talking about me," Mimi ranted.

"No, Miss Mimi," King conceded. "But it wouldn't hurt to have a safe place that can act as a hospital if needed far away from here until this guy is found."

"Mac, it sounds like a good solution," I agreed.

"I don't think you have a better option tonight," Dan conceded.

Running his fingers through his hair in frustration, Mac finally sat, his body slumped in exhaustion.

"Do we have a choice?" I asked.

"Not when it comes to your safety," Mac mumbled as he squeezed my hand.

"Fine." Mac pulled four agents into the study for orders. "Here's the plan. Momma and Mimi go back to Autumn Valley and pack. I'll have agents pick them up. Alert the nurses at their station, but *only* those nurses. Celia?"

"Yes, baby."

"Call your dad and let him know what's happening. I'll need him to check on the house, but I'll have agents staying here to be on the safe side."

"Okay," she stumbled. "You sure you want me to go?" Celia asked.

"You're my second mother. I'm not taking any chances. And before you ask, Polly, you're going too. Sorry for the inconvenience."

"It's okay," Polly sighed. "We're family. Right?"

Mac nodded in her direction. "Everyone is traveling wherever they go with an agent at their side. You can use the bathroom alone, but that's it. And don't take too long. We've been known to knock down doors if we think something is wrong."

Mac walked away to talk in private with Dan and I went to Mimi after taking Katy from Celia's arms. "What have I done, Mimi?"

"Sweetheart, you haven't done anything. But I think Mac is right. We've got to get out of here."

"My entire family is in danger." My voice broke with fear and Mimi could see the terror in my eyes.

"Let's not get to worrying when we don't need to. All worry does is give a big shadow to little things."

"This isn't such a little thing."

"It will be when it's all said and done."

"What about the house?" I asked as if everyone in the room was thinking in my head.

"What do you mean?" Mac asked.

"My house. Mimi's house. Polly was watching over it while we are on our honeymoon. Now what?"

"Should we call your parents?" Mac asked.

"God no," I lamented. "They were leaving the country tonight."

"What about your cousin? The one who came into town for the wedding?" Mac continued. "Richard."

"The Dick?" Mimi interjected. "I don't trust him as far

as I can throw him."

"Mimi," I pleaded. "You know he's the only one."

"Like hell I do."

"Then what do you suggest?" I asked.

Mimi gave me a heavy sigh and pushed herself off the couch with her walker, shooing away the men who came to her assistance. "I suggest you go back to the house and put everything of value in the hidden safe. If he's coming into the house, he's not robbing us blind."

"I guess that's settled," Mac quipped.

"I'm coming too, Mac." King declared.

"There's no need."

"It's my house. I'm going."

"Can you get away from work that easily?" I asked. "It's not that I don't want you there. I do. I just hate to use your house, make you leave Shadeland. I mean, just for us."

King glanced at Mac and walked to me, taking my hand. "I'm not going to let anything happen to you, the kids or the ladies."

"Nice," Mac chided.

I noticed Polly smirk in the corner and when our eyes met, she came to sit with me as I rocked Katy to sleep. "Why don't they just drop their pants and let's see whose dick is bigger," Polly uttered under her breath.

"I'm so sorry, Polly. I had no idea you were going to get entangled in this mess."

"Hey, I'm going to New Orleans with a hot doctor who told me I was beautiful. I mean, aside from the fact that a crazy Mexican drug pusher is looking for us, it's almost like a vacation. But with a weird and amusing little family."

"Polly?" Mac interrupted. "Go pack. Dan's gonna set you up with an agent. Meet us back here. Celia?"

"Yes, baby."

"Dan's gonna give you an agent too. Get home and pack and get back as soon as you can. We'll need help packing up the children."

Celia nodded and walked to the door to meet her agent.

"King, go back with Momma and Miss Mimi and get them settled in. Have a nurse to help them pack. If they can't, I'll buy them clothes when we get there."

King stood still, clearly unhappy that Mac was dishing out orders to everyone, including him.

"Do you need to pack, King?" I asked, feeling horrible about the situation and how Mac was treating everyone.

King shook his head in quiet disgust. "I have clothes there. I'll need medical supplies but I can find them at my office. I'm fine by myself. I don't need an agent."

"If you're going with us," Mac ordered, "you're taking a agent with you tonight. End of discussion."

"Mac," I gasped. "Quit telling everyone what to do. We're not your field agents. You can't just boss us around."

"Sam, follow directions like everyone else. Okay?"

I kissed the baby and asked Dax to stay with Polly. He was already half asleep on the couch. "Dax, I'm gonna pack you up for the honeymoon."

"You mean I get to go too?" he asked sleepily.

"Yes, you do. We're all going."

I shot Mac a look as I walked out of the room. In one day I'd gotten married to the man of my dreams and had my worst nightmare come true.

"Sam, wait up," Polly called to me as I climbed the stairs past three FBI agents. Suddenly I was amazed at the number of agents who were at the wedding in an official capacity. The house was teeming with them, and as I passed each one I became more angry and afraid.

I wanted to get my suitcase, go to Dax and Katy's room and pack. I knew Miss Celia needed to pack for herself and not just the children.

I stalled on the landing and gave a heavy sigh. I was afraid if I opened my mouth the tears would begin to flow and I wouldn't be able to stop them. I nodded to Polly and waved my hand for her to hurry. "I'm so sorry," I whimpered as she hugged me.

"What do you have to be sorry for?"

"Everything. Nothing. I don't know anymore."

"It's all going to be okay. Everyone is safe, you are finally married and we all get to go on vacation."

"Yeah. Some honeymoon," I lamented as we climbed the stairs together.

"If I know Mac Callahan, and I think I finally *do* know Mac Callahan, you'll still have your honeymoon. It'll just be a little later than you planned."

"Take the kids while I shower?" I pleaded. "I'll be quick. I feel terrible leaving you and Miss Celia to pull the kids' things together."

"Shower? Why –" she began as we walked into Mac's bedroom where we were immediately overwhelmed with agents dusting the room for prints. The flashes of light from the bathroom let me know right away I'd have to find another place to shower and change.

"I know why you need a shower," Polly whispered with a grin. "You guys were up here doing the deed while creepy-ass Hector was writing on the bathroom mirror with lipstick. Can I see it?" she asked, barely taking a breath between thoughts.

"I guess," I sighed. "I really haven't looked at it that closely. Mac had me out of here before I had a chance to do anything."

Polly and I pushed our way past the three agents in the doorway while the two that were escorting us stood in the bedroom and waited.

"*Remember me?*" Polly read from the mirror. "Where's the lipstick?"

"I don't know. I didn't look for it," I uttered, trying to catch my breath. The whole evening had riddled me with anxiety and I didn't know how much more I could take or how much more I wanted to know. I was furious with Mac for not telling me the truth, but at the same time now that I was completely immersed in Hector's games I didn't know how I would've reacted while pregnant.

My body shook with the adrenaline still pumping through my veins.

"Where's the lipstick?" Polly asked the agent who was dusting for prints on the mirror.

"We haven't found it yet. Mrs. Callahan?"

"Sam?" Polly nudged my arm as I stared at the mirror.

"I'm sorry," he continued. "I just want to make sure we have everything we need from you since Agent Callahan is taking you off grid."

"He's taking me where?" I asked.

"Mrs. Callahan?" he patiently asked again.

I paused, thinking that it was the first time anyone other than Mac had actually referred to me as Mrs. Callahan. Standing in the middle of a crime scene wasn't the way I pictured the lovely moment would happen.

"Sam?" Polly urged me again.

"I'm sorry." I was in a daze. None of it seemed real to me. My heart was racing and my vision was blurry. "I need to sit down," I murmured.

I walked to a skirted seat in front of the vanity mirror in the large bathroom and sat, putting my head between my knees. "Just give me a minute."

"Someone get Agent Callahan up here. Pronto!" someone shouted from the doorway.

I lifted my head and stared at the words on the mirror. What did Hector really want? Did he want to kill me? And why had did he wait almost a year? Maybe he just wanted to scare us. Maybe he just wanted to ruin my wedding day. So far he was two for three.

"Sam!" Mac shouted from the doorway. "Baby, are you okay?"

I nodded as he knelt at my feet. Taking my tear-stained face in his hands he lifted my chin. "Samantha, look at me."

I stared into the eyes of the man who was my dream come true. He was everything I'd ever wanted and I suddenly worried that our life together wouldn't be as long as we'd planned.

"Samantha, I promise you everything will be alright. I'm not going to let anything happen to you or the kids. I've waited my whole life for this. Nothing and no one, especially a hood like Hector Quintes, is going to ruin that for us."

He pushed the falling curl from my face and nodded until I joined him.

"Are you okay?" he asked.

"I just feel, I don't know—overwhelmed."

"Sir!" an agent shouted from the bedroom. "Sir, I think you need to see this."

Mac kissed my forehead and stood with me. My legs were quivering, but Mac stayed with me until I was stable on my feet.

"I'm coming," he said over his shoulder. "You okay for

a second?"

"Mac, I want to shower before we go. You can stay in the room with me, but I'm showering before I get on that plane."

"Sweetheart, I'd love to watch you soap up," he whispered into my ear.

I shook my head as he turned to meet one of the many agents now covering the house from top to bottom.

"What's the plan?" Polly asked, coming back to the bathroom to check on me.

"I'm going to shower and then we're going. I guess."

"Sam!" I heard Mac shout from the other room. "Sam, can you come out here?"

Polly took my hand and together we went back into Mac's bedroom to find him standing by the writing desk that sat like a distinguished gentleman in the dark corner of the room. I knew he rarely used it as he'd made himself at home in the study.

"What is it?"

"Sam, is this your lipstick?"

I looked down to the table and saw the black tube as it caught the light of the bright chandelier overhead. Chanel. I knew it was Chanel by the top of the cap with its connecting and mirrored C's. The golden tube lay on its side, the tip ruined.

"What color is it?" I asked.

"Red," the agent replied flatly.

"I can see that," I smirked. "I need to see the bottom of the tube to tell if it's mine."

"What?" asked Mac.

"It's true" Polly agreed. "She wears ninety-eight. I wear ninety-seven."

"It's a different color," I explained.

"Red's not red?"

Polly and I looked at each other and shook our heads. "No," we replied in unison.

"Get me some gloves!" Mac shouted.

"I've got it, sir," said an agent.

Turning the tube on its side, it was easy to see the ninety-seven in gold on the bottom. It was not my lipstick. It was Polly's.

"Where did you leave your things today, Polly?"

"In the bedroom where Sam and I dressed."

"Where your mother stayed later today?" I asked.

"No. She was in an empty guest room."

Polly curled her bottom lip inward and held it with her teeth. I knew something was wrong.

"Mac," Polly stated calmly. "I didn't bring that with me to Lone Oak today. That lipstick is from Sam's house."

I backed away from the table and sat on the bed, putting my head back between my knees. "We've got to go. We've got to get out of here. He's been everywhere."

Mac picked up his phone and started making calls. I looked to Polly and shook my head. "I'm so sorry, Polly."

"He's been at your house *and* Lone Oak today, Sam. He's been…" Polly trailed.

"He's been busy," Mac finished her sentence. "Polly, is there anything you must have from Sam's house before we leave? Any prescription meds? Anything?"

"I need my clothes and makeup," Polly replied.

"If you had to, could you survive on what you have with you and buy clothes when we arrive at our destination?"

"You mean New Orleans?"

"If that's where we go."

I could tell Mac was going to fight King's offer tooth and nail, but he knew it was the best option for Mimi and his mother.

"I guess," Polly mumbled, clearly shaken by the idea that someone had been going through her things.

Mac nodded, silently thanking her for taking one thing off his plate for the evening.

"I've sent a team to sweep your house, Sam. In the meantime, let's keep moving. I want us out of here. Where's King?"

"He left with Mimi, Nancy and his agent to pack and get medical supplies," Polly sighed. It was clear that the events of the day were wearing thin on everyone.

"Polly, can you help Miss Celia gather the kids' things?"

"Sure," Polly said flatly.

"Mac, may I please take a shower?" I begged.

"Let's go," he conceded as he grabbed an agent to tag along. "You can stand watch outside the door."

"Yes, sir," he said.

9

MAC

Sam and I took the elevator from the second floor to the basement. The most modern floor of Lone Oak, it was equipped with a gym, weight room, indoor pool and steam shower.

"Do you have to have your gun out and ready to shoot?" Sam's voice trembled. As she grabbed my hand, I felt even worse about the events of the day.

"Yes."

As we reached the large bathroom, I turned on the lights and watched them illuminate the dark marble floor. The room seemed cold and masculine, and I immediately kicked on the under floor heating system. Sam had been padding around in my old sweats and in bare feet. It was no way for my bride to have to exist. Especially on our wedding day.

I walked through the room and checked each corner. Opening the shower door, I turned on the water for Samantha and turned to give her the best smile I could muster.

"It's all clear. Get your shower."

She nodded to me and then tilted her head to the agent still looking around the room.

"I'll take it from here," I ordered.

"Yes, sir. I'll be right outside the door."

I nodded to him and shut the door.

Turning to Sam, I watched as she leaned against the vanity and looked at her own tear-stained face in the mirror. "How did this happen, Mac?"

I walked behind her, slipping my arms around her waist and pulled her close to me. I looked at her reflection and had an overwhelming urge to beg for her forgiveness. But I didn't. "Hector's a bad guy. That's all. I've dealt with assholes like him for a long time."

"Not one who wanted to kill your wife."

Sam's tears were more than I could handle.

"And I thought my biggest fight was going to be keeping you out of my panties on a seven hour flight to Paris. Instead it's staying alive."

"I think Hector is long gone."

I turned Sam to face me and pulled her close for a tight hug. I could feel her breath in short bursts as she wept. "Hector's got a lot going on and a lot of territory to cover. I'm sure he's still trying to get his drug operation secured. I think he just wanted to ruin our day. But I'm not going to let him."

"It's too late for that," Sam whimpered as she wiped the tears from her eyes, smearing what was left of her mascara.

"Oh no," I chuckled, taking her hands in mine. "Nothing and no one can change the fact that I married the woman of my dreams today. Nothing. Now get in the shower."

Sam nodded and quickly slipped the sweatpants that swallowed her tiny frame to the floor while simultaneously pulling the old shirt of mine over her head.

"Baby, even with a crazed drug dealer hot on your trail, you are *fine*," I drawled, hoping to lighten her mood.

She didn't return my smile and merely nodded, dropping her head as she stepped into the shower roaring with steam.

I paced the room with nervous energy. I knew I needed to be with my family, but at the same time I needed to stay here or go back to headquarters in D.C. to oversee the takedown of this bastard.

By keeping Hector's notes from Sam, I'd saved her months of anxiety. Now I had no choice but to find him and put him away.

The door to the shower opened and Sam appeared, wet and glistening. Her toned body was beautiful and I couldn't help but smile.

"What?"

"Can't a man be proud?"

She shook her head at me. "You'd better take a quick shower too. Give me your gun. I'll guard *you*."

"I'm getting in. But you won't need to guard me for the one minute I plan on being away from my gun."

I placed my Glock on the marble counter and quickly dropped my pants. I walked closer to her wearing just my t-shirt.

"Get that thing away from me," Sam quipped.

"What?" I asked as I pulled the towel from over her shoulder off of the warming rack.

"Oh. Sorry. I didn't. I thought–"

"'Get that thing away from me' is exactly what every man wants to hear on his wedding night, Sam."

I pulled the shirt over my head and dropped it to the floor.

"I'm sorry."

"No. I'm the one who should be sorry," I apologized as I pulled her close and removed her towel to briefly nuzzle her nakedness.

Kissing her shoulder, I nodded to the corner where two large fluffy robes hung. "You can wear that back upstairs to get dressed."

"I'm not leaving without you."

"Give me one minute."

I was in and out before Sam could even get a robe on and skipped the towel, opting to go straight for my own robe.

"Let's go. We've got a plane to catch."

We were dressed and downstairs in ten minutes. Sam and I went to the study hoping to find most of our family. It was almost ten o'clock and we were scheduled to leave at nine thirty for Paris. I wanted to keep with the original flight plan as much as possible. I wasn't taking any chances.

"Where's Miss Celia?" I asked as we wheeled our luggage into an open corner.

"Just got a call," Dan explained. "She's on her way. Dr. Giles is en route as well."

"What about my mother and Sam's grandmother?"

"The agents are with them. We're going to Autumn Valley to collect them. It'll be the last stop on the way to the airport."

Polly walked in carrying Katy and walking a sleepy Dax to the couch to lie down.

Sam took Katy in her arms as she yawned and stretched

her tiny body. At least one Callahan wasn't on edge tonight.

"Mommy, when are we leaving?" Dax asked, rubbing his eyes. "Polly said I could wear my jammies."

"I think that's a grand idea," Sam sang softly, trying to conceal the fear in her voice.

"Mac," Dan continued. "We're going to need to spend some time at Sam's house. Is there someone who can meet us there?"

"Sam's cousin Richard came into town for the wedding. Have you called him yet?" I asked Sam.

"No."

"Sam, honey," I sighed. "Let's tie up loose ends. And quickly."

"Fine."

I took inventory of the room and did my best to show a calm exterior to the crew. It was going to be an interesting few days. I needed to get everyone settled and make my way either back to Shadeland or D.C. to follow up. FBI would be working with DEA and I wasn't missing the party.

As Celia walked into the study with an agent by her side, Sam finished her call to Richard and turned to me with a nod.

"What kind of detail did you give him, Sam?"

"What do you mean?"

"Did you tell him what was going down?"

"Did I tell him a crazed drug lord that I shot to save our lives has been after me for over a year and just surfaced again at my wedding reception to scare us and cause us all to leave for New Orleans?"

Polly stifled a laugh and looked away from me. She knew I wasn't amused.

Dropping my head, I placed my hands on my hips, wanting to be angry but knowing Sam had every right to be upset.

"Yeah. Something like that, I guess."

"Yes. He knows there's going to be an agent at the house too."

"There'll be more than one," I muttered as I turned to begin packing the cars. "Let's get everyone loaded. We'll get Momma and Mimi on the way."

"We can't leave," Polly interrupted. "King's not here yet."

"King…" I mumbled with an air of disgust. "Someone needs to track him down. It's time to go."

"I'll call him," Sam volunteered.

"Load the kids, Sam. Someone else can get his whereabouts."

She raised her eyebrow at me in distaste and I knew the next few hours were going to be touchy.

"I just spoke with him," Dan blurted. "He's meeting us at the airfield."

I picked up the bags in the doorway and the other agents followed suit. We would be locked and loaded in minutes.

"I'm sending Z with you," Dan announced as I tossed the last bag into the van carrying the luggage, guns and supplies.

"Z? Leo Xanthis?"

"He's the best man for the job, Mac. He's flying in from Quantico and will meet you at Lakefront."

Leo Xanthis, nicknamed Z, was a ball-buster of an agent. Older than me by maybe a year, I knew him from the Academy in Quantico. He was from New Orleans, Greek, and most of the female agents thought he was a descendent of the gods. Part of the Behavior Sciences Unit, Z was smart as hell and twice as scary. I didn't know how Sam would react to him.

"Why Xanthis?" I asked, almost taken aback.

"Dammit, Mac. Hector's off his damned rocker and you know it. The fact that you're acting as if he's not is frankly pissing me off. Get to New Orleans, get everyone settled and get caught up."

"I know what's going on, Dan."

"Do you? Because I'm starting to think you believed the line of shit you fed your wife."

I wanted to punch Dan in the face but instead held my tongue and gritted my teeth. No one was going to lay a hand on my family.

"What the hell is Lakefront? Does King know we're flying out of Kershaw in Montgomery?"

"It's the airport in New Orleans, Mac. I suggest you get your shit together. King seems to know more than you do."

I shook my head in disgust. "It's my wedding day. I've got other things on my mind."

"Get the family settled and I'll see you back at the office. We'll need to coordinate with DEA," Dan said, giving me a handshake and a slap on the back. "I'm staying here and cleaning up. Z will meet you in the Big Easy."

I nodded again, filled with so much rage and disgust over Hector, the end of my wedding day and myself. What kind of agent was I if I couldn't keep my own family out of harm's way?

We arrived at the private airfield in Montgomery and the Gulfstream was fueled and ready to go.

I'd called ahead and spoken with the pilot to let him

know the plan. He made all the arrangements necessary to land in New Orleans and had all the paperwork in order. I was thankful that one thing was easy tonight.

The ground crew loaded all the suitcases and supplies. The guns were checked and bagged at Lone Oak and loaded in with everything else in the cargo hold. Our trip that was to consist of two people had expanded to seven adults and two children. The plane would accommodate ten comfortably, but I had a feeling this wasn't going to be a comfortable journey in any way.

It was nearly midnight and the gang was growing weary. With everyone on board, I joined the group and closed the hatch myself. They stared blankly at me and I felt as if I needed to say something to ease their minds, but nothing came to me immediately.

Instead I nodded, hoping that with one small gesture they would know I wasn't going to let anything happen to them.

I took my place next to Samantha and buckled in. I pulled her hand to me, brushing my lips across her knuckles and gave Katy a kiss on the forehead. It hadn't been the day we'd carefully planned and it definitely wasn't the wedding night *I* had planned. The Belle Etoile Royal Suite at Le Meurice on rue de Rivoli would be empty tomorrow, but the vacation home of King Giles would be full.

10

SAMANTHA

I was ready to drop from exhaustion as we walked into King's Lake Pontchartrain home. Located in the middle of nowhere, we were definitely *off grid*.

"Sorry, ladies," King sighed as we walked through the doors and he began to disarm the alarm system.

"Sorry for what?" Polly asked.

"This house was built for the men. There's not one feminine thing about it. And I apologize in advance for the urinals in all the bathrooms."

"What?" I was tired and unsure of what King had just said.

"The urinals. They're in all the bathrooms."

"What's a you-n-all?" Dax asked, still half asleep.

"More man stuff, Chief. I'll show you later," Mac explained as he picked up Dax and began to carry him through the house.

I smiled, thankful that Mac was beginning to take things in stride.

As I looked around I had to laugh a little. The house was the biggest man cave I'd ever been in. More like an old-fashioned hunting lodge than a lakefront home, I'd counted two large screen TVs and we hadn't even made it past the front door. I looked to Polly and whispered, "I hope there's a kitchen."

"I just hope I don't have to stand to pee," she replied.

"King, I need to set up and make a few phone calls. Is there somewhere I can do that?"

"Sure, first door on the right down the hall. It was Dad's man cave," said King.

"The whole place looks like a cave to me," Mimi chimed. "I just need a place to lay my ninety-nine year old butt for a few hours. I'm not as spry as I used to be."

"I should get Miss Nancy to bed too," Celia agreed.

"I'll show you to the room," King gestured as he walked past them to follow him. "I know you're used to being in a room by yourself, but we're gonna be tight on space. Especially if we have FBI agents too."

"Sweetheart, I don't give a damn. Just point me in the right direction so I can rest my eyes for a spell," Mimi said.

King disappeared for a few minutes while the rest of us wandered the great room that connected to the kitchen. I opened the refrigerator and found it completely stocked. We'd have breakfast in the morning for sure, if we could just get to bed.

I grabbed a bottle of water and twisted the top, taking a long cold drink. Nothing had ever tasted so good to me. I felt guilty as I watched Katy, Dax and Polly lying like ragdolls on the sectional couch.

"Polly?"

"What?" Her voice cracked with exhaustion.

"Are you thirsty?" I asked as I carefully inspected the side of the house that was completely glass. In the dead of the night it was hard to imagine what was beyond, but I assumed it was the lake.

"No. I just want to go to bed. This has been the longest day of my life – like, ever."

"Mine too," I agreed.

"Polly?" King called to her.

"Yes?"

"Let me show you to your room."

"I need the bassinet from the car. I'm keeping Katy with me tonight," Polly explained.

"I've got it," Mac offered as he came back through the front door.

"How'd you get past me?" I asked, looking down the hall and back to the front entrance.

"There's a door off the office. I took a look around and set up the agents outside," he said as he sat the wicker bassinet on the floor.

King raised his eyebrows and cocked his head. I knew by the expressions he'd had enough of Mac. "I should show you how to work the alarm if you're going to be in and out tonight."

"It can wait," he replied. "Let's just get the women and children to bed. I'll worry about security."

King nodded and looked back to Polly. "Your room is ready, Polly. You'll be next to Miss Celia. The two rooms share a bathroom. I hope that's okay."

"Sure," Polly yawned. "Do I have to share a urinal with them too?"

"Don't worry. There's a toilet in the bathroom and it's stocked for you."

"Stocked with what?" Polly laughed. "Booze? Cause if there's a cocktail waiting for me I might have to kiss you."

"If I'd known that, I would've set you up downstairs in the guestroom near the bar."

"Damn," she laughed, picking up the bassinet and following King. "Just my luck."

"Polly," Mac jumped to get her attention. "Give me the bassinet. You take Katy."

Mac and I kissed her on the head. I'd fed her in the car on the way to the lake house. At least I knew she'd sleep for a while. Dax was another problem.

As King led Polly and Mac down the hall, I fell back onto the couch and cuddled with Dax, wondering how he'd react to not being close to Polly and Katy.

When King and Mac returned, Mac gave me the tiniest smile letting me know we were next.

"Where's Dax sleeping?" I asked.

"There's a little bed for him in Miss Celia's room," King replied.

"I'll carry him back, honey. Celia's getting Mom and Mimi settled and into their pajamas."

"Tomorrow Aurelia will be here to help with the older ladies. She's a nurse, among other things. She'll be a big help... to everyone," King offered with a tired sigh. "Sam, I showed Mac where you will be sleeping."

"King has graciously given us the master suite," said Mac.

"Oh, King. No," I protested. "You've left your practice in Shadeland, brought this circus into your lake house and now you're giving up your bed? It's too much."

"Look, Sam," King replied. "I would never want to spend my wedding night in a house on Lake Pontchartrain, but you are. Just let me do this for you. Besides," he confessed with comical grimace, "I didn't have a chance to get you a wedding gift."

"Okay," I agreed, dropping my shoulders. I couldn't fight anyone anymore. I was done. I was beyond done.

"C'mon babe," Mac said, taking my hand and leading me up the stairs to the bedroom.

"Goodnight," King waved as we took the wooden spiral staircase up and onto the second floor.

I looked to Mac and shook my head. As soon as we were alone I let down my guard and began to sob.

"Shhhhhhh," he whispered into my shoulder as I cried uncontrollably.

Picking me up, Mac carried me down the hall and to a set of double doors. Leaning down to open them, I sniffed and turned my head to watch as Mac carried me over the threshold of the bedroom.

Still holding me in his arms, he flipped the light switch and illuminated the dark room. I rubbed my eyes, unable to believe what I was seeing. There were roses everywhere. But how?

I looked to Mac as he laid me down on the turned-down bed. "Did you do this?" I hiccupped, still crying.

"King helped me," Mac confessed. "His housekeeper came and stocked the kitchen and made sure all the rooms were ready. I asked him if she could put some roses by the bed for you. I didn't know he'd done all this."

I pulled Mac close. I was mentally and physically exhausted. "I love you, Mac. I do. But you can't keep anything from me ever again. Do you understand?"

"I hope you understand *why* I kept things from you."

"I know you want to protect me, but we're a team — a family. I'm no longer on a need to know basis. I *need* to know," I insisted as I lay down on the enormous down-filled bed. I released the tension in my body and the soft pillow-top enveloped me.

"Agreed," he said as he moved a pillow behind my head. "I'm going to get your luggage in case you want to freshen up. Then I'll check with King and give some orders to the agents on guard about securing the house for the night."

I nodded, groggy from the tears and closed my eyes. "Don't be long," I begged softly.

I awoke to the smell of bacon and sunlight through a wall of windows. Looking to my right, I hoped to find Mac. What I found instead was a warm spot, letting me know I'd just missed him.

I rolled over, searching for my phone to check the time. Seven-fifteen seemed early and the three hours of sleep had only made me feel worse.

I rolled out of bed dressed in only Mac's t-shirt. Too tired last night to even begin to sort through a suitcase packed for Paris, Mac had graciously given me the shirt off his back. He slept naked – as usual.

Surprisingly, I didn't even mind that I didn't get to wear the fancy Carine Gilson chemise and kimono set my mother had given me as a gift. I loved sleeping in Mac's shirts. They always smelled like him.

Pulling on the jeans I wore last night and a sweatshirt, I glanced at myself in the mirror and made a face. My hair was scary. The leftover curls and hairspray from my wedding day were a hot mess. Running my fingers through my hair, I pulled the mop that was once a masterpiece into a tight ponytail. As I searched my purse for a hairband to secure it, I heard a knock.

"Come in."

"Sam?" Polly asked, peeking around the corner.

"Hey," I sighed.

"What the hell? Where'd all this come from?" she asked as she turned in a circle, admiring the hundreds of roses covering the room.

"Mac asked King to help make our night special. This is what King's housekeeper did."

"Well, she's a little creepy, but at least she comes through in a pinch."

"Creepy? What do you mean?"

"Nothing." Polly quickly changed the subject. "How are you?"

"I'm fine," I said, shaking my head. "How are *you*? Did Katy sleep through the night?"

"Of course. Not a care in the world. Miss Celia's feeding her now."

"Mimi and Nancy?"

"They're both up and eating breakfast. Mac's mom is a little confused. She tried to leave the house. Said she was going home."

"Did Mac stop her?"

"He was on the phone. Speaking of which, he took mine."

"Took your what?"

"My phone. He took everyone's. King was none too pleased."

"Why?"

"Something about us being tracked. I dunno. Also, there's another agent on his way here."

"I'm so confused. Slow down, Polly."

Polly took my hand and led me to the bed to sit. "Let me make it simple. We are trapped in a testosterone-filled man house, unable to go anywhere and unable to call anyone. We're fucked."

"We're not staying here forever, Polly. Just until we

know Hector's whereabouts. Then we can go home…or something," I trailed off.

"Look, I really hate bitching to you about all of this. You're supposed to be having day and night sex in the city of love, and instead you're here with us."

"No," I agreed. "Bitch. Maybe it'll make us both feel better."

"C'mon, Sam. Don't you just wanna scream your head off? This is so unfair."

"Yeah, well we both know life's not fair." I stood and walked to the bathroom. "Tell Mac I'm taking a shower and I'll be down in a bit."

Polly paused and dropped her head. "I'm sorry."

"Don't be. This sucks."

"This sucks ass," Polly murmured.

"I heard that," I shouted over my shoulder.

I made my way down the stairs to find everyone was present and accounted for. Mimi and Nancy sat on the couch and watched a morning news show on the big screen TV while Dax colored at the huge table in the dining room.

The table was made for a crowd of at least twenty, and I immediately thought that maybe it had come from an old tavern somewhere. Dax was dwarfed by the size of the table and looked like a little elf hard at work.

The house was even bigger in the daylight, and I took it all in. On the walls were animals from what had to be big game hunts, including a warthog and a zebra head.

The house was open, one area easily moving into the other. The gaping two-story great room had a bridge that went across the top floor between bedrooms.

The hand-hewn beams were massive and only added to the lodge atmosphere. I walked the staircase down, thankful that the children were on the first floor and would have no need to navigate the curling and intricate wooden spiral.

"Good morning," I said as I kissed Dax on the head.

"Mommy, your hair's wet."

"I know. I couldn't find a hairdryer. What are you drawing?"

"That's me," Dax explained as he pointed to the small figure. "And that's Coco."

"Who's Coco?"

"He's been drawing the agents all morning at their posts," Mimi chimed in.

"Sorry about the hairdryer, Sam," King apologized, walking into the great room. "I don't use one and..."

"It's fine, King. And thank you for arranging the flowers last night," I said as I stood on my toes to give him a hug. "It was a nice touch."

"Just trying to help out."

"You always seem to help out, King. When are we going to find you a nice Southern girl?" I asked.

He smiled and shook his head. "I don't know."

"Good morning, Mrs. Callahan," Mac chimed as he walked out of the office door and into the great room. He whisked himself between King and me very impolitely, picking me up and kissing me on the lips. I gave him a scowl to let him know he was being rude and he quickly gave me one of his wicked half grins, hoping any angry thoughts I might have would fly right out of my head. I couldn't blame him. It had worked in the past. But not today.

"What's this I hear about you taking everyone's phone?" I asked.

"Can't take any chances. If someone needs to make a call, they can use mine. I've taken all the batteries out of the phones. They're completely dead. I'll get you a burner phone today, Sam."

Mac looked over his shoulder to King. "You and Sam can share it. Okay? But no calls until we have a plan."

"When's that going to be?" Mimi asked. "Don't get me wrong, I'm old and no one is looking for me other than my poker buddies at the old geezer's home – I make four. But I would like to know how long we're going to be locked up in the henhouse. What did Polly call us? Man slaves?"

"Man cave, Mimi. Man cave," Polly shouted, making sure Mimi heard her correctly.

"Well, you don't have to yell about it. I'm old, honey, but I'm not deaf."

Polly looked to King and grimaced. "Sorry."

"No offense taken," King smiled. "It *is* a man cave. It was designed to be."

"To answer your question, Mimi," Mac continued, "another agent will be here any moment. We have a conference call with Washington in an hour, and I'll know more then. I promise I don't want any of us to be here any longer than we have to be."

"Who's the other agent?" I asked.

"Leonidus Xanthis. They call him Z."

11

MAC

I waited for Z to report and began going over the information the D.C. office had sent to me, including a new and disturbing photograph.

I dialed my old office, hoping to hear a familiar voice. I needed to ask some questions and I knew who might have the answers.

"Micah, old girl. How's it going? Have you threatened to rip anyone's throat out today?"

"Fuck off, Mac," she rasped. "Do you know I had to drag ass in here in the middle of the night? No. Do you care? No."

"I've missed you too," I teased.

Micah had been my assistant at the Bureau from my start. She was thirty, attractive but wore too much makeup and jewelry and was from New Jersey. Micah acted like a man, worked like a dog and cursed like a trucker. We fought like brother and sister, but loved each other the same way. I'd do anything for her and she'd do the same for me. She was the perfect Betty Bureau – married to the job.

"What a shit-storm, Mac. Have you talked with Dan this

morning?"

"What's going on?"

"The cartel. We got confirmation that Hector Quintes has been cut off."

"He's rouge?"

"He's fucking nuts – that's what he is. DEA sent over the intel last night. Hector's own cartel is looking for him, and when they find him I have a feeling they plan on sending him home in pieces."

I took a deep breath and sat back in the old creaky chair. Hector had been pegged as Halcones, or falcon long ago. A term meaning he was the eyes and ears of the street. After his affair with the now dead Autumn Valley CEO became public, he provided unwelcome exposure and plenty of leads for the DEA and the FBI.

"What's the report say? Is there a hit out on him?"

"I'm putting you on speaker. Dan's here," Micah rasped.

"So is there a hit out on him?" I repeated.

"Latest phone tap led them to believe so. We're trying to confirm with our agent inside. Listen," Dan lowered his voice. "The report says they've killed Hector's son."

"The photo," I uttered as I took a long look at the picture of the bloody boy lying face down on a dirt road. I was used to seeing heinous crime scene photos. The ones involving kids were always the most disturbing. Now that I had children of my own, they were unbearable.

"He had a kid. The cartel got to him. Five year old boy named Diego," Dan sighed. "Maybe we should let Hector go and allow the cartel to take care of him."

"No way," I blurted.

"They think he's loco. And now that his son and lover are both dead, I would tend to agree with them," Micah added.

"He's crazy, armed, and set on revenge. That's just another day at the office, Micah."

"Like hell it is," she quipped.

"What are you trying to say? That I'm rusty?"

"No, Mac. You're not rusty. You're soft."

"Bullshit!"

"Okay, you two," Dan interjected. But Micah wasn't having any of it.

"Remember, I've known you from the beginning," Micah continued. "I knew the Mac who was the gentleman on the outside and underneath it all didn't give a shit about anyone or anything. You were balls out, all day, every day. Now you've got Sam and a family. Believe me, I think it's nice and all. You're just not the same person."

"Enough!" Dan shouted.

I clenched my teeth and leaned into the phone with disgust. "I'm *not* soft, Micah. Hector shouldn't be afraid of his drug lord. He should be afraid of *me*. I'll have this fucker's balls in my back pocket before this is all said and done. Don't…" I lowered my voice, mad as hell. "Don't fuck with me."

"*That's* the Mac I'm looking for. Where the hell has *he* been?" she shouted.

"I'm right here. Bring it on."

"I'll tell you who's bringing it," Dan interjected. "Z. He's on his way."

"Yeah, why are you sending BSU?"

"This is a Behavioral Sciences Unit case now," Dan explained.

"Micah, didn't you have a thing for Z at one time?" I asked, trying my best to ruffle her feathers for goading me.

"No. Although I've never understood how a man as fucking hot as Z has gone all these years without a woman.

God knows there've been plenty who've thrown themselves at him."

"Including you?" I prodded.

"You know I don't go for all that Southern gentleman crap. Give me an Italian stallion who's tan, works out, loves his mother and goes to Mass."

"Don't forget the tattoos, Micah. I know you love a man with a good snake, barbed wire cuff or crucifix on his body."

"You know it," Micah rumbled.

"Z should be there any time," Dan added, trying to deescalate our attitudes.

"Try to keep your women off of him," Micah added.

"I'll do my best," I said. "I'll check in later."

"Hey, Mac. You coming to D.C. or staying in the boonies?" Dan asked.

"Don't know yet. I'll keep ya posted."

I hung up and saw a black SUV kicking up dust as it roared up the long lane. I watched the car, windows down, music blaring, roll to a stop at the front door. Only one agent would travel in such an overt way. Leo Xanthis.

I could hear the knock at the door. Everyone had retired to various parts of the house as the morning came to a close. Sam was on the couch reading a magazine and sat alone in the room.

She rose to answer the door and I shook my head and shouted. "No one answers this door – no matter what, no matter who you think it is, no one answers this door but me."

"Fine," she protested as she quickly sat back down.

I opened the door and there he stood.

"Z," I nodded as I shook his hand.

"How y'all doin' out here in the middle of nowhere?" he asked, his accent dripping with the Cajun drawl he'd attracted so many girls with over the years.

"It's good to see you," I nodded.

I'd always liked Z. We'd been a little bit of a dynamic duo during our time at Quantico. The FBI Academy was never the same after we left.

"Samantha, darling," I said as I turned to her and shut the door. "I'd like you to meet Leo Xanthis, better known as Z."

I watched Sam light up with charm as she always did. Dressed in a pink skirt and blouse, she was clearly ready for a day on the Champs-Elysées in Paris and not King's lake house.

"Z, it's so nice to make your acquaintance."

Z took the hand Sam offered him and gave it a kiss without losing eye contact. "The pleasure is mine, cher," he drawled. "Please, call me Leo."

"Z," I continued. "This is my *wife*, Samantha."

"Wife? Isn't that just the cat's pajamas," Z continued, not taking his eyes from her. "When did *that* happen?"

"Yesterday," Sam blurted, seemingly taken by his charms.

Z snapped his head to meet me. "You should be off honeymooning with your gorgeous wife."

"Don't I know it," I sighed, running my hands through my hair.

"You look good, man," Z continued. "I mean to be on your honeymoon with a psychotic drug dealer hot on your trail."

He was dressed in a perfectly cut, dark blue three-piece suit and yet he wore no tie. Obviously tailored specifically for his muscular frame, he looked like he worked for the mob more than the FBI.

At six foot five, Z was a menacing presence and his dark, Greek skin made him look dangerous. Part of that was his hair.

Black, wavy and to his shoulders, he pulled it back in a ponytail most of the time. The women swooned over his hair. The other agents, including me, generally gave him a hard time about it. True to his Greek heritage, he wore it long and told everyone at Quantico he was really Samson and if he cut his hair, he'd lose the ability to kick all our asses.

Z wasn't a run of the mill agent, but he'd have to be a little crazy to work in BAU. It was the worst of the worst. Criminal minds were one thing, but sick criminal minds? That was another world and the idea that Hector had now been lumped into that category made me uneasy on more levels than one.

"Leo," Sam smiled. "May I get you something to drink? Sweet tea, perhaps?"

"Thank you, darlin'. You surely know the way to a man's heart," he sighed as he clasped his hand to his chest in gratitude.

"Have a seat, Z," I gestured to the large sectional couch that covered the open room. "Catch me up. I need to know."

"Thank you, cher," Z said as Sam handed each of us a tall glass of sweet tea.

"If you don't need anything else, I'm going to check in on the baby."

"Thank you, sweetheart," I smiled, leaning up to kiss

her cheek.

Z watched Sam glide from room to room with elegance. I knew the look on his face and witnessed it many times in the weeks we trained together at the Academy. He approved of her.

"You did a damn fine job there, Mac."

"Thank you. I'm the luckiest man in the world."

"And you have a new baby?"

"Yes. I guess that was in the file."

"No, she just said she was going to check on the baby. I just assumed it was yours."

"Sorry, Z," I sighed. "I'm just a little more than on edge right now. Before I never cared. Now I have a family to protect."

"I understand," Z said coolly. "You're only willin' to die for what you're livin' for."

I nodded.

Z shifted in his seat and took a long sip of his sweet tea, leaving it to rest on the table in front of him. "Hector Quintes has gone off the rails. He's considered armed and dangerous. He's been using aliases and classic stalking techniques, but at the same time he's not stalking in a possessive manner. He's not seeking to control Samantha or you."

"What then?"

"What fuels the soul like love but isn't as sweet? Revenge."

I sat quietly taking it all in. Z had a PhD in psychology, was smarter than hell, and tough as nails.

"Here's the whole story. Hector was sent into Alabama to set up part of a drug route from Mexico. The larger cartels have been using smaller towns to move through. They feel it's safer, they blend in with some of the migrant seasonal workers and no one really bothers them. I doubt anyone would've bothered Hector had you not exposed his love affair with the CEO of Autumn Valley."

"I agree."

"What we didn't know was that the CEO, James Miller, had been funneling Hector money. Whether it was a pay off or he was just funding his lover – pay for play, we don't know. That money has allowed Hector to remain mobile even after the cartel cut him off."

"And they cut him off because of me," I added.

"You and your takedown. Although if Hector had just kept his mouth shut and his hands to himself, he might've continued to fly under the radar, but he couldn't."

"He kidnapped Sam to kill her, blaming me for Miller's suicide," I added.

"He came from a poor, abusive family. Whether his immediate family knew he was gay or not, who knows. He found recognition and a sense of belonging in the cartel. Maybe he thought he and Miller would live happily ever after. Maybe not. As far as I can see, Hector Quintes wants Sam dead to make you pay for what happened to Miller. And in turn what happened to his kid."

"Yeah," I sighed, leaning back and running my hands through my hair. "I saw the photo. What was his son's name?"

"Diego." Z nodded. "In the beginning it was his rage that fueled him. When he didn't kill you, it became a game. Now that they've killed his son, well…"

"He blames me."

"Who knows, man? He's got nothing and nobody. And he's got nothing to lose."

"And I have everything."

"Unfortunately."

"Z, I need to get to D.C. I feel like I'm trapped here in the middle of nowhere when I need to be out there, looking for this man."

"I will say this," Z laughed. "You're off the beaten path. Hector would be hard pressed to find you here."

"I want him to find me, dammit. I want to blow his head off."

"I think you're too emotionally involved in the case, Mac. Besides. He's not looking for you."

"I'm looking for *him*," I ground through my teeth as I stood and began to pace the room. "Z, you know me. Hell, we're cut from the same cloth. Put yourself in my place. What would you do if a psychotic man was threatening your family and somehow, even though you've got the best trained agents watching your back, still finds a way to get to you? What would you do?"

"I'd find him."

"Exactly. So don't start your pyschobabble bullshit on me now, because you know what I'm going to do. And you'd do the same."

"Fine, but you've got to make some changes around here."

"Like what?"

"We need to get the elderly folks back to Shadeland. In the thick of it last night it was a good idea to just clear everyone out. But let's make a plan and get them under heavy supervision back at their nursing home."

"Agreed. What about King?"

"The doctor who owns this place? Let's get him home and out of harm's way as well. What about Sam and the children?"

"I'm not sending them back to Shadeland to be sitting ducks. And Sam won't leave them."

"Based on the notes sent by Hector it's Sam he's targeting, although I don't think at this point he'd pass up an opportunity to blow *your* head off."

"Lower your voice," I cautioned. "Sam is upset enough as it is."

"Where would you move them? Or would you stay here?" Z asked.

"I don't want them in the middle of nowhere even if I do surround them with agents. Hell, it'd take forever to get back up out here in the boonies."

Z sat back and took a long draw on his sweet tea and sighed.

"I'm sorry," I heard over my shoulder.

Polly walked into the room wearing a sundress, no doubt part of Sam's honeymoon trousseau.

"No, no, cher," Z's deep voice dripped with charm as he stood in Polly's presence. "The pleasure is mine."

"Polly, this is Leo Xanthis. Z, this is Polly, Sam's best friend."

Polly extended her hand to him and as expected, Z lifted it to his mouth for a kiss.

"So is it Leo or Z?" Polly asked. "I'm confused."

"And *I'm* smitten," Z drawled. "Z is my nickname, but you can call me anything you'd like."

Polly giggled a little and I watched the two have a moment that I promptly broke up. "Did you need something, Polly?"

"No. Not really. I... ah...no. Nothing. It was nice to meet you, Z."

"I'll see you soon," he smiled. "You can count on it."

Z watched Polly all the way out of the room and I shook my head. "You've not changed a bit."

"You used to be just like me. And you know it. We're cut from the same cloth. Remember?"

"I want to get to D.C. by morning. I can make arrangements for my mother and Miss Mimi to go back to Shadeland and I'll send King and Celia with them. I'll have Dan coordinate security at the nursing home, Sam's house and Lone Oak."

"Who does that leave here?" Z asked. "Your wife, your baby and her best friend?"

"And my son."

"You've been busy, my friend."

"Dax is Sam's son from her first marriage. She was a widow. I adopted him — day before yesterday as a matter of fact," I sighed, putting my face in my hands.

"Look, Mac," Z offered as he came to my side. "No one would fault you if you left this up to Dan and the boys in D.C. You know they're more than capable of handling this. It's been an emotional rollercoaster for you and it's not going to get much better until Hector's in custody."

"Yeah," I agreed, looking to the floor. Z had been a good friend over the years and I knew I could let down around him. "If we get the first group back to Shadeland, all that's left is Sam, Polly, Dax and Katy."

"I'll take them to my house in New Orleans. The place is a fortress. You know my family's history. There's more surveillance at the house on Third Street than Fort Knox."

"You'll watch over them while I go to Washington for a couple of days?"

"Of course."

"We need more agents than you, Z."

"I agree. How else would I have the time to get to know your friend Polly?"

"Dude, my family is in danger. Can you keep it in your pants until Hector is dead or behind bars?"

"They'll *all* be in good hands," he gruffed. "You take care of you. I'll take care of the rest."

12

SAMANTHA

I heard the front door close and decided it was safe to come back to the great room.

"How'd it go?" I asked.

Mac walked to me and whisked me off my feet, bringing my face to his for a long, drawn out kiss. I felt his hands rise up my back as he slowly brought my feet to the floor. "Have I told you how much I love you today?" he asked, leaning his forehead to mine.

"No. But we haven't really seen each other that much this morning," I confessed. "I take it that things went well with your friend Z?"

"We got some things worked out anyway. I'm going to send Mimi, Miss Celia and Momma back to Shadeland with King tonight."

"And then what?" I asked.

"And then we're going into New Orleans to a secured location with more agents and lots of surveillance."

"What location?" I asked as he took my hands in his and kissed them one by one.

"Z's home in the Garden District."

"And what does his home have that this one doesn't?" I asked. "I mean, I thought we were trying to hide."

"We're not hiding. We're staying safe. Believe me, I want Hector to think it's cool to walk around in the world and look for us. That's how we'll nail him."

"Really?" I smiled. "Because so far that tactic hasn't worked worth a flip."

"How do *you* know what we've done to look for him? Until yesterday you didn't even know he was out there looking for you."

"So it *is* me he wants," I whispered.

"He wants me," Mac corrected, pulling me close to make me feel safe. It wasn't working.

"Then why the notes about *me*?" I asked. "Why the lipstick? Why make sure I knew he was in *my* house?"

"He was in Lone Oak too, sweetheart."

"You know what I mean, Mac. I read the note." I inhaled, holding in the fear.

"What note?"

"I read the note from Hector on your desk. The one where he wanted to crush me like a butterfly or something. What he's *dreaming* of doing to me? I mean…"

"He's crazy, Samantha."

"I don't care what he is. He's after *me*. Not you."

"He wants to hurt anyone and everyone. He's no longer under the protection of the drug cartel he was working for. They were like his family, his stability. He had Miller *and* the drug cartel. Now he has nothing. He wants us, you and me, to feel his pain."

"Mac," I sighed as I began to pace the room with nervous energy. "I want this to be over."

"Don't you think I'd rather be sipping champagne with you in Paris? You know I would. And we will. Once Hector is gone for good, we can breathe easy and get on with our life."

"Can we? Because the last time I checked I believed he *was* gone. Then yesterday there's lipstick on my mirror making sure I never forget him."

"Samantha, I'm never going to let anything happen to you. You know that."

"I just wish things were different."

"Look at it this way," Mac smiled as he sat and pulled me into his lap. "If Miller hadn't been funneling money to his secretary to keep quiet about the affair with Hector, I would've never come to Autumn Valley and we wouldn't have met."

"You would have come to visit your mother and you know it," I insisted, unconvinced of how his logic worked.

"Everything happens for a reason, Sam. We were supposed to meet. We had a once in a lifetime chance of meeting and we did. Now we are married and have a new baby. All things that were never going to happen to me until I met you."

"Are you actually thanking Hector for bringing us together?"

"I'll thank him with some handcuffs on his wrists," he continued. "I'm saying we were meant to be together and someone like Hector isn't going to take any of that away from us. You, the kids, my mother and Miss Celia are all I have in this world. I'm not going to let anything happen to any of you. You have my word."

I sighed, knowing he meant everything he said. Mac Callahan was the most loyal, genuine man I'd ever known. The fact that he was as beautiful on the outside as he was on the inside was icing on the cake for me. He was my everything.

"It's not your word I want," I smiled. "It's my honeymoon and I want to *act* like it's my honeymoon. I've waited so long to be with you."

"Tonight, baby. Tonight," Mac growled.

Looking for Mimi, I found her and Mac's mother in their room together. Mimi was reading to Nancy as she'd done many times before at Autumn Valley.

"How's Miss Nancy doing?" I asked.

"It's just hard for us older folks to pick up and go like you young people. We have a routine and we like to stick with it. It makes us feel safe. Nancy and I are both a little out of our routine."

"Not for much longer," I smiled. "You're going back to Autumn Valley tonight. You and Miss Nancy both."

"And what about you, dear? Aren't you coming along?"

"Mac and I are staying behind with the kids and Polly."

"You're staying *here*?"

"We're moving into New Orleans. Another agent has a home there. Apparently it's a fortress of security. Mac's not comfortable with us going back to Lone Oak just yet. He wants to see if Hector makes a move."

"Well, you don't hit a hornets nest with a short stick, that's for sure."

"I don't think we're provoking Hector. Do you?"

"Honey, I think Hector's bat-shit crazy. His cheese slid off his cracker a while ago."

"I don't want to talk about it. Are you and Nancy doing okay? Has Nancy said anything?"

"Honey, I've been reading to her this morning, but I

think she's so confused as to where we are and what's going on. The only thing she's said today is the word *man*."

"Maybe she's referring to the décor of King's lake house," I joked.

"Did someone say my name?" King asked as he knocked and walked into the open door.

"I was just remarking on the testosterone-laden decorating style. That's all."

"Sam, are you making fun of my man cave?" he quipped with a dazzling smile.

King could somehow always make things seem okay. When Mac raided the office last year and Miller killed himself, King was there as a shoulder to cry on. When the FBI was questioning me, King was there offering support. For goodness sake, he was on duty in the emergency room the night Hector shot Mac and we both came in by ambulance. Now that Hector was back, he'd once again come to the rescue and offered a place to hide until we could make plans. King Giles was more of a guardian angel than a man.

"No, King," I replied as I stood and walked to him for a hug. "I was just thinking to myself that you are truly a guardian angel."

"Not really. I just seem to be in the right place at the right time. Or maybe it's the wrong place at the right time," he smirked as he hugged me tightly.

"Well, I'm thankful for you every day, Dr. Giles," Mimi chimed in. "It does an old woman's heart good to see a man so pretty on the outside have a good heart. Us old folks sometimes think the world has gone to hell in a hand basket based on how men act these days. You surely do an old Southern woman's heart good."

"Well, that's kind of you, Mimi," King drawled. "I think

mostly I just do my job."

"She's right, King. I just don't understand why you're still on the market."

"Maybe I've just not met the right girl yet." King uttered, looking to his feet to hide the redness that had crept into his face. "Speaking of Southern girls, how are my two favorite doing today? Aurelia told me everyone had their meds this morning on schedule."

"I'm fine, but I worry about Nancy," Mimi confessed. "She doesn't do well with change. But Sam says we're all going back to Shadeland tonight so maybe that will be better for her."

"We're going back to Shadeland?" King asked, raising a suspicious eyebrow.

"Mac is sending you home with Mimi, Nancy and Celia." I explained.

"And the rest of you?"

"Mac, Polly, the kids and I are going to New Orleans. Another FBI agent has a place there and security is tight – tight enough that we can breathe a little until Hector makes a move."

"And how long will that be?" King continued with the questioning.

"I don't know. A couple days, a week."

"It would've been nice to hear this from Mac."

"I know. I'm sorry you're hearing it from me. The other agent, Z, just left. This all just happened."

"What time are we leaving?"

"I don't know. Do you want me to ask Mac?"

"No, thank you," he dropped his head. "I think I feel emasculated enough for one day."

As King left the room, I dropped my shoulders. He didn't deserve this. He'd only been trying to help and all

Mac had done was keep him in the dark. I knew Mac respected King. They'd grown up together. I just think because King was, once upon a time, sweet on me as Mimi said, it still bothered Mac. I just needed all the men in my life to come together and help right now. King was doing his part. Mac was making me a little crazy.

I sat back down and took Mimi by the hand. "Will you be okay without me in Shadeland?"

"Hell, yes. I can keep an eye on that no good rotten Richard a lot better down the street instead of on the bayou. I just worry you're putting yourself in danger and you don't need too. Scum like Hector will always turn up. He doesn't know any other way."

"Like I said, Mimi, just until we know what Hector is up to."

"Humph," she protested.

"What are you trying to say? Spit it out."

"I'm saying you can't keep trouble from coming, but you don't have to give it a chair to sit on."

"We're just laying low until Hector makes a move, Mimi. That's all."

"Just make sure the next move he makes isn't check-mate."

I walked through the house looking for Mac. I wanted to tell him to be extra nice to King. I climbed the stairs and with each step felt worse about all that had transpired. We'd trampled through King's house and all over his feelings in the last two days. As I called for him, Polly found me in the master bedroom.

"Hey," she smiled. "Mac is outside on the phone. I didn't want you to walk all through the place."

"Thanks," I replied as I took a seat on the end of the bed. The red roses that covered the room had a fragrant but overwhelming smell.

"What's wrong?" Polly asked, sitting beside me. "Let me rephrase that. I know what's wrong. I guess I should ask what can I do for you?"

"Nothing," I sighed, throwing myself backwards on the bed, my feet still on the floor.

Polly did the same and we looked to the ceiling where I noticed for the first time mirrors.

"Ooooo," Polly sang. "Dr. King Giles just officially became Dr. Kinky."

I couldn't contain my laugh and we both burst out in giggles.

"I wonder what else King's got in here," Polly continued as we looked at each other in the mirror.

"Polly…" I said with disgust. "He's a gentleman. But—I'd be lying if I didn't say I was surprised."

"I'm not. He's hot. There's probably a red room up here somewhere. There's a door hidden in that knotty pine wall over there that leads to his red room of pain and submission," she jeered.

"Stop it, Polly. You've been reading too many erotic novels in your free time," I laughed. "It's funny, though."

"What?" Polly asked.

"I don't remember it this way last night. I thought there were windows over the bed. You know, like a huge skylight kind of thing. It matched that wall of glass. Maybe I was just too tired."

"No," said a deep voice from the door. "It *was* windows last night."

Polly and I both shot off the bed and stared in embarrassment and I wondered how long he'd been standing at the door.

I quickly filled the silence. "Hi, King. Ah, yeah. It wasn't like this last night. I mean I didn't *think* it was."

"Someone must've hit the button," King confessed with a sly smile as he walked to the bedside and pressed a recessed button on the side of the huge rustic bed.

The mirrors quickly changed to windows and I became red-faced. "Sorry. We weren't trying to snoop," I confessed.

"No problem," he continued as he sat down in the huge overstuffed chair by the bank of windowed walls. He looked like Gaston in *Beauty and the Beast* as the chair had a set of antlers at the top. Its mate sat cattycorner to him.

"I feel badly about taking your room, King."

"Don't. This room was meant for more than one person to enjoy."

I was at first taken aback by King's behavior. I wasn't used to seeing him like this. And then it occurred to me as he gave Polly a smile he wasn't talking about Mac and me—he was speaking directly to Polly.

"Polly, did I overhear you asking about a room of submission?"

"I'm sorry," Polly laughed nervously. "I was just making a joke. You know, trying to cheer Sam up."

"Okay then," he shrugged as if he had a secret and he rose from the chair. "I didn't mean to bother you girls. I just came in to get a few things from the closet. I want to take some things back to Shadeland. If you'll excuse the interruption."

"By all means," I insisted as I took Polly's hand and helped her from the massive bed. "We'll give you some privacy."

"No need," he continued as he moved toward the walk-in closet where I'd stored my luggage. "You never know, you might see where the secret door is hidden in the knotty pine...Polly."

Polly giggled nervously and I shoved her out the door, knowing we'd been caught. "We'll leave you to it."

I heard him laugh soft and low as we walked the hallway. "Oh my Lord," I winced. "What was that?"

"I don't know," Polly smiled. "But Dr. King Giles just got a *lot* more interesting."

"What do you think he wants to take back with him to Shadeland? Fishing gear or something?" I asked.

"I was thinking handcuffs and a riding crop."

13

MAC

"Yeah, Micah," I muttered as I paced the grassy area behind the lake house. "I understand. I just want to make sure each house is completely watched."

"We've got more agents covering the grounds of Lone Oak than before. No one can get in or out without being seen," Micah rasped.

"What about Autumn Valley?"

"There are agents guarding empty rooms. Meals have been delivered as if your mother and Mimi Peterson were actually in the room. Only the nurses and attending physician know the truth."

"Good. And how's it looking at Sam's house? No one is going back there, but I want to make sure it's secure."

"Yeah," she continued. "The guy, Sam's cousin? He's a dick, but other than that it's fine."

"That's funny. Mimi says the same thing about him."

"Tell Mimi I agree."

"What's going on?"

"He's giving the agents a hard time. I guess he wanted

to have some people over for something and they told him no and it turned into a shouting match. The agents held their ground. I didn't want to mention it. You're supposed to be on your honeymoon."

"Thanks for the update," I sighed as I rubbed my day-old beard with my hand and continued around and through my hair with frustration. "I met with Z. We're moving to the Garden District tomorrow in NOLA. He's there now making the arrangements."

"Good. You'll have secure phone lines from there."

"Speaking of phone lines. Now that I've heard Richard is trying to throw parties while we're away, let's just get a tap on the phone in the house at Sam's and get NSA to track the bastard. If Mimi doesn't trust him, we probably shouldn't either."

"Agreed."

"I'll check in tomorrow after we've changed locations."

"When are you coming to D.C.?"

"After tomorrow. I've not told Samantha yet that I'm leaving. She'll understand."

"If you say so."

"C'mon, Micah. Not you too."

"All I know is if I were supposed to be on my honeymoon, I'd be a bitch on wheels if you left me behind."

"Well, maybe that's the difference between you and Sam. She understands me."

"If you say so," Micah repeated.

"Yack at ya later," I sighed.

"Only if you're lucky."

I turned to find my bride waiting for me in the doorway of the front entrance. "Mac, sweetheart. Can you please fill King in on what's going on? I had to tell him he was leaving tonight. I think he feels bad enough. He's only been trying to help."

"Come here," I growled at her as I climbed the steps to the expansive porch that encompassed the house. I pulled her in tightly. The stress of the case was starting to wear on me and I was horny as hell. I looked around the lake house to see if there was a tool shed close by. I was *that* desperate.

I'd had a taste of Sam yesterday after the wedding, but it wasn't enough. It would never be enough.

"I need to get you alone. You look so sexy in your little spring dress," I whispered in her ear. "I want to clear this house out and have you all to myself."

"Don't forget Polly and the children will still be here," she sighed as I tickled her neck with kisses and felt her melt in my arms.

"I can handle your best friend and our children in the house," I whispered into her. "It's just a little much with the entire clan hanging around."

"I know," she agreed. "But if we get some quiet later tonight, I might have a little surprise for you."

Her words worked through me like a spark to a flame and I pressed my eager manhood into her as hard as I could manage.

"Not here," she whispered. "Not now."

"I can't wait much longer, blue eyes," I confessed as I caressed her long beautiful chestnut hair. "You know you can't tease me like you do and then walk away."

"Why?" she giggled.

"Because I have a hard time walking away – literally. Seriously, Sam," I murmured, pressing my face into her neck. "I'm dying here. Give me something."

She tilted her head back and pursed her lips. I pulled her close, uncontrollably grinding myself into her hip as I began to kiss her sweet lips.

I wanted more and felt my shoulders heave as I took a breath and pressed my tongue deeper into her mouth.

She met my passion with a vengeance and I felt my manhood ache to be released. As I pulled away to tell her we'd go for a drive – anything, just to have a few moments alone, she sucked my lip into her mouth, releasing it in a raptured slow motion, leaving me hungry for her body. As I bent my knees and picked her up and off the ground, she put her legs around me as I pressed her back to a post supporting the porch.

"Sam?" Polly sang as she threw open the door, catching us in a precarious position. "Oh!" she exclaimed as she turned her back and yelled, "Sorry!" slamming the door behind her.

"Well, shit," I blurted as Sam unwrapped her legs and slid back to the ground and our reality.

"At least it wasn't Miss Celia," I joked, trying to make light of the situation.

"Really, Mac. It was just Polly."

"Just Polly," I repeated and I pulled my hands from her body and adjusted the ache in my crotch. "Just Polly."

I looked to Sam as the tears began to well in her eyes. "I'm sorry." She shrugged her shoulders and looked to the ground.

"No, baby. I'm sorry," I apologized as I kissed her forehead and tugged at her neck to move closer to me. "It'll all work out. We've waited a long time to be together again. I can wait a little longer. I want it to be perfect."

"But…" Sam began as I shushed her.

"The quickie after the wedding doesn't count. I want to completely possess you for hours on end," I said, kissing her nose. "And I will."

We walked to the door together and as I began to open

it, Polly emerged again.

"Hi. Is it safe to come out now?" she asked with a smile.

"Yes," Sam grimaced, giving my hand a squeeze. "Were you looking for me?"

"Mac." She answered.

"You're looking for *me*?"

"It's your mom. Miss Celia is worried."

"Momma?" I asked as I came into the makeshift hospital room. "What's wrong?"

"She began to weep, Mac." Mimi explained. "I don't know why. We were reading for a while and when she didn't seem to respond I read to myself."

"May I have a moment alone with her?" I asked.

"Of course, darlin'," Mimi chimed as she used her walker to push herself from the chair.

"Mimi, let me help," Sam said as she rushed past me to get to her.

"We'll be just outside in the great room if you need anything," Sam explained as she shut the door behind her.

I turned to my mother and took her hands in mine. "Momma?" I begged. "Momma, it's Mac. Can you look at me?"

She looked away, staring out the window focusing on a slow-moving boat on Lake Pontchartrain. "Momma, please. I need to know you're okay."

I laid my head in her lap and released the air in my lungs, defeated. Helpless, I knew there was nothing I could do for my mother. There was no way to comfort her when she didn't know who I was. The confused look on her face broke my heart. I knew that she would never want to be this person. She loved life too much to end her days scared and confused.

I was actually thankful my father was gone. He loved her so much his heart couldn't take the life my mother now lived.

I turned my head in her lap and listened to her shallow breathing. "Momma, I just wish you could tell me if something is hurting or if something is wrong."

I felt her hand on my head as she began to stroke my hair. I didn't move, not knowing if it was more therapeutic for her or me. It'd been a tough couple of days on everyone and I loved that somehow she understood me. Maybe I just wanted to believe she was with me in the moment. Regardless, I loved feeling the connection with her.

"Mac," she whimpered.

"Yes," I breathed.

"Be careful."

"I'm always careful."

"Be careful," she repeated.

I looked up to her face and found her still staring out the window.

"Momma?" I asked, taking her face in my hands. "Look at me. Will you look at me?" I pleaded.

She turned her face and looked into my eyes. "My sweet boy."

"You know me," I gasped.

"Mac."

"Yes." I stood and pulled a chair to sit and face her.

"Mac," she said yet again, looking me in the eye. "Tell Mac to be careful."

"I'm Mac."

"Tell Mac to be careful," she said again, looking out the

window.

"I'll be careful," I whispered as I stood.

She was gone, and I hated myself for taking her from Autumn Valley for the wedding and then dragging her to Louisiana. If my dad were here, he would've told me to leave her where she was comfortable – where she knew more of her surroundings. He would tell me to think of her and not what I wanted for her.

I wanted to protect her the way she always wanted to protect me. I felt as if I was failing on so many fronts –as a son and a new husband. It occurred to me that I'd not held Katy or Dax all day. Too caught up in the FBI case, I'd let my new life fall by the wayside while pursuing Hector filled my every thought.

I told myself that I should go to D.C. and hand over the case. Tell them everything I knew and come back to be with my family.

My mother had always been such a source of strength for me. In my thirty years she'd never steered me in a wrong direction. Using a combination of gentle guiding and reminding me who I was when we were together helped me make big decisions in my life after Dad was gone.

Even though she'd really not said much, she knew what I needed to hear. I needed to be more careful. And I would.

I kissed her on the head and closed the door behind me, hoping she would be able to get some sleep in the middle of the whirlwind. I found Sam, the kids, Miss Celia and Mimi all waiting for me in the great room as I emerged.

"Is everything okay?" Sam asked as I walked to her.

She could tell by the look on my face I was upset. Standing immediately as I came closer, I hugged her tightly, almost squeezing the breath out of her body.

"Mac," she gasped. "What is it?"

"I just love you. That's all."

I watched Mimi and Celia give each other a nod as I closed my eyes, feigning off the lump in my throat.

I pulled away and took Katy from Celia's arms and sat on the large couch.

"I'm going to turn the case over to Dan and Z."

"What?" Sam asked.

"I'm turning it over. I'm too close. Hector's too volatile. My place is with you and the children."

"Are you sure you can handle having an arms-length distance from all that's going on?" Sam continued.

"Yes. Of course. Why wouldn't I?"

"No offense, Mac," Mimi began. "I know you, son. You're gonna stick to it 'til the last pea is out of the pod no matter what your mouth is sayin'."

"I'll be fine. It will be better if I'm here —with my family. Dax," I smiled, changing the subject. "Why don't you get a book and let's read a little so Miss Celia and Mimi can pack to leave tonight."

"Okie dokie," Dax said, running to his backpack hanging on the back of the dining room chair where he'd been coloring all day.

"Here," Dax said, tossing the book in my lap.

"Be careful. We don't want to knock your sister in the head."

"Sorry," he cried as he climbed onto the couch and scooted back to rest against the cushions.

"*I'll Love You Forever*," I remarked, giving the dog-eared paperback book the once-over.

"It's Mommy's favorite," Dax replied.

Sam looked at the book and smiled. "It *is* my favorite, but while you read I'm going to help Mimi and Miss Celia pack."

"Okay," Dax smiled. "Read, Daddy."

Before I could begin, Dax spoke up. "*I'll love you forever, I'll like you for always, as long as I'm living my baby you'll be.*" Dax looked me square in the eye. "I know this one. You'll like it."

14

SAMANTHA

We kissed Mimi, Nancy and Celia goodbye at the door as night had taken over the bayou and the frogs were singing in harmony on the water. One of the agents on post would take them to the airport in New Orleans where Mac had arranged for the jet to meet them.

I kissed Mimi on the cheek and noticed that Mac was having a hard time letting his mother go. Nancy was confused but kept a smile on her face, continuing to nod at everything Mac said. I took a deep breath, holding in my own tears. I knew it was so hard for Mac to see his mother this way – I was worried about the toll the last couple of days had taken on both her and Mimi.

"I love you, Momma. Do you understand?" Mac asked Nancy as he held both of her hands.

She nodded and kissed him on the cheek. "Be good," she smiled.

"I think everything's loaded," King announced as he came back through the entrance. "Mac, if you have any problems or questions about the house, let me know. I'll have Aurelia come back and secure it tomorrow after you've gone."

Mac smiled one last time at Nancy and nodded. He shook King's hand and slapped him on the back. I knew Mac appreciated everything King had done for us over the last twenty-four hours, not to mention watching over the older ladies and safely escorting them home to Alabama.

"King, I can't thank you enough," Mac nodded.

"I'm glad I could help out," he acknowledged. "I'll let you know when everyone is back at Autumn Valley safe and sound. A limo from the nursing home is coming to meet us on the tarmac and your man Timms is picking up Celia."

"We appreciate it, King. Thank you," I added, give him a hug.

"Here are the phones," Mac said as he handed the three phones back. "My only request is that you not speak or text of our whereabouts on your phone or otherwise. Understood?"

"Not a problem," King nodded. "Sam?"

"Yes?" I turned to him as I hugged Celia.

"I didn't get a chance to say goodbye to Polly. Will you let her know I'm sorry we didn't have an opportunity to…ah, talk," King fumbled.

"I'll let her know," I assured him. "She's putting the children to bed. I'm certain she'll be sad she missed saying goodbye."

"Tell her to take good care of my babies," Celia added.

"Don't worry, Miss Celia," Mac smiled. "We won't spoil them too much while they're away from you. I'd hate to return an unruly bunch back to you in Alabama."

"Just get *back* to Alabama. That's all I ask." Celia's voice cracked as she tried to hide her worry. "Come home soon, baby."

"We will."

Mac and I stood on the porch and waved as the black SUV drove away into the lonely night.

Mac shut the door behind us and gave me a long and tight hug. I felt his arms grow heavy around my waist and I knew he was as emotionally spent as I was.

"It's almost eight o'clock," he said, holding me tightly by the waist. "Are you hungry?"

"I've had such nervous knots in my stomach since we left Lone Oak, I don't know when I ate last."

Mac took me by the hand and led me into the kitchen. "Let's see what King's girl left us in the fridge. I could whip up a little something for my wife for dinner."

"Since when do you know how to cook?" I asked with a laugh.

"Since always."

"Miss Celia practically spoon feeds you. I've never, and I mean never, in the last year I've known you seen you cook."

"I barbeque," he protested.

"Cooking a steak or a hamburger doesn't count," I smiled, trying not to hurt his ego.

"I've been a bachelor so long, baby," he smiled. "I can made dinner out of almost anything. Now," he paused, sexily cocking his head to one side. "Whether or not you'll eat what I fix is another thing."

"I'll take my chances," I grinned.

"I was hoping you'd say that." He turned his attention back to the refrigerator. "Aha, I think King's kitchen help left us a little present."

"What?"

Mac pulled his head out of the refrigerator and present-ed a cast iron pot with a lid. "This looks like something…."

Releasing the lid, he leaned in and took a whiff. "Thank you, Jesus, it's shrimp étouffée. There *is* a God," he smiled.

Mac turned on the gas burner and sat the cold covered pot on the stove. "I'll give this a little stir and some heat and we've got dinner."

I nodded and dropped my head, suddenly overwhelmed. It was too much and I couldn't control the tears now that the older folks were gone and the children were tucked in for the night.

"Come here, baby," Mac whispered.

I buried my face in his chest and did my best to keep from sobbing. Biting my lip, I calmed myself as he rubbed my back without uttering a word.

After three big breaths, he kissed my forehead and whispered into my skin, "Let me draw you a bath, sweetheart. We can eat later."

I could only nod, knowing if I uttered a word I would crack – completely.

Turning off the stove, Mac left the etoufee in its covered pot on the burner and began to walk me out of the kitchen and up the twisted stairs.

As we neared the top, I saw Polly out of the corner of my eye. Mac gave her a nod and Polly smiled back. I wanted to say goodnight, but the word got stuck in my throat. I knew Polly understood my fears. She had them too. She was too good of a friend to let me know we were both scared.

The old cast iron claw-footed tub was a nice feminine addition to King's manly master bath. I looked around at the candles Mac had lit. The soft light bathed the pine-covered walls with warmth. After seeing the skylight change from windows to mirrors earlier, I knew that King's man cave was no doubt also used as a love nest. Southern gentlemen liked to woo their women and I was pretty sure King had wooed his fair share – especially from this quiet little location on the bayou.

I couldn't help but wonder as I soaked away the last twenty-four hours if King was joking or being serious about his secret room in the house. Part of me believed he was telling the truth. The other part thought that maybe he was just teasing Polly – knowing Polly would love the tease.

Music began to waft through the room and I opened my eyes as I slid down into the warm soapy water. The hidden speakers in the walls were playing a simple solo piano piece and the beauty of the music helped me to unwind a little bit more.

I sank deeper into the water and wondered what else King's little love nest contained.

The huge bathroom was covered in mirrors. More mirrors, I smiled to myself. Either King was really into himself or he liked to see exactly what he was doing.

The long marble vanity contained his and hers sinks and there were separate water closets for the toilet and the urinal.

There wasn't a television in the master bedroom, but a flat screen TV was built into the mirror in between the two sinks. King could shave, have sex and watch a football game all at the same time. I was beginning to rethink the love nest idea and moved back to man cave.

I giggled to myself as I pictured the scene.

I secretly hoped Mac wouldn't get any big ideas after being in this testosterone-laden haven. I loved the old world charm of our home. Massive in its size, Lone Oak had felt like home to me immediately.

I pictured Hector destroying the house or the grounds as catastrophic thinking took over my garbled mind. Then again, he seemed more intent on hurting me.

I thought back to the note I read in Mac's stack of papers and calmly reminded myself that Hector probably didn't just want to kill me—he wanted to torture me.

"I've brought you some wine, my dear," Mac said, breaking my thought and shutting the door behind him. All day Mac had worn an old pair of jeans and a plain t-shirt that hugged his chest in all the right places. He was sexy when he was dressed to the nines, as his muscles always seemed to stand out even under his clothes, and he was hot in his old jeans where I could gaze at his biceps as they stretched the band around the arm of his shirt. Not to mention the sexy bulge that always seemed to be just a little more accentuated when he wore jeans.

He carried two wine glasses, one bottle and a wicked grin.

"I hope you didn't raid King's wine cellar," I breathed into the bubbles, causing them to separate, revealing cleavage.

"Whatever we drink, I'll send a case of the same when we return."

I shifted in the tub and came to the edge. "That sounds like a fair trade."

Mac twisted the corkscrew, and I watched the muscles in his arms tense. With each turn I became mesmerized as his tan skin glistened in the candlelight.

"Baby," I uttered. "You are so sexy."

He shook his head at me and pulled the cork from the bottle.

"Don't be stealing my lines, love," he rasped, his voice deep and full of intention.

He poured the dark red wine into the glasses and came to the edge of the tub, placing my glass in my soapy hand. He sat on the floor.

"Aren't you going to join me?" I asked with a pout.

"I'm going to let you relax with your wine. I promise," he grinned. "I'm more than happy just to watch you."

I giggled, and it felt good to release the tension in my body. This was what my honeymoon was supposed to feel like.

"Here's to my beautiful wife," he said as the crystal glasses chimed with his toast. "My sun…"

"My moon…" I continued.

"And all my stars."

Mac leaned in and before kissing me gave my lips a fleeting lick with his tongue.

"Mmmmm" I moaned. "You're going to make me think dirty thoughts."

"You're on to me."

"It's so quiet. Is everyone tucked in?"

"Polly is reading, the children are fast asleep and there are agents at each door – the lane leading to, and all sides of the house."

"Geez," I swallowed. "How many agents?"

"Eight."

"That's a lot," I confessed.

"It will never be enough where you and the children are concerned. I'll take every precaution, use every agent they'll give me and take no prisoners when it comes to your safety."

"Wow," I whispered into my wine glass as I took another sip. "That's kinda sexy."

Mac laughed soft and low and the sound echoed off the glass ceiling. "Wanna see my big gun?" he teased.

"In a little while."

"Want me to wash your back?" he asked, picking up the sea sponge that hung on the wall with a loofah and an assortment of bath gels.

"Sure," I agreed, leaning forward and hugging my knees.

As Mac washed my back, I continued to relax. The combination of wine, candlelight and warm water was putting me in a trance. Mac began to hum to the piano music playing through the sound system as he filled the sponge with water and slowly squeezed it across my back.

"What are you singing?" I asked.

"*Fly Me To The Moon.*"

I smiled and turned around to see his face as he sat on the edge on the tub, humming.

"I'm finished washing your back," he said softly. "Want me to wash your front?"

I nodded and came to my knees as the water and bubbles dripped from my body.

"Samantha," he moaned as he stepped back from the tub. "You are the most beautiful thing I've ever seen. Ever."

"So are you," I agreed, standing up completely.

Pulling a towel from the rack behind the tub, in one motion he wrapped it around my body and lifted me from the water and into his arms.

"I hope you were finished with your bath," he whispered into my neck as he began to carry me into the bedroom.

I twisted the knob on the door and gave it a gentle push and we crossed the threshold into the bedroom.

I looked around in amazement. Mac had lit candles everywhere. The entire room was filled with them.

"How?" I asked as I looked to him in disbelief.

"All part of Dr. Love's stash," Mac smiled. "He let me

know where to find everything."

"So he knows you're planning on ravishing me in his bed tonight?"

"He knows I'm in love with my wife and I can't wait to show her just how much."

Mac sat me on the edge of the bed and toweled me off, quickly brushing any unwanted foam from my body.

I slid into and under the sheets quickly as the air was beginning to chill my skin.

"Am I on my own to undress?" Mac asked.

"No," I smiled. "I'm going to watch."

15

MAC

The room was aglow as Sam reclined in the bed waiting for me.

My first instinct was to get the hell out of everything as fast as I could so I could feel her naked body against mine. But I knew she wanted something else.

Slowly I reached for the collar of my shirt at the base of my neck. I pulled the t-shirt over my head in one protracted motion. Sam made a purring noise that got me hard in an instant, and I had to remind myself to go slow – for her.

As the shirt dropped to the ground, I paused and put my hands on my hips and gave her a smile.

She giggled and threw herself on her back, pulling the sheet up and over her eyes, squealing like a teenage girl.

I chuckled, embarrassed by what she was making me do, but refused to go any further until her eyes were on me again.

She returned to her side and propped her head up on her hand. "Continue," she whispered. "Please."

I began unbuttoning the front of my jeans, taking my time that each button was open completely before moving to the next.

A tiny gasp escaped Sam's mouth as she came to realize I wasn't wearing underwear.

"You're so naughty," she purred.

My crotch ached and I grabbed myself from the outside of my jeans and adjusted as Sam gave me another soft moan.

"Mmmmmmmm," she whimpered.

Placing my hands inside the waistband of the old Levis, it took only a nudge to get them past my rock hard erection.

They slid to the ground and I took zero time stepping out of them and kicking them to the side of the bed.

"You're beautiful," Sam sighed.

"You're stealing my lines again. You know how mad that makes me," I grinned.

Sam opened the sheet and held it for me to slide in beside her. Her perfect body was soft and warm and I pulled her close, pressing myself into her. I wanted her. It was desperate. Yet I didn't rush. I refused to hurry the moment. We'd bolted from our own wedding and shuffled through the wedding night surrounded by too many friends and family. I had Sam all to myself and tonight I was making it happen.

Hector himself could come crashing through the bank of windows flanking the master bedroom wall and I would end him with one shot and continue to make love to my wife.

I felt compelled to be inside Samantha. It was an uncontrollable need. I pressed my hard-on into her taut stomach and felt her shudder, fueling my desire to be inside her.

I encompassed Sam's tiny body under mine and as she writhed against me she let out a whimper. I could barely hold myself together and I hadn't even begun to make love to her. With each beat of my heart my shaft ached. I took a deep breath and began to kiss her body as I counted in my mind the many ways that I wanted to possess her.

I started with her lips—the taste of the woody merlot still lingered and I parted her mouth with my tongue to taste all of her. She moaned and I moved to her neck where she dropped her head to the side, inviting me in for more.

Taking a deep breath, I inhaled her sweet scent and traced the line of her collarbone with my tongue, feeling her body shudder under me. As I moved down to her beautiful breasts, I lightly stroked her soft skin and rolled my tongue along her tight nipple.

Samantha arched her back and I slid my hands and mouth lower to kiss her from hipbone to hipbone. Pulling up on my knees I stopped and looked at the beauty that was mine. Samantha was mine – all mine.

I pushed her knees forward, moving between her thighs. I knew what I wanted and she relinquished any control, opening herself up to me.

Throwing her arms over her head in surrender, she began to search the side of the bed as if she'd lost something.

"What is it baby?" I gasped.

She strained and I heard a click. "Look up," she whispered.

I turned my head and looked to the ceiling. The once tall and expansive skylight that revealed the stars was now nothing but mirrors.

Our naked bodies shone in the candlelight and my burgeoning erection throbbed.

"How?" I asked.

"King showed me where it was."

I couldn't contain the wickedly sexy thoughts running through my mind. "King, you ole dog, you."

"Mac Callahan," she purred. "Welcome to your honeymoon."

I kissed Samantha and quickly rolled her over on top of me. "This is amazing," I sighed as I gazed upon her beautiful body astride mine.

"What do you think King does in here?" Samantha asked as she leaned down and kissed my chest, running her fingers lightly across my nipples, sending a chill down my spine and driving me crazy.

"I don't care what King does in here," I ground through my teeth as I looked over Sam's shoulder and into the reflection of her beautiful body astride me.

I know what I'm gonna do in here.

Sam moved down and kissed my body as she positioned her head between my legs. My first instinct was to close my eyes, enjoying the intense feeling of Sam's lips on my straining shaft, but at the same time I couldn't look away. I'd never in all my days as a bachelor had an experience like this. It was fanfuckingtastic. I was mesmerized as Sam's head moved back and forth, bringing me in and out of her mouth. I was on sensory overload and I wanted more.

"Yes," I said, urging her on her performance.

Bringing me to the edge, I was dangerously close to climaxing when I pulled away from her. "No," my throat caught in a hoarse timbre from the desperation in my breathing.

"No?"

"Come here," I growled.

She smiled as she began to kiss her way up to my lips, stopping only for a moment to run her tongue across my hard nipple. I caressed her perfect bottom and my pulsing core tingled as I watched my hand grab her. I was watching my own private sexy-ass movie starring Samantha.

I lifted her hips and eased myself inside her as she gasped for air. She tossed her head back and caught her own reflection.

"I know why you want to be on the bottom," she whispered as she lay on me, brushing her hard nipples against my chest, driving herself forward.

"Oh God," I moaned as I watched and felt her move with fluid perfection. As she rocked her hips in slow, insistent circles, I nearly lost it and ended our perfect connection.

"Slow, baby," I begged. "I want this to last all night."

She lowered herself closer to me and positioned her beautiful breast over my mouth. I kissed her body, lifting my hips to meet her measured insistent rhythm.

As she moaned, I could feel her grip my body tightly from within and I quaked, unable to control the electricity arcing between our bodies.

"Oh noooo," I called aloud, unable to control the volume in my voice.

"Yes!" she responded as she leaned forward and began to give into the waves of passion.

I lifted her off the bed with my legs and turned her on a dime, laying her flat on her back without leaving her. I swayed her body back and forth with mine as I put my hands on her hips and pushed my way up and in, reaching for the bottom and the height of her soul. We arched in a frenzy of yearning.

"Ooooobaby," she cooed. "This is so hot."

Samantha grabbed my ass and opened herself deeper to me as I shook our bodies uncontrollably, exploding deep inside her and collapsing in a heap of spent flesh.

"Oh my God, I love my wife," I panted.

"Yes, you do."

We lay in silent perfection, naked on top of the sheets, staring at our bodies.

"You, my darling, are a rock star."

"You certainly make me feel like one," Samantha smiled, turning her body into mine, curling her leg across my hips and pulling me closer. "That was incredible."

"These mirrors are fantastic," I sighed with a smile as I caressed her bottom from her waist, down to her thigh and back up again.

"Don't be getting ideas, Mac," she smiled. "We are not retrofitting the bedroom at Lone Oak with ceiling mirrors."

"A man can dream, can't he?" I joked.

"Was it really that much better with the mirror?"

"Sweet Jesus. I loved watching you make love to me. It was hot. Like amazingly hot."

Samantha laughed and buried her face in my chest. God, I loved this woman. She indulged my fantasies, made me feel like a man and let me show my emotions without being judged. I wanted her to know every day for the rest of our lives how lucky I was to have her.

"Men are so visual," she murmured.

"Are you saying that when I turned you over and you could see me making love to you it wasn't sexy?"

"No," she agreed. "It was amazing. I loved watching your rock hard butt. It's just I love it when you stare through me with those beautiful green eyes of yours."

"Honey, I couldn't agree more. I love seeing your face when I take you places that no man has taken you before."

"I've never known a love like this. But then again, I'm not as experienced as you."

"What's that supposed to mean?" I teased.

"You know what I mean," she smiled. "Don't get me wrong. I feel as if I benefit from your years of learning how to do everything…right."

"Baby, none, and I mean none of those women ever meant anything to me. I love *you*. I've loved you from the moment I laid eyes on you in the hall at Autumn Valley."

"Mac, what if they don't catch Hector? What if he's in our lives forever? What if we are always looking over our shoulder waiting for him to show up?"

"That's not going to happen," I promised. I pulled her close and watched her body entwine with mine from above. "Hector's not going to lay a hand on you or anyone else. I promise."

"And you don't make promises you can't keep," she added.

I nodded in agreement, brushing my chin against her silky hair. "That's right."

We lay in silence and I felt her body twitch as she slowly fell into a deep slumber. I flung the sheet and thin blanket over our bodies, doing my best not to disturb her and sighed with contentment. I was so thankful that she would have a good night's rest. Tomorrow we would change locations with the children and Polly, and I would make my plans to return to D.C. It would be one of the hardest things in my FBI career, but I needed to be a husband and father first and a crime fighter second.

I watched Sam sleep as I gazed into the mirrors above. I finally had everything I'd ever wanted in life. I wasn't about to lose it.

I heard her scream. I ran to the window and saw him in the distance. I ran out of the room and down the stairs, grabbing my gun from the dresser. I shoved the magazine into the handle as I ran to the front door. I flung it open and there he stood. Alone in the grass, Hector held Samantha at arm's length, gripping her long brown ponytail and jerking her to attention as our eyes met.

"Who's in charge now?" he shouted. "Who?"

"Mac," Sam begged. "Tell him!"

"Hector," I shouted as I walked toward them. "Don't do anything stupid."

"Don't come any closer," he yelled.

Reaching behind his back, he pulled a gun from his pants and held it high in the air for me to see.

"Who's in charge now?" he shouted again.

"You're in charge!"

I watched Hector shake his head at me in disgust. "You piece of shit. You can't even protect your own family!" he yelled.

"Don't hurt my wife!"

"I decide who lives and who dies. Not you!"

"Please," I begged. "Let her go. Take me. Take me!"

Hector held the gun to Sam's head as she screamed, "Please!"

I heard the gunfire.

"NOOO!" I shouted.

I sat up in bed in a pool of sweat. Samantha was gone and I immediately began to call to her as I pulled on my jeans from last night. Without buttoning them, I grabbed my gun and ran down the spiral staircase shouting her name loudly. "Sam! Where are you?"

"Mac?" Polly shouted as she walked out of the kitchen carrying Dax on her hip. "What's wrong?"

"Where's Sam?" I shouted again.

"She's with Katy in the bedroom. Why?"

"Sam!" I shouted as I ran down the hall and into the guestroom.

She rocked slowly, feeding Katy a bottle.

"Oh God," I sighed, dropping my shoulders at the sight of her. She was safe and I was a wreck.

"What's wrong?" she whispered. "Katy's almost asleep."

Walking to her I fell to my knees, dropping the gun to my side and laying my sweating head in her lap. "I'm sorry, sweetheart," I apologized. I gripped her legs as she moved Katy to her shoulder and began to stroke my head.

"What's going on?" she whispered, the fear in her voice showing through.

I sighed, trying to catch my breath. "It was just a dream," I told myself aloud.

16

SAMANTHA

"Mac," I shouted up the stairs. "Polly and I have the kids packed."

"Be right down."

"Sooo," Polly sang with sarcasm as she walked in holding Katy in her arms and Dax by the hand. "How was your evening?"

"It was very nice, thank you," I replied, giving Dax a smile.

"I'll bet," Polly continued.

I shook my head at her, knowing she wanted details. I had to admit it was unfair for Polly to live with us the way she did. She'd not had a real date in a long time. Shadeland, Alabama was no place for her and we both knew it. She'd been the best friend a girl could ever have after Daniel died and we moved home to be close to Mimi.

I wasn't looking for a relationship, let alone a new husband, but I seemed to be the one who hit the jackpot. I knew Polly wanted a man of her own. I also knew that Mac made it hard for any other man to seem good enough. In my heart I felt Polly's days with us would be numbered. She'd talked about going back to school to get her Ph.D. and even talked about criminology now that she'd spent the last year living vicariously through Mac.

"King said to tell you he was sorry he didn't get to say goodbye and he was looking forward to spending some time with you once you made it back to Shadeland," I quipped.

"He did not," Polly smiled.

I tucked both of my lips in tightly and gave her a sarcastic head bob as I led Dax to an agent who would put him in the car.

"Sam," she begged, handing Katy over to me after Dax had cleared the room.

"I'm serious. If I didn't use the exact words I was pretty close."

"Really?" she asked with a smile.

"Really what?" Mac descended the spiral staircase with both our suitcases held high.

"I was just filling her in on what King said as he left last night."

"Based on what I know about King," Mac began, giving me an all-telling grin. "I don't know if he's the man for you or not, Polly."

"What?" she wailed as we all moved to the door and another agent gave Mac a nod to let him know we were ready to move out.

"You heard what I said," Mac continued as he passed the last of the luggage out the door.

"Is this about the mirrors on the ceiling?" Polly asked, deadly serious as she turned and walked back to the dining table to retrieve her cosmetics bag. "Because if it is, I'd like to draw my own conclusions about who and what kind of man is right for me."

Agent Leo Xanthis walked in as Polly raved on, her back

turned to the door.

"Believe it or not, Mac," she continued to rant. "It's been longer than I want to admit since I've had sex. And I'm not settling for just anyone. I want a real man who's kind and supportive. One who will sweep me off my motherfucking feet and make me feel like a goddamned Cinderella. So if King Giles wants to show me the mirrors on the ceiling of his bedroom or what's in his red room of pain, I think I might just have a look. Do you feel me?" she finished with gusto.

Turning on her heels, Mac, Leo and I stood at the door waiting.

"Well now," Leo uttered in his thick Cajun drawl. "I think I like this girl. C'mon cher, let's roll."

Leo walked to Polly and offered his arm to her. "I think the Big Easy and Miss Polly are gonna get along just fine," he smiled.

Polly remained silent, and I watched the heat of the moment fill her cheeks with embarrassment. I bit down on my bottom lip and tried not to smile. If I went there, a laugh was going to follow and I didn't want to embarrass Polly any more than she'd already embarrassed herself.

Polly took his arm and the silence in the room became uncomfortable. Everyone was thankful when Katy decided to give a little cry as she stretched her arms out of the blanket she was tightly wrapped in.

Leo and Polly walked to the cars and Mac smiled and shook his head at me. "Can't take her anywhere."

I walked out the door of King's lake house, never looking back.

With Mimi and Nancy secured in Shadeland and Celia and Richard taking care of our homes, all we needed to do was sit tight, let the FBI find Hector and then we could all go home and live happily ever after.

Mimi told me once to never look back, and I hadn't. I wasn't going that way.

We pulled through the gate of Z's home in the Garden District of New Orleans.

The Third Street home was like a beautiful jewel set in an amazing string of pearls along the neighborhood streets. The two story neoclassical home was about one hundred and fifty years old and contained everything an old Southern home should – pillars, a garden and charm.

The perfectly manicured lawn made me long for Lone Oak and the home I was anxious to make for us back in Alabama. The magnificent white manor Leo called home had always been known as Jackson House and was covered in ornate ironwork – a sign of wealth from years gone by.

As we pulled through the gate and into the circular cobblestone driveway I couldn't help but be impressed. I stepped out into the warm Louisiana sunshine and took a deep breath. The azaleas were in full bloom and the entire area was warm and inviting. It was like coming home to a place I'd never known.

A butler met us on the porch and gave Leo a "good day" bow. "Mr. Leo," he smiled. "It's good to have you back."

"Hello, Oscar," Leo smiled as he took a deep breath. "It's good to be back."

I unhooked Katy from the car seat as Polly did the same for Dax and looked up as I took in all that was the grounds of Jackson House.

"C'mon in, folks. Let's have a little sweet tea and talk over what's to become of us," Leo laughed as he waited at the door for us to make it into the entrance hall.

"I hate to miss the sweet tea, *y'all*," Polly interjected, giving the Southerners a little jab. "But I need to put a little girl down for a nap and a little boy probably needs some downtime too."

"Not a problem, cher," Leo replied with a smile.

"Oscar, will you escort Miss Polly to her guestroom and please tell Adelay that Polly will require her assistance."

"Oh," Polly breathed. "I don't need any assistance."

"Miss Polly," Leo drawled as he moved closer to her and took her hand. "We've some safety issues to cover, and I'd like to only go over them once. If that's alright with you."

"Sure, I mean, sorry." Polly's voice dropped.

"No, no," he smiled. "I'm the one who's sorry, cher. Just get the babies settled and come down directly."

"I'll help you, Polly, and then we can get back down for the ah…security briefing even sooner," I nodded with a smile, taking Polly's free hand in mine and urging her up the stairs with Katy in my arms and Dax in hers.

We followed Oscar to the second floor of the magnificent home. The white walls of the entrance made it seem even larger.

"Mr. Leo has you in the Golden Room, Miss Polly," Oscar explained as he opened the door and ushered us in.

It was warm and breathtaking in its ornate décor. Every single thing in the room was gold and the space reverberated in the color. The walls were covered in an ancient golden fabric that matched the bed and drapes. The mirrors were gold as was the furniture. The large canopy bed was draped in miles of gold fabric. It was as French and fancy as any photo of the Versailles home of King Louis.

"It's magnificent," I remarked.

"Wow," Polly smiled. "Can we bring in a bed for the baby and Dax?" she asked as she looked to the ceiling, admiring the crystal chandelier that was the center masterpiece of the room.

"No need, ma'am," Oscar smiled. "The golden room is connected through the washroom to the nursery. I hope that suits."

"It's wonderful, Oscar," I nodded. "I feel as though we are putting everyone out,"

"No, ma'am. Mr. Leo gave specific instructions that Miss Polly was to have a private room."

"Okay then," Polly smiled as she let go of Dax's hand and sat in an ornate chair by the window.

"Where am I sleeping?" Dax asked Oscar.

"Follow me, Master Callahan," he smiled, ushering him through a hidden door that led to the large marbled bathroom.

As he led us through, Oscar opened the door on the opposite side and looked to Dax. "You, fine sir, will be staying in the White Room."

We walked through the door Oscar held open into a blinding light. Like the Golden Room, everything in the White Room was white – the furniture, the bed and the crisp linens. A mound of white roses sat on a center table between a bed and a bassinet.

"It's a big boy bed," Dax smiled.

"Your sister has a bed as well." Oscar motioned toward a beautiful round bassinet complete with a white satin bow.

"It's beautiful," I smiled.

"Good day, everyone," a cheerful voice said from the door. We turned and a young girl of no more than twenty stood in the doorway in a khaki skirt and polo shirt. "I'm Adelay, and you must be Dax."

"I'm Dax!" he shouted, excited that someone knew his name already.

"Can you say Adelay?" she asked with an inviting smile.

Dax looked up to me as if to ask permission and I gave him a nod, letting him know it was okay to speak to her.

"Ad-ah-lay," he sounded out.

"Wonderful!" she shouted with enthusiasm. "We're going to have such fun, you and me. What do you think about that?"

"Polly's gonna make me nap," he scowled.

"It's up to your mother." Polly shook her head, making me the heavy.

"Katy needs a nap, but if you can play quietly and not wake her, I think that would be just fine."

"I have crayons," Dax announced to Adelay. "I'm a good draw-ler."

"C'est magnifique!" she smiled.

"What does that mean?" Dax asked.

"It means that is great," Adelay laughed.

"Great," he repeated.

I put Katy down in the bassinet for a nap and looked to Adelay for a sign that everything was okay.

"Mrs. Callahan," she smiled. "Here's a monitor to the room," she explained as she handed me a small hand-held television. It was the size of my phone, but the screen clearly showed the nursery and the attached bathroom.

"You'll be able to watch from this," Adelay assured me. "Don't worry. We'll be just fine."

I walked out of the room and looked to Oscar. "Don't worry, Mrs. Callahan. Adelay is wonderful with the children."

"No...no," I stuttered. "I'm sure she's great. I'm just feeling...relaxed for the first time in a couple of days."

"I understand, ma'am. The Big Easy will do that for you. Shall I show you to your room?"

"Absolutely."

Polly and I followed Oscar down the hall, giving each other looks as if we'd just checked into a luxury hotel that was too good to be true.

"Ma'am, you and Mr. Callahan will be in the Blue Room."

As he opened the door, I expected floor to ceiling blue, but was completely surprised. The room was a steely grey with silver accents and white linens. Beautiful, it opened onto a balcony that overlooked the back yard of the home.

The white curtains flowed into the room, catching the afternoon breeze with a vengeance.

"It's beautiful," I sighed.

"It is," Polly agreed. "I just expected it to be blue."

Oscar nodded but gave no explanation. I didn't want to push it, as it was more than what we would need for the next few days.

"Oscar," I smiled, taking his hand. "Thank you for getting us settled."

"My pleasure, Mrs. Callahan."

"Please," I begged. "Call me Sam."

"And I'm Polly."

Oscar nodded. "I think Mr. Leo wanted me to escort you back into the front parlor so you can join the discussion. I'll have some sweet tea brought in for you."

He escorted us down the grand white staircase and motioned for us to go left and into a beautiful parlor. Mac and Leo sat on the couch, file folders and legal pads in their hands.

I watched as Leo dropped a thick file folder on the coffee table.

"Leo," I smiled. "Thank you so much for taking us in like this. Your home is lovely."

"It's my pleasure, cher. I know if I were in the same position, Mac wouldn't hesitate to take me to Lone Oak. How you gettin' along at the old homestead anyway?"

"Sam just moved in. We were making it official after the honeymoon," Mac explained.

"I see," Leo sighed. "Well maybe *petit Paris* will do for a couple of days until we can get things under control and you can head to the other city of lights and love."

I nodded and he looked past me to catch Polly's eye.

"Do you prefer Leo? Or Z?" Polly asked as she took a seat in the room and made herself comfortable.

"Either," he smiled. "Most of the household calls me Leo. It's what my parents called me. But I've always been Z at the Bureau. I'm pretty sure Mac made sure of that."

"Yeah," Mac joked. "Because no one wanted to say Xanthis all the time. It made you sound like an evil comic book character. Z was easier."

"And what did they call you, sweetheart?" I asked Mac sarcastically as I sat on the couch beside him.

"Mac," he said flatly.

"We didn't want him to think he was Dirty Harry," Leo smirked.

"What?" Polly asked.

"You know, Clint Eastwood in *Dirty Harry.*"

"His name was Callahan?"

"See Mac, chicks just don't dig a man with a gun."

"Sure they do." Mac smiled my way as he picked up the folder.

"Ladies," Leo began as he pulled up a chair. "I've been

filling Mac in on what I've learned about this case in the last forty-eight hours. Mac will get more in Washington himself when he gets there tomorrow—"

"Wait. What?" I interrupted. "Mac, is there something you want to tell me?"

Mac gave a heavy sigh and stood and began to pace the room. "I was going to tell you this morning but didn't get a chance."

"Tell me now."

"I'm leaving for D.C. Just a couple of days to wrap things up. I'm still handing over the case, but I need to do it in person. I need to meet with Dan and not on a conference call."

I shook my head. "You're leaving us here?"

"You're in the best hands I know, Sam. Z's house is a fortress and no one is getting in or out."

"Including us," Polly sighed.

"Well, that's not entirely true, cher," Leo interjected. "I was hoping to show you around New Orleans while you were here."

I was confused and scared. I didn't want Mac to leave me in a strange city in a stranger's home while he ran off and played FBI agent. "Mac, I don't understand."

"I'll be back before you know it. I can work faster from D.C. where I'll have access to the DEA's records and everything the CIA might have on Hector."

"I don't know if you understand this or not, Samantha," Leo drawled. "But spooks and G-men aren't a house on fire."

"What?" I asked.

"CIA and FBI don't play nice in the sandbox," Polly explained.

"Nicely done, Miss Polly," Leo smiled.

"I'm going back to D.C. to do as much of the legwork as I can for Dan. The last thing I want is for Hector to go back into hiding and show up in six months to terrorize us. I want Hector caught, but as I promised I'm going off the case," Mac assured me.

"How are we going to make sure he doesn't go back into hiding?" I asked, looking to both of them.

"We're going to bait him a little, Samantha," Leo explained.

"What? How?"

"His drug cartel has all but abandoned him. We know this because we have a man on the inside."

"You mean inside the drug cartel?"

Mac and Leo both nodded calmly.

"What can *he* do?" I asked.

"Get word to Hector that his scare tactic didn't work and hope he'll be eager to make a move," Leo continued.

"Then what happens?" I asked.

"We track him and arrest him," Leo continued.

"Just like that?" Polly asked. "If it's that easy, how come it's taken until now to get to him?"

"Hector was not welcomed back into his drug family with open arms after trying to kill me. They knew the FBI would track him to the cartel. Frankly, I'm surprised they let him live. He had to lay low while they hoped the case would be filed away and they could find another avenue to run the drugs through the South. Small towns like Shadeland are a perfect hideout for drug runners. Local police don't know what to look for. They can fly under the radar, establish legitimate employment – like at Autumn Valley – and set up the exchange from the suppliers to dealers," Mac explained. "Problem was, Hector fell in love."

"With my boss."

Mac nodded. "Unfortunately. Hector fell in love with a sixty year old man who was living two lives. One as a pillar of the community with a wife and grown children and the other the unsuspecting gay lover of a drug dealer at the wrong time," Mac continued.

I listened and felt like for the first time I truly understood the whole story.

"Hector has probably repressed his homosexual feelings most of his life," Leo explained as he stood to pace the room. "Before Miller, we don't think he expressed his sexuality. That's why it made it all the more devastating when Miller committed suicide."

"And why he wanted some sort of retribution," Polly added.

"Yes," Leo agreed.

"Sam," Mac pleaded as he took my hands and pulled them to his mouth for a quick kiss. "You know I wouldn't leave you unless I absolutely had to. But I feel it's the best way to wrap the case quickly."

I nodded and looked to the floor.

"And then we can go to Paris for our honeymoon," he added.

"I think I might need a vacation from all this vacationing before we make plans to leave the country," I confessed.

"Whatever you like, baby."

"Hector's probably psychotic, Sam," Leo explained. "Now whether that's due to some past emotional trauma before he ever made it to Shadeland and his affair with Miller, or it's a result of a combination of lots of things, Miller's suicide, the death of his son Diego, schizophrenia, bipolar…" Leo trailed.

"Wait." I stopped the conversation and stood. "Hector had a son? And he's dead?"

"I wasn't going to tell you that," Mac frowned in Leo's direction. "But yes. We think the cartel killed his young boy. It's part of why he's off the rails."

"He's certainly delusional," Polly offered.

"Interesting diagnosis, Polly," Leo nodded.

"Polly's a psychologist. We went to Princeton together," I mumbled as I watched Leo give Polly the once over from head to toe as I wrapped my head around Hector's loss. I felt bad for Hector. Even though I knew he wanted me dead, somehow I felt bad for his young son.

"Jersey girl, huh?" Leo drawled.

"Where did you go to school, Leo?" Polly asked.

"Stanford," he drawled.

"But you live in New Orleans?"

"I live in Fredericksburg, Virginia. Just outside of Quantico."

"Z's part of the Behavioral Analysis Unit," Mac added.

I watched as Leo and Polly maintained eye contact. We talked around them as if they were part of our conversation. They weren't. They were carrying on their own tête-à-tête with their eyes.

I gave Mac a frown as they looked at each other without saying a word. Leo with his dark skin and eyes was as mysterious as I would expect a psychologist from New Orleans to be. His shoulder length hair was always tied back in ponytail, but it gave him an edginess that I knew was a turn-on for Polly. He was far from the FBI norm, wearing dark jeans, black ankle boots and a white linen shirt that remained untucked. He was badass, and I could tell by the look in Polly's eyes she thought he was hotter than hell.

In return, Polly's long legs and Midwestern charm seemed to be working on the gentleman from Louisiana.

"Z," Mac finally spoke. "What do the ladies need to

know about the grounds here?"

"Yes," Leo continued as he broke his stare on Polly and moved to the other side of the room. "It's pretty simple. I come from a long line of bootleggers in the South. My family immigrated long ago from Greece and my great grandfather and grandfather made the family– ah, fortune – so to speak, in providing illegal alcohol for more than a few decades."

"That's interesting," Polly chimed as she sunk deeper into the oversized green chair.

"It is," he agreed. "Of course the family diversified as prohibition came to a close and now we're primarily involved in textiles."

"Except for you," Polly added.

"Correct," Leo continued as he paced the room. "But the surveillance system has remained in the house and has been updated year after year. It was something my dad was fanatical about, and well, my mom..." he trailed.

"What Z's saying," Mac interrupted. "Is that this place is Fort Knox. No one gets in or out without being seen. This house is secure."

Leo turned to us and nodded. "It's why we brought you here. I want you to feel safe and I want you to make yourself at home."

Leo smiled and turned to Polly. "As much as you possibly can."

17

POLLY

For the first time in a long time I didn't feel like the third wheel. I wasn't the extra person in the room. It had been at least two years since a handsome, intelligent man seemed interested in me.

The beautiful Leo Xanthis had been watching me all day. Maybe it was because he overheard me talk about the mirrors on the ceiling at King's house, but I didn't care. I'd been appropriately embarrassed and went on my way.

Z. What a sexy name. Although as he walked the room and explained the security system of his beautiful home I rolled the name Leo over and over in my mind and fantasized about what his dark wavy locks would look like out of the ponytail.

I didn't stop there. I wondered what his body looked like under the form-fitting jeans he was wearing ever so sexily. And I fantasized he had an unusual tattoo only a very few lucky ladies had seen.

Who was I kidding? This man's body had been seen and satisfied by plenty of women. Besides, he was probably not even into blondes.

I dropped my head, disgusted with myself. In two short minutes I had a man drooling over me, analyzed him, wondered what he looked like naked and told myself he wouldn't be interested in me. I was a psychology major that needed psychological help.

I took a big breath and decided, as with most in the mental health field, I was nuts.

"Is something wrong, cher?" Leo asked.

"I'm just tired. The children were up early and I didn't want to disturb Mac and Sam," I smiled as I looked at them all happy, newly married and fresh from a night's worth of hot sex and mirrors on the ceiling.

"If you're havin' a sinkin' spell, let me take you up to your room to rest," he cooed.

Was he coming on to me? Or was this genuine concern? I looked to Sam for a cue and she only smiled.

"That would be nice," I agreed.

Leo took my hand and balanced my body as I pulled myself from deep inside the chair. "Thank you."

"My pleasure, cher. Mac, I'll return momentarily. Please make yourselves at home."

Sam gave me a smile and Mac raised one suspicious eyebrow in my direction to which I promptly scowled when Leo wasn't looking.

"Come this way, cher."

I held onto his arm as we walked the long staircase up to the second floor.

"So I'm curious, Z."

"Please, call me Leo." He spoke soft and low. "That is, unless you want me to treat you like one of the boys from the Bureau."

"So I'm curious....Leo," I corrected. "Why all the *cher* business? Like French, chéri?"

"It's just a term of endearment. Like darlin' or sweet-heart."

"I see. And you call all women *darlin*?" I asked, punch-ing the word with as much Southern drawl as I was capable.

"No, ma'am."

"What?" I laughed. "Of course you do. I've heard you say it the entire time I've been around you."

"I've only said it to you. But I won't if you don't like it, Polly."

"I didn't say *that*," I stuttered as he opened the door to the Golden Room. "This room is exquisite, by the way."

"I wanted you to have it especially," he smiled as he looked around the room.

"Really?" I asked with nervous anticipation. "Why?"

"The room faces due west. It's a beautiful sunset in the afternoon. It glows like your own personal ray of sunshine around five-thirty," he drawled.

"Really?" I hung onto the word, conforming my speech to match his.

Leo walked to the French doors and opened them wide as a burst of light and fresh air entered the room. "This is a wonderful place for a mint julep in the evening," he mused as he looked over the western end of the property.

"How do you go from Stanford to the FBI?"

"I didn't. I went from Stanford to Yale for my Ph.D. Then Quantico and the Academy."

"I don't understand guys like you and Mac. Your fami-lies have everything. They can give you everything. I mean, you don't need to work. And you *really* don't need to work in a job where you have a badge and a gun."

"Everything you say is true," he agreed.

"So why?" I asked. "I mean, if I'm not getting too per-sonal."

"Why stop now?" he smirked.

Leo stood in the doorway, and I watched his rugged face as the wind blew his hair. He was all sex with obvious intelligence. I didn't know what I wanted to screw first – his mind or his body.

"Mac and I are alike, I suppose. Two men with everything and yet willing to risk it all for a job they don't need."

"What do you think that says about you?" I asked.

"Are you analyzing me, Miss Benson?"

"How'd you know my name?"

"Polly Benson, twenty-seven from Montana. Your dad was a banker and your mother a homemaker. They died in a bus accident while vacationing in Chile. You're an only child and you met Samantha at Princeton. You've got a degree in psychology, and you stayed with Samantha after her husband died and she was pregnant. I doubt that helping your best friend raise her two children now that she's remarried is your idea of a challenge, so I'm wondering what might be next for you."

"Jesus," I sighed. "I guess when you work for the FBI you can find out pretty much anything you want to about a girl."

"Why don't you take a rest? I'll have someone wake you so you can dress for dinner," he smiled as his dark eyes twinkled in the sunlight.

"What about the sunset...the mint juleps?"

"We'll do it another night," he nodded and turned to leave.

I watched him all the way out the door. He pulled the door shut and didn't look back. I didn't know what had just happened, but I was pretty sure even though Leo Xanthis hadn't touched my body, my mind felt a little violated. And as I lay down on the bed and stared out the window, I sighed. I had to admit, I liked the feeling.

"Polly?"

I opened my eyes to find Samantha sitting beside me on the bed.

"Did you have a nice nap?" she asked.

"How long have I been asleep?"

"Just a couple of hours. I wanted to wake you in case you wanted to shower before dinner."

"Sam?" I asked as I sat and rubbed my puffy eyes. "What do you think of Leo?"

"Leo," she paused.

"He's different. I mean he's beautiful and all, but I get the feeling he likes to get inside a woman's head as much as he enjoys getting inside her... you know."

"What did he say?"

"I don't know. He knows a crazy amount of information about me. Why do you think that is?"

"I'm sure he's got files on all of us. If he's invited us into his home he's checked us all out. Mac says he's brilliant. All I know is if he's the key to bringing Hector out of the woodwork so we can put him away for good, I'm all for it."

"I agree," I sighed as I flopped onto my back and re-called my *cher* conversation with him.

"If you don't like the extra attention, I'll tell Mac. He'll have him back off."

"God no," I wailed. "Do you know how long it's been since a man has paid *any* attention to me? Years."

"If I remember correctly, someone was canoodling with Dr. King Giles at my wedding not three days ago."

"Yeah, well. That was probably the champagne and the deep voice."

Sam laughed and I joined her. It felt good to release the

tension by giggling with her again.

"You really aren't interested in King?" Sam asked.

"There's something about being with a man that knows more about my vagina than I do that is a little off-putting."

"He's not a gynecologist, Polly."

"He's a doctor, for crying out loud. And I suspect he's spent a little off-duty time down there anyway."

"Every man thinks he's a part-time gynecologist," Sam laughed. "Really though, I think King is looking forward to you coming back to Shadeland when this is all said and done."

"And what will I do in Shadeland, Sam? Miss Celia's going to raise the kids and you know it."

"You'll always be their *Polly*. Dax won't ever let anyone take your place."

I smiled knowing that my little Dax and I had a special bond that time and distance would never erase. I loved Celia and I was glad that Sam and Mac had her to raise the children at Lone Oak, but I wasn't sure if Shadeland was the place for me anymore.

"I'd never leave your life for good. But after this is all over and Hector is in jail, I might need to find my own way. You've got a wonderful husband, two beautiful children and an amazing future ahead of you. My work here is done," I smiled.

"I know I shouldn't be selfish and want you to stick around. I know this."

"And you won't be."

"What do you want to do next?"

"I'm thinking I want to go back to school. Get my Ph.D."

"I guess Leo has his, huh?"

"Yeah, he's Dr. Leo Xanthis," I sighed.

"King would call him a paper doctor. Polly," Sam remarked as she sat up in bed next to me. "You could have two doctors pining away for you. What do you think about that?"

"If that's true, I'm wondering why my life was void of men for so long and all at once two amazing men show up?"

"When it rains, sister. It pours."

We giggled and I heard a knock at the door. "Come in," I shouted.

Mac opened the door and immediately shook his head.

"Don't be jealous, Mac," Sam laughed as she bounded off the bed and into his arms.

"I'm not jealous, baby. But I am here to let you both know cocktails are in one hour and we have been requested by the host to dress for dinner."

"How fancy," I remarked. "I'll look great in the jeans and t-shirts I brought with me. Although that's probably good since whatever the children are eating will be on me anyway," I laughed.

"Adelay is feeding the children now, Polly. Z wanted to make sure you would be ah...unoccupied at dinner," Mac explained with a sly smile.

"See?" Samantha chimed. "I told you."

"I don't have anything to wear," I stammered.

"I have lots of dresses. They were all for the streets of Paris. We might as well wear some of them."

"Sam, I don't want to wear your wedding trousseau. That's a little weird. Just tell Dr. Leo that I appreciate his offer, but I don't have anything to wear."

"C'mon, Polly," Sam lamented. "You know I don't care."

"Fine. I'll take a shower and just leave me something on the bed. Whatever you like the least in your suitcase will be fine."

Sam rolled her eyes at me and turned to leave. "Whatever," she sighed.

"You girls work it out. Sam, I'll see you in the bedroom," Mac smiled.

I shook my head as Mac left and gave Sam a smirk. "I know what *that* means."

"Get in the shower, and I'll come back with a dress. You'll have to wear your own shoes," Sam grimaced.

I nodded knowing my size seven feet would never fit into Sam's tiny size six shoes. "Hope no one minds my sandals."

"I'm sure it'll be fine. It's hard to be a fashionable girl when you're on the run from a psychotic stalker," Sam added.

She closed the door and I went to my suitcase to have a quick look. Maybe something would do and I wouldn't have to bother Sam. Alas, there were only jeans, t-shirts, sweatshirts, pajamas, and flip-flops. I probably didn't even have enough clean underwear to last the next couple of days. I shook my head and began to undress, dropping my clothes at the tall armoire by the bed.

I felt like a princess in this room. It was so ornate and lovely. If only I had a wardrobe to match it, I thought as I stared at myself in the mirror.

I walked naked to the bathroom and flipped on the light. The crystal chandelier that lit the white marble room was delicate and beautiful. I looked around and found soap and shampoo. The question was whether I wanted to soak in the huge tub or quickly shower in the huge walk-in that encompassed the corner of the room.

I shut the door and opted for the quick shower, knowing it might take some time to do my hair. I could at least look decent in the face if I wasn't going to have anything to wear.

I noticed the thick fluffy robe on the back of the door

and pulled it off for closer inspection. There was a monogram over pocket. It was a large X. Xanthis. It was kind of hot how beautiful and smart he was – maybe too beautiful and smart for me.

I showered quickly and pulled on the robe as I stepped out and onto the plush mat that enveloped my toes.

I began to comb through my long blonde mane, thinking that I needed a haircut. I pulled the dryer from its holster on the wall, sat at the small white seat at the vanity and began to dry my hair. The cushion was embroidered and had a skirt that fell to the floor around it. I felt incredibly ostentatious as I sat in the robe as the breeze from the window high above the tub blew softly into the room.

"I'm ready for my close up, Mr. DeMille," I said to my reflection as I finished with the dryer.

I walked back into my golden room and the french doors were once again open. Leo was right. The entire room radiated a vibrant warm hue. It was breathtaking.

I walked to the doors to admire the setting sun and noticed on the table beside the door a note and a glass filled with what looked to be a mint julep, complete with a sprig of mint.

I gasped and grabbed the note, hoping it was from him.

Miss Polly,

I trust you had a nice rest. This is to help you unwind before dinner and I've left a little something for you on the bed. Looking forward to this evening.

Yours truly-
Leo

I could see from across the room the pillows had been rearranged and the linens fluffed from my afternoon nap. On the bed was a large white box. Next to it was a pink dress I'd helped Sam pick out for the honeymoon, but what was in the box?

I untied the white bow on the lid and tossed it aside. Tissue paper flew with the breeze as I opened it to find a blue silk Zac Posen dress –size two. Underneath the remaining tissue were a pair of nude Valentino pumps – size seven. But how?

My first thought was to be angry with Sam for telling him I didn't have any clothes to wear tonight. My second thought was how beautiful the dress was.

A tiny envelope was taped to the lid.

Sip your drink, get dressed and join me downstairs, beautiful lady. Leo

My heart skipped a beat. How was I supposed to respond to this? It'd been a long time since a man paid so much attention to me and I was unsure of how I felt about it. Sam was raised Southern, I was not. Men didn't act this way. I wondered immediately if it was just an elaborate scheme to get me into bed with him quickly. I'm sure the routine had worked on plenty of girls.

I grabbed the curling iron and plugged it in. If he wanted to play, I'd give him a run for his money. I'd wear his dress and shoes. I would put on a dog and pony show he wouldn't soon forget – hair, makeup and red lipstick – Chanel 97.

"You wanna play this game, Leo?" I said to my reflection as I began to doll up. "You're on."

I began to roll my hair and then remembered the mint julep on the table.

"I'm gonna need this," I muttered as I thought of Dr. Leo Xanthis. Dr. Hot-Ass-What-The-Hell-Am-I-thinking Xanthis.

18

MAC

"Dan Kelley's office."

"Hey, Micah. It's Mac. Sorry to be calling so close to quittin' time. But you know me."

"Yeah, I know you," she rasped. "What's up?"

"I'll be in tomorrow. I'm coming off the Quintes case. Z and Dan are going to take it from here."

"Are you fucking kidding me?"

Micah wasn't known for her tact, but at the same time, I didn't know how much I wanted to hear from her right now.

"I'm not –" I paused, taking a deep breath. "Kidding you."

"Just when it starts to heat up you're going to walk away?"

"Something like that," I replied, trying my best not to lose my temper. I knew Micah meant well, but her delivery needed some work.

"Well, I throw my hands up to you," she spat.

I lowered my voice and turned my back in case Sam might walk into the room. "Look Micah, don't you think I want him? I want him bad. But now I'm married and I have Dax and Katy. You were right. My mind just isn't in the right place anymore."

"You're actually going to let someone else wrap this case and take down this psychotic piece of shit—who by the way has sent more than a few notes in the past year—to let you know what he intends to do with your wife when he gets her?"

"There's no need to remind me, Micah. For Christ's sake, you're making this even harder."

"You think I'm hard on you now," she preached. "Wait until you get here tomorrow and I junk-punch some sense into you."

I shook my head and looked to the floor. I had a lot of respect for Micah, but the emasculating way she spoke to me was no longer amusing. It was pissing me off.

"Wait," she continued. "There's no need to junk-punch you. Seems as if you don't have any balls between your legs anymore."

"Enough, Micah," I ground out.

As I waded through the many women in my career as a bachelor, Micah was the one stable female force in my life. That role was now Sam's and Micah hadn't adjusted to it very well.

"Thank God I know you love me. Otherwise I'd be inclined to tell you to fuck off," I hissed.

"Tell me why you really called," she hacked through her smoker's cough.

"I need you to pick my sorry ass up from the airport tomorrow."

"Fine. Send me your itinerary."

"And I need you to check the surveillance at Autumn Valley. I want updated reports from the agents guarding my mother and Mimi Peterson."

"Okay," she agreed. "Anything else?"

"Yeah. I want an update of Richard Peterson. You know, you'd get along with him just fine," I teased.

"Who? They guy your wife calls The Dick?"

"Her grandmother calls him that. Sam would never stoop to using those words."

"Whatever, asshole. I'll see you at the airport tomorrow."

"Great. And Micah?"

"What now?" she complained.

"Yak at ya later?"

"Only if you're lucky."

Sam breezed into the room after delivering Polly a dress to wear for dinner. She was fresh from the shower and her soft body that smelled of soap and fresh perfume was making me feel like a giddy drunkard. I sat after hanging up the phone and watched her move around the room gracefully without saying a word.

She finally caught my eye and realized I'd been watching...staring.

"What?" she asked, tilting her head and driving me wild.

"Can't a man just admire his beautiful wife from afar?"

"I suppose," she sighed, turning to sit at the vanity and brush her long chestnut hair.

I continued to regard her beauty, not taking my eyes from her. Each movement was fluid, as if it had been carefully choreographed. She was elegance incarnate.

"Seriously, Mac," she murmured. "You'd better finish

getting dressed. They'll be waiting on us."

I stood and walked to her, kneeling behind her chair and wrapping my arms around her tiny frame. I kissed her neck and breathed her in.

"You are so beautiful, baby. I mean truly beautiful."

She looked at me in the mirror and I smiled as a warm blush filled her cheeks.

"Are you blushing?"

"You make it hard not to."

I pulled her in tighter and slipped the silk robe down, revealing her soft shoulder. I couldn't help myself. I breathed her in again.

I leaned down and kissed her arm, working my way to her shoulder and around her collarbone. She closed her eyes and dropped her head back, giving me better access. I watched her face in the mirror as she moaned with each brush of my lips.

Her breathing became shallow and I was at once memorized by the rise and fall of her beautiful body.

"It's hard for me to concentrate while you're half naked," I confessed.

"I'm half naked because you took my robe off," she giggled as I kissed her throat and proceeded to lick the side of her neck up to her ear.

"Mmmhmmm," I mumbled. "We could be a little late. It would give Z and Polly a chance to chat alone."

"What are you suggesting, Mac Callahan?"

I spun her little chair around and pushed her legs apart, causing her loosely tied robe to separate, leaving her naked body partially exposed. "I'm merely saying we could be a little tardy for dinner."

She leaned in and kissed me, pulling on my tie and moving my body between her legs. I was immediately ready to go. She'd teased me with her beauty, intoxicated me with her smell and lured me with her gentle voice. I wasn't going anywhere until I had her.

I stood and took her with me, picking her up off the chair and immediately holding her by her bottom. She was so tiny in my arms. She barely weighed anything.

"Would you be so kind?" I nodded to my pants, bulging with anticipation.

She leaned back in my arms and quickly unhooked my belt and unzipped my suit pants, allowing them to drop to the floor.

"And again?" I requested between kissing her neck.

She giggled, "I can't. I can't get them down with only one hand."

I adjusted her weight and held onto her with one arm, pulling my boxers down just enough to free myself, leaving my shirttail hanging.

I shuffled, pants around my ankles, briefs around my thighs, to the wall beside the ornate vanity where Sam had sat. In one motion I pinned her against the wall, pressed up and inside, filling her completely.

"Oh God," I moaned at the rush of warmth around me.

Sam gasped as I collided our bodies into the wall again, thrusting slowly and with deliberation.

"Beautiful Sam," I whispered into her ear as I moved again, slowly dipping down and back up as the silk robe finally fell to the floor.

"Yes," she breathed into my neck, seemingly unaware we were shaking the furniture on the wall with each propulsive charge.

"I can't stop," I gasped. "I'll never stop."

My body took over as the urge to climax came upon me with lightning speed and I felt her squeeze her thighs together, narrowing my position and sending shock waves through my core. I didn't want to leave Samantha behind and slowed my pace.

"Yes," she begged again.

I kissed her delicate neck leaving a damp trail.

As we moved in unison I could feel her pleasure build, and I pressed into her sweetness and nearly spiraled out of control.

"Oh God!" Sam shouted as I quickly placed a finger to her lips.

I expected her to smile, but instead she pulled it into her mouth and began to suck, quickly sending me into a spasm.

"Oh Jesus," I gasped, my passion cresting as I held my breath and groaned between thrusts.

I felt Sam's body collapse in my arms and I was suddenly weak in the knees. Turning, I sat her back on the chair and dropped to the floor, pants around my ankles, exhausted and elated.

I rocked back on my heels and slid my head into her lap. I was spent.

"I'm sorry, baby," I apologized.

"For what?" she choked out, still trying to catch her own breath.

"For making us late."

She pulled my head up, gripping my hair and turning my sweaty face to meet her.

"I'm going to shower...again," she smiled, rolling her eyes and taking a deep breath.

"I'll join you," I agree, kicking off my shoes to quickly lose the pants and shirt.

"No," she held up a hand. "I need to do this quickly and you won't let that happen."

"True," I confessed as I folded my suit pants and laid

them on the bed. "I'm right behind you."

"We can't leave them down there alone too long. I think Leo has a thing for Polly."

"What?" I asked, taking off my shirt and following her naked body into the bathroom.

As she turned on the water, she looked to my still hard erection and laughed. "Put that thing away."

"I can't help it, baby. This is what you do to me."

"You're a mess," she giggled, breaking her serious tone. "Shirt, no pants and lipstick on your collar."

"Oooo," I cooed. "I love it when you talk dirty to me."

I pinched Sam's perfect behind as we hurried down the staircase and into the front parlor. She swatted at me and I noticed we were fifteen minutes later than we'd been expected.

"Oh yes, he did," I heard Z laugh in his booming voice.

"Who did what?" I asked as we burst into the room, our faces still flushed from our lovemaking.

"Well, well, well," Polly smirked. "The newlyweds decided to join us after all."

"Sorry we're late," Sam blushed. "I had a hard time finding something to..." Sam paused and gave Polly a confused look. "...Finding something to wear. Polly?"

"Yes."

"I left you a dress on your bed."

"I had a dress brought in for Miss Polly," Z drawled.

"How nice," Sam smiled, giving Polly an eyeful.

"Wasn't it?" Polly agreed.

"Now that we're all accounted for," said Z, his eyes

cautiously eyeing Polly's backside as she stood to show Sam her new dress. "Let's continue to the dining room. That is, unless the newlyweds need a cocktail before dinner to cool them down."

"I'm sorry we're tardy," Sam apologized again.

"No need for a cocktail, Z," I shook my head.

"Let's go," he smiled as he strolled to the double doors separating the parlor from the dining room.

In one swift motion, he slid the pocket doors into the wall, revealing the opulent blue dining hall.

Polly let out a gasp as she walked into the room, and I had to admit it was grand.

"It's beautiful," Sam remarked as we took our places around the ornate table.

"Everything is so French and Louis the Fifteenth," Polly remarked.

"It is quite something," Sam agreed.

"I can't take any credit for it," Z explained as he held Polly's chair and waited for her to sit. "It was all here way before I ever came along."

"That's what I always say too," I laughed.

"Right?" Z continued. "Mac knows what I'm talking about. I've been to Lone Oak. It's the same. Old South, old families, old..." Z paused, looking to Polly again and seemingly losing his train of thought.

"Furniture?" Polly asked.

"Yes," he smiled.

I gave Sam a look and squeezed her hand under the table. I had a feeling that my old friend might be smitten with Polly.

"I can't thank you enough, Leo," said Sam, her voice beginning to crack with emotion. "This could've been just a horrible day. Between not being on our honeymoon and moving from place to place at a moment's notice? Your home? Miss Adelay taking over the children as soon as we arrived? This beautiful dinner? It's just —"

Z gave her a huge smile and nodded. "Please, Samantha. There's no need to go on. I'm glad I could be of help. Jackson House is always open to you."

Sam nodded and I leaned in and kissed her on the cheek, hoping to calm her.

"Thank you," she continued.

"It's been my pleasure meeting..." Z paused and confirmed he had Polly's attention. "All of you."

19

SAMANTHA

"**I** hate it that you're leaving. But I understand why," I said as I folded the last of Mac's things and closed the suitcase for his trip to Washington.

Mac hurried from the bathroom with his dopp kit, unzipping my handiwork and placing it in the suitcase. He immediately turned to me, bending his knees to come face to face. Placing his hands on my cheeks, already warm with the anxiety of being alone, he looked me in the eye and leaned into my forehead. "I don't want to leave you, baby. You know I don't. But I want Hector out of our lives and as soon possible."

I nodded, afraid if I spoke I'd begin to cry.

"Z's gonna take excellent care of you and the children while I'm gone. And it's just for a couple of days. I'll go through everything with Dan, turn the case over to him and I'll be back."

"Then what?" I mumbled. "We can't stay in New Orleans forever, Mac. I want to go home. Dax misses home. I miss home. Katy's off her schedule…"

"Shhhhh…" Mac kissed my forehead and pulled me in for a tight hug. "It's all gonna be over before you know it. Hector will soon be a distant memory."

"Promise?"

"I promise."

"I'll call you when I land."

"I love you, Mac."

"Don't worry. I'll be back, this will all be over, and we'll be sitting on top of La Mer á Boire overlooking the Parc de Belleville sipping café au lait."

I nodded, thinking of where we were and where we were supposed to be as I held back tears. "Did you say goodbye to the children?"

"Yes," he dropped his head. "I didn't think anything could be as hard as leaving you, but telling Dax and Katy goodbye this morning just about killed me."

I smiled, understanding his separation anxieties.

"I feel like both of them are growing so fast, and I don't want to miss any of it."

"They are," I sniffed. "And you won't. As long as you hurry back."

I followed Mac as he rushed down the stairs. A black car was waiting in Z's driveway and I knew he was anxious to get on the road.

"Who's picking you up from the airport in D.C.?"

"Micah," he said, dropping his bag and shoving a file into his briefcase.

All I could do was shake my head.

"What?" Mac said as if it wasn't a big deal.

"It's just…she doesn't like me," I confessed.

"She likes you fine."

"That's not true. And you know it, Mac."

"Sam," he consoled. "She's just had a hard time adjusting to me being out of Washington and getting married, having a baby…"

"Those are the exact reasons she doesn't like me."

"C'mon, honey," he whined. "I can't do this now. I need to leave. I'll deal with Micah. She's like my sister. She's just mad because she doesn't get to work with me anymore and she has to work with Dan. He's not as easy as I am."

"Easy, huh?"

"Samantha…" he droned.

"Go. I don't want to hold you up."

Mac leaned in for one last kiss. "You're not holding me up. We're holding each other together," he whispered.

"I love you," I smiled.

"I love you."

Mac climbed into the car and just like that, he was off.

It was the fourth day of my honeymoon and I was all alone.

"Let's do something."

I looked up from my book and found Polly standing in the doorway of my room.

"Like what?" I mumbled.

"Let's go shopping." Polly was unusually glib for it to be so far away from happy hour.

"What?"

"C'mon," she insisted as she walked to me with a little skip in her step. "I need some clothes if we're going to stay here much longer. All I packed were shorts, jeans and t-shirts."

"Apparently Z didn't want you to have to wear anyone

else's clothes last night."

"Well…" she drew the word out. "It was very nice of him, don't you think?"

"I think Leo is a very kind man."

"He is, isn't he?" Polly sighed as she threw herself into the chair opposite me.

"What's this all about?" I asked, closing my book and setting it aside. "Polly, you didn't sleep with him, did you?"

"No!"

"Leo," I repeated. "Is he a Leonard?"

"Nooo…" Polly chided. "Leonidus."

"Like, Greek warrior king of Sparta? Leonidus?"

"He's a Greek god. Don't you think?" she asked, all aflutter.

I nodded, happy that Polly had something to be excited about. "He *is* very handsome."

"His hands are so big, Sam," she smiled.

"What's that supposed to mean?"

"I dunno."

"What? You think because he has big hands he might have something else that's big?"

"He's just so manly. I like that he's a badass FBI agent, but I also think he's the kind of man who would feed a hungry kitten if he found it," Polly giggled as she bit on the end of her index finger.

"What?" I laughed. "Look who's been fantasizing."

"Can you blame me?"

"I'm a married woman, Polly. I only think naughty things about my own hot and handsome gentleman."

"Leo *is* a gentleman, isn't he?" she continued, oblivious to my comments.

"He is that. And a kind one. What would we be doing if he hadn't taken us in? I mean Hector will never find us here, and the surveillance in this place is pretty scary."

"Do you think he has cameras in the bedrooms to watch us?"

"What? No!" I cried. "Do you *want* him to be watching you all the time?"

"Maybe," she admitted with a smirk.

"You're such a dirty girl," I laughed.

"I am not. Now let's go shopping," Polly whined. "I don't wanna wear these awful clothes around this beautiful home."

"I don't even know if we *can* leave. I'd have to ask Z."

"Leo," Polly corrected.

"You ask *Leo*," I mused. "I need to call and check on Mimi and the house in Shadeland and I need to make sure we aren't just dumping on Adelay."

"*Adelay* was the one who told me to get out of the house and enjoy NOLA."

"Really..." I drawled, wondering if Adelay had ulterior motives on behalf of her dear Leonidus.

"Yes," Polly nodded. "Can we go? C'mon. Can we go?" she repeated, reminding me of Dax begging for a new toy.

"Calm down." I giggled at her nervous excitement and thought that perhaps a little retail therapy might help to cure my honeymoon blues as well. "Fine. Get dressed while I call Mimi and Richard."

Polly cleared her throat at me with frustration. "Didn't you hear me the first time? This *is* what I have to wear."

I shooed her out of my room and yelled, "Go. I need fifteen minutes."

I watched Polly skip out down the hallway and went to the bedside to call.

As the phone rang in Shadeland I looked over the beautiful grounds that were Leo's home and wondered how the lilacs were blooming at my own.

"Richard Peterson home."

The words threw me and I looked at the display to make sure I'd called my own house.

"This is Samantha Peterson Callahan. I'm looking for my cousin Richard who is currently staying there in *my* home."

"Yes, Mrs. Callahan," said the pleasant voice on the other end. "Hold for Mr. Peterson."

My first thought was who is this woman who's answering phones in my house, and my second thought was that Richard had only been there three days and had apparently moved in for good.

"Samantha?" Richard breathed heavily as if he'd been far away from the phone.

"Richard, what's going on?"

"Nothin', darlin'. I can't just up and leave Biloxi to watch over the house without bringing a couple of people into town to help me with my business."

"What do you mean?" I asked. "There're others staying in my house while you're there?"

"Now Sam, don't go gettin' your panties all in a wad. You asked me to watch over Mimi's house and that's what I'm a doin'. I can't help that the real estate market doesn't take vacation. That means that your ole cousin Richard can't either."

He was making me angry every time he referred to my home as *Mimi's*. Richard was well aware that Mimi had signed the deed over to me when she moved into Autumn Valley. That house was mine.

"I didn't realize we'd inconvenienced you so. I'll have Mac send a couple of agents to stay at the house instead."

"No, darlin'," he gruffed. "I think it's best that family

take care of family. Besides, there are plenty of agents combing the place. Surely we don't need anymore black suits around here. It makes the whole place so depressing."

I paced the floor, pulling and twisting the old phone cord in nervous strides. I didn't want to be hateful, and I didn't want to call Mac and complain that there were too many people in my house when I knew twice as many were at Lone Oak. Furthermore, *we* were staying in someone else's home.

"I suppose," I conceded. "Just don't let anyone steal anything. Okay?"

Richard cackled in a smoker's cough before trailing off. "Darlin', I'm sure the ole girl Mimi has everything hidden around here. You probably don't even know where half of her things are."

"No," I replied. "I know *exactly* where everything is in that house. So don't make me come shake the pockets of your so-called help for the good silver when I return."

There was a sudden silence that made me feel a tiny bit guilty that maybe I'd been too crass. But as soon as he opened his mouth again, it was gone.

"Speaking of returning home. Where the hell are you?"

"New Orleans."

"What's in New Orleans besides freaks and drunkards?"

"I wouldn't know. I've not been out of the house."

"Well, it's nice someone is extended their Southern hospitality to ya. Anyone I might know?"

"An agent friend of Mac's. That's all."

"Must be pretty cramped, all y'all in one little house together."

"It's a huge estate in the Garden District, Richard. Don't worry yourself over us," I snapped, tiring of his questions.

"I've got some friends in the Garden District," he continued. "That's a pretty pricey area. Does the property have a name?"

"Jackson House," I sighed. "Listen, Richard. While you're working out of my house, it would be nice if you would check in on Mimi from time to time. She *is* ninety-nine, you know. She's not going to be around much longer."

"I'd be delighted to have a visit with Mimi, darlin'. But Mimi isn't too delighted to see me when I call on her."

I met his comment with silence. I knew he was right. I was Mimi's favorite. Always had been. Always would be.

"Maybe you need to mend fences while you're in town," I suggested, knowing Mimi would probably throw something in his direction if she found out he'd brought friends with him to stay in the house.

"We're not all as well liked as you are, Samantha," he drawled. "Anyway, darlin', just take care of yourself. What am I sayin'? I'm sure Mac is taking very good care of you."

"Mac's in D.C." The words escaped my mouth before I had a chance to rethink them.

There was another uncomfortable lull in the conversation and I regretted even calling Richard.

"Mac's not with you?"

"He'll be back…tonight." I lied.

"Hmmmm," Richard groaned. "Well, just know that everything is just fine and dandy here in Shadeland. And don't hesitate to call if you need anything else. Family first," he sang.

I didn't know how to respond so I said the only thing I could. "Thank you, Richard."

"Bye now."

"Goodbye."

I hung up the phone and at once thought I should call

Mac and tell him to have his agents watch my smarmy cousin, but I knew he had enough on his plate at the moment. Richard was a greedy beast, that was for sure. But I was pretty certain he was harmless.

Instead of calling Mac, I called the other rock in my life.

"Hello."

Her voice cracked over the line and I swallowed hard, worried that the past few days had taken a toll on her.

"Mimi?"

"Sam, honey, how *are* you? *Where* are you?"

"I'm with an agent friend of Mac's. His name is Leo. Leo Xanthis."

"Are you okay, baby girl?" The concern in her voice was shining through her usual *roll with the punches* attitude.

I sighed. "I'm fine. How are you? Are there agents around you twenty-four-seven?"

"Well, they aren't as handsome and sweet as your husband, but they're at least dressed nicely and seem to have manners."

"Well, that's *something*," I agreed. "As long as you're safe, that's all I really care about."

"I'm finer than frog's hair split four ways and sanded."

"I'll just assume that means you're okay."

"I'm probably better than I think I am. Speaking of…" Mimi hesitated. "I hate to trouble you, darlin', when you've already got so much going on, but Pete Peterson came to see me yesterday."

"I'm sorry, Mimi," I laughed, amused at not only the name but also the way it rolled off her tongue. "Is this someone I should know?"

"Pete? He's a distant cousin on your grandfather's side. He's the family attorney. You've met him, I'm sure."

"I'm fairly sure if I ever met a relative of ours that had

the same first name as our last I'd remember it."

"Maybe you've only met his son, Petey."

"Please tell me there aren't two of them in the same family."

"Of course. Pete Peterson and Petey Peterson…" she paused. "Jr."

"So nice they named them twice," I mumbled.

"What's that, honey?"

"Never mind. So what was it he wanted?"

"Richard's been to the courthouse asking for a legal description of the house and land."

"Whose house and land?"

"My house and land. Your house and land, darlin'. Do you know any reason the dick would be poking around?" She laughed a little at her own words. "No pun intended."

I didn't want to worry Mimi any more than she already was. "I have no idea, but I will ask him."

"Ask whom? Petey or the Dick?"

"Richard."

"I don't trust him, Sam. I just don't. He'll steal anything that isn't too hot or too heavy to carry."

"Don't get yourself all upset. Just be a good girl for the agents Mac's assigned to watch you."

"Good girl, huh?" she quipped. "I guess that means I should keep my hands to myself."

"What?"

"Well, like I said, they're not as handsome as Mac, but I've never been one to look away from a man in a well-cut suit that's carrying a nice piece."

"Mimi!" I gasped.

"Well, they do have nice equipment. One even obliged me and pulled it out."

"What are we talking about exactly?"

"His gun, Samantha. His gun," she scolded. "Where is

your mind, young lady?"

I searched for words and all I could come up with was "Sorry."

"Kiss my great-grandbabies for me," she replied, ignoring my apology.

"I will. You're an ornery ninety-nine year old woman. Do you know that?"

"Hell yes, I know it. You don't think God let me live this long to make everybody's life easier, do you?"

"You make *my* life easier," I replied. "I know that much."

"I mean it, Sam. Keep an eye on Richard," she cautioned. "You can't trust a hungry dog to watch your dinner."

"I understand."

"Check in again soon, dear," she requested as her voice trailed. "And Sam?"

"Yes?"

"Just remember what Liz always said."

"What's that?"

"Pour yourself a drink, put on some lipstick and pull yourself together."

I knew she was tired from the events of the past few days and I again felt guilty for putting her through so much. She was older and more fragile than she'd ever let on. As long as she could muster a smile and have some lipstick handy to brighten her face, she'd go on as if everything were just fine. Even if the world was falling down around her, Mimi displayed only grace and charm. She was the perfect combination of Scarlett O'Hara and Elizabeth Taylor and I hoped that someday, someone would think as fondly of me as I did of her.

"Yes, ma'am. Please take care of yourself and I love you."

"I love you too, baby girl."

20

POLLY

I breezed through the house looking for Leo. Sam was making me ask permission to leave the house. My first thought was to be angry for feeling like a child in a game of Mother May I, but that was quickly replaced with the idea of chatting Leo up.

He was dark and brooding with a hint of danger, but when he opened his mouth he was smooth as silk and I found myself hanging on his every word.

Leo made me feel soft and sweet, even though that wasn't my nature and I'd become what I'd teased Samantha about for over a year now – a swoony girl.

I rounded the long and winding staircase that led from the second floor guest rooms to the main vestibule of the house. Downstairs the windows were open, and a cool breeze flowed through the delicate curtains that breathed in and out with the wind. The house smelled of sweet honeysuckle, no doubt from the beautiful garden outside. They didn't call this part of New Orleans the Garden District for nothing.

I stopped for an instant and shut my eyes, allowing the

warm smell to wash over as I breathed it in.

"I trust you're enjoying your stay at Jackson House?"

I jumped, startled from the voice, but knew immediately Leo was standing behind me. "Yes," I replied without turning to face him. "I can't imagine being more comfortable anywhere else while we're hiding from a psychopath."

"Is that your official diagnosis?"

Leo walked around me, staying close without touching me. I could feel the heat from his body and I was immediately turned on.

"What?" I stuttered. "You mean my diagnosis of Hector?"

He stepped away from me, and his casual nature and adorable grin made me a little weak. For a moment I lost myself, but with one breath recovered and came back into reality.

"Why do you think Hector is a psychopath?" he asked as he motioned for me to join him in the parlor we'd shared drinks in the night before.

"He lacks a moral compass," I began as I took a seat on the small sofa.

Leo shrugged his shoulders at me unconvinced. "Sociopaths lack that too."

"Both sociopaths and psychopaths are incapable of sympathizing with the feelings of others."

"True," he replied. He drew a breath before continuing and I promptly cut him off.

"There's no real diagnosis for Hector. But he is more of a psychopath than a sociopath."

"Why?" Leo interrupted.

"He's crossed the line of moral behavior. He's tried unsuccessfully to kill Sam and Mac. He's dangerous."

"Are you aware of Hector's past?" Leo asked as he

walked to a table across the room and shuffled through papers.

"No."

Leo selected a folder and presented it to me. I looked at the tab and saw the name Hector Quintes and gazed back to him. "Am I allowed to even look at this? I mean, this is official FBI, right?"

He shrugged his shoulders and turned around to take the seat across from me.

"Read it. Tell me what you see."

"You mean right now?"

"Keep it for the day."

I dropped the folder into my lap and sat back and into the comfort of the sofa. Another strong breeze swept the gossamer fabric of the curtains into the room.

Leo said nothing but never took his eyes from mine.

"I wanted to thank you again for my dress. I'm a hot mess most of the time, and I didn't get to pack to go on the run after the wedding."

"You're welcome."

He was deliberate in everything he did. The way he spoke, the way he moved, and the unnerving way he always continued to make eye contact.

"Actually," I began, breaking his gaze to look at my feet in embarrassment. "Sam told me I had to ask permission to venture out into New Orleans today. I wanted to buy some more appropriate attire for...well, for as long as we might be here. I'm a little embarrassed by my old jeans and t-shirts."

"Don't be," he smiled.

I waited for him to continue with another thought. I expected a follow up *you look fine*, and even wished for a *you're sexy in your soft jeans and oversized shirts*, but it never happened. I watched in vain for the next words to cross his lips. Instead he held his unwavering gaze upon me.

"Still," I uttered, breaking the silence. "I'd like to venture into the city to do some shopping and Samantha said I needed to ask you first."

"I'd be happy to accompany you," he smiled.

"I was planning on taking Samantha with me."

He pursed his full Greek lips and shook his head no.

"So it's you or nothing at all." I stated flatly.

"It's me or no shopping. Samantha needs to stay here. The house is being guarded from the outside. I'll bring an agent in while we're gone."

It was my turn to be silent. I didn't know how I felt about being watched while I tried on sundresses and sandals. I stood and began rocking on my heels. I felt like I was back in high school and the cutest boy in the class was asking me out. I shoved my hands into the back pockets of my jeans, bit my lip and shrugged my shoulders. "Okay."

We drove through a historical area not far from Jackson House and I took in the eclectic shops that lined the street. The weather was beautiful and Leo let me choose the car we drove from a well-kept collection in a garage behind his home. I picked the red Mercedes 500 SL convertible. If I was going shopping with a hot man at my side while wearing grungy clothes, I was going in style.

"This is Magazine Street," he explained as he adjusted the aviator sunglasses on his tanned face. "We can shop here and get something to eat."

I watched him with intent and thought how he fit and then again didn't fit the FBI M.O. He was tall, visibly muscular under his suit coat and expensive designer jeans and held that quiet mysterious calm and badass confidence one would expect from a federal agent. Yet he had a side that seemed dangerous, off the grid and unconventional. Maybe it was the hair. Yes, I told myself. It was the ponytail that was throwing me. I smiled, wondering what happened to Z when Leo let his hair down.

We parked on the street and he jumped from the car to open my door. When he offered me his hand, I took it. "Thank you."

"My pleasure."

"Leo, I feel bad," I began as soon as my feet hit the pavement. "I could've done this on my own. I really just needed someone to point me in the right direction and give me a ride." I giggled nervously and tried to ease the unspoken tension that hung heavily over our heads.

"It's a beautiful day, Polly," he replied, looking to the sky. "Who wouldn't want to spend it outside and in the company of a beautiful lady?"

I felt the heat rise from my chest and into my face. He'd done what no man had ever done for me before. He'd caught me off guard and caused me to blush.

Not wanting to be seen, I fanned my face and gave him my best Southern belle drawl, "Why, Mr. Xanthis, you *do* go on."

He smiled and under his breath gave me a low and guttural chuckle. Even his laugh was dark and sexy.

"So where are we going?" I asked, hoping to move on and away from my flushed cheeks.

"There are a couple of small boutiques I know the ladies like. We can start there." He motioned with his arm to walk under a decorated awning and into a store.

The front door was open and I walked in as he waited

for me.

"Good afternoon," sang the salesgirl. Her hair was long, black and pulled into a sleek ponytail. She was beautiful. She was, for lack of a better term, immaculate. Her hair, lipstick, nails, shoes and body were all perfect. She almost looked airbrushed.

I watched as Leo nodded to her, acknowledging her greeting as he removed his sunglasses, revealing his beautiful dark brown eyes.

"Hello, Leo," she oozed as she came closer and he smoothed back his hair. It was apparent they'd met before.

"How are you today?" he asked her as I stood beside him and nervously picked at my fingernails.

"Better now," she replied with a wink.

He gave her no reaction, which made me happy. I would hate to think he was only cool with me.

"What can I help you with?" she asked, still not acknowledging my presence.

"My good friend Polly has been stranded here in the Crescent City without her luggage and we need to find her some appropriate items for the next few days."

The Kim Kardashian lookalike stared at me and I watched the smile fade from her face. "Of course," she replied, exuding false warmth. "What size are you? A six?"

"I'm a two," I smiled, cocking my head to the side while I thought of ripping hers off.

"Let me pull some things for you."

She eyed me up and down and I had a *Pretty Woman* moment, suddenly feeling like a Julia Roberts prostitute in Beverly Hills. I thought for a split second to say, "Hey, I've got good money to spend in here," but I held my tongue and instead gave her a crusty glare.

Turning to Leo, I dropped my head in embarrassment after she'd left us, shading my eyes with my hand. "I don't know if this was such a good idea," I breathed as I rubbed my forehead in frustration. "I would've been perfectly happy to find a Saks somewhere and just afford myself some retail therapy."

He lifted my chin and bent his knees so his tall body met my face head on. "She, my dear, is of little consequence. Choose whatever you'd like. She works on commission. By the end of this, she'll want to be your best friend."

"Leo," I sighed. "I'm not Samantha and Mac, and I'm not you. I don't have the kind of money it would take to shut her up. And I'm certainly not going to start anything I can't finish."

She walked back into our conversation and placed her hands on her hips. "I've put some things in the first dressing room...ahhh—" She looked to Leo for direction.

"Polly," I interjected quietly.

I wasn't one to feel inferior, but at this moment, standing in front of a well-bred, handsome man and a woman hell-bent on making me feel like trash, I was beyond mortified.

"I've got to step outside to make a couple calls, Jill," Leo said to her. It was all becoming a little too much to take. He knew her by name and I wanted to sink further into my shell.

"Whatever she wants, box it up and have it sent to Jackson House."

"Wait. What?" I asked as Leo began walking to the door.

"Whatever you want, cher," he smiled. "I'll be right outside if anyone needs a second opinion."

I looked to Jill and shrugged my shoulders. Her attitude changed quickly as she smiled at me and took me by the arm to lead me to the dressing room.

"Get started and let me know if there's anything else

you need or if you want another color or style."

"Thank you," I muttered, still in disbelief of what had just transpired.

"What size shoe do you wear? We have some cute sandals that just came in. I'll pull a couple things for you."

"Seven."

I closed the pink and white striped chintz curtain that separated me from the boutique and looked at all the clothes hanging there for me to try. I immediately took a good long look in the mirror to see how badly I must look to have been treated so poorly. I did have dark circles under my eyes and my hair was flat, but my cheeks were still rosy from the convertible ride and I could tell I'd lost some weight in the past few days.

I pulled my t-shirt over my head and began to unzip my jeans. Just as I dropped them to the floor, Jill without warning whipped open the curtain.

"Oh!" I jumped. I was already twitchy and on guard, but the last thing I expected was to be accosted in the dressing room.

"Sorry to scare you," she smiled as she handed me three shoeboxes and gave me a second head to toe inspection.

"I'll get you some lingerie," she sighed.

"I think I'm fine in that department."

"Honey," she sighed putting her hands on her hips. "If Leo Xanthis is calling you *cher*? You need to be wearing better panties."

I looked down to my sweatshirt-grey cotton panties and t-shirt bra, and before I could utter a word she continued.

"I'll take care of it. Leo prefers silk," she volunteered as she closed the curtain.

"Wait!"

I looked at myself and spoke aloud. "What just happened?"

21

MAC

I walked into my old stomping ground at 935 Pennsylvania Avenue. The J. Edgar Hoover building was buzzing with activity. Dan was allowing me to use my old office while I was in town and I had to admit—it was good to be back.

"Micah!" I shouted into the intercom.

"Jesus," she shouted back. "You don't waste time sliding right back into dickhead mode, do you?"

"Can you come in here…please?"

I didn't mean to be a dick, but I was frustrated that I wasn't on my honeymoon and worse, I was horny because I wasn't on my honeymoon. In general I was grumpy but Micah was used to it.

"Hey," Micah blurted, sticking only her head through the doorframe. "You've got bigger problems than me, asshole. Dan wants to see you. Now."

"Stop calling me asshole. I might not be your boss anymore, but I'm still a hired operative, and as such you need to treat me with respect."

"Yeah. Well," she began, unimpressed with my self-righteous declaration. "I'm sorry you're a dick in deep shit. And I'm sorry Hector is raining on your wedding and honeymoon parade. But I think your deep shit just got deeper."

"When did this come through?" I barked at Dan as I paced his office. It was a room I was familiar with. It was where I came to get bitched out for screwing up or going out on my own on a case when I wasn't supposed to.

"The transcript from the wire tap came in this morning," Dan replied, taking a deep breath and pushing himself away from his desk in frustration. "Look, Mac, there are a couple different ways to play this and if we don't pick the right one, we could be putting Sam and the children in danger. Now they're already in protective custody and I'd trust Z with the lives of my own wife and children."

"Danger?" I shouted as I threw my hands into the air in disgust. "I think we're way past danger."

"Does Samantha's cousin Richard know where she's located?" Dan asked.

"When I left yesterday she hadn't spoken to him. When was the conversation picked up?"

"The time and date stamp *is* from yesterday," Micah added.

I walked behind Micah as she held the transcripts in her lap. "Read it again," I demanded.

"Mac," she began in a soothing voice that wasn't her norm.

"Again, goddammit!"

I watched Micah look to Dan as he nodded.

"Richard: I have news for you.

Unknown male: Yes?

Your package has been sent.

Where?

Not on the phone.

Fine. Meet me.

This needs to be worth my while. Do you understand?

Meet me.

I'll be in touch. Soon.

End transcript."

"It's Hector," I insisted. "Who's contacted Z?"

"We don't know it's Hector, Mac," Dan sighed. "This guy's a businessman. He's in real estate. The phone call could've been to anyone."

"Where did it trace?"

"If it's Hector, he's probably tossed the phone and purchased another one at the drugstore," Dan replied, keeping in pace with Micah's calm demeanor. "The signal was over a network provider, so we're tracing the locations."

"And how long before we have that information?" I asked.

"You know NSA. It could be this afternoon – it could be in a week. We've made a high priority request."

"I want every record known to man pulled on Richard Peterson," I said, picking up the file and walking to the door. "That bastard is up to something. And I know because someone smarter than me thinks so." I pointed at Dan.

"Don't look at me." Dan shook his head. "We don't have evidence to link Richard to shit right now."

"No, but Sam's grandmother doesn't trust him. And now neither do I."

"Jackson House."

The voice from Z's home in New Orleans was pleasant, but not enough to knock the edge of rage I'd carried with me from Dan's office.

"This is Mac Callahan with the FBI. I need to speak with Agent Xanthis."

"Mr. Leo is out at the moment, Mr. Callahan. This is Adelay. May I take a message?"

"I'll call his cell phone, thank you, Adelay. May I speak with my wife, Samantha?"

"I believe she went out with Miss Polly and Mr. Leo, but if you'll hold, I'll double check."

"I don't want to hold, but if she is there, would you please ask her to call me?"

"Yes, sir."

I hung up and called Sam's cell from mine. The phone rang once.

"How is D.C?" Samantha asked, immediately forgoing the usual hello.

"Sweetheart, where are you?"

"Where you left me yesterday. Why?"

"Why isn't Z there?"

"I didn't realize he wasn't. I also didn't know I was supposed to keep tabs on your agent. Why?" she asked a second time.

"I don't want you leaving the house, okay? I don't want the children out of the house. Do you understand me?"

"Mac," her voice dropped. "What's going on?"

"I'm not sure yet. But I'm going to get to the bottom of it."

"Mac, you're scaring me."

"You *need* to be afraid, Sam. I want you on your guard. If anything seems fishy, assume something is wrong. Okay?"

"Okay." Her voice trembled with unspoken desperation.

I felt terrible. What I'd tried so hard to spare her from was now falling down around her while I was away.

"I miss you," I whispered into the phone as I put my head into my hand on the desk.

"I miss you too."

"I'm not going to let anything happen to you Samantha – or the children. Ever."

"Mac," her voice shook. "Please tell me what's going on."

"Have you spoken with your cousin Richard?"

"Yes."

"Did he ask where you are?"

"I'm pretty sure I told him I was in New Orleans. Why?"

I pulled out the transcript again and read through the conversation.

"When?"

"Yesterday. I wanted to check on the house."

"It's probably best if you don't speak with anyone. Don't even answer your phone. I'll have Z get you another burner."

"Okay," she deadpanned. "May I ask why?"

"I just don't trust anyone right now," I explained.

"You and Mimi both."

"What's happened with Mimi?"

"She's mad Richard's brought in some of his business-people to work there while he's in Shadeland."

"I knew that. I get an update from his agents twice a day. But business is business."

"He wants Mimi's house. I mean, he wants to live there."

"How do you know?"

"Apparently he's pulled the title and deed to the land at the county courthouse – which I find interesting because I'm not giving him that house. First off, Mimi's name is still on the deed with mine and if she died…well."

"What?"

"She's promised to come back and haunt me if Richard ever sees a dime from her."

"I'm with Mimi."

"He's not a criminal," Sam continued. "He's a selfish, greedy asshole."

"I'll have him watched more closely," I repeated.

"I wasn't going to say this, but…"

"What?"

"I'm scared, Mac."

"Everything's going to be fine," I said, unsure of who I was trying to convince.

"I really need you to hold it together in case I decide to fall apart."

"I'm tired and I miss you. And I'm tired of missing you," I replied, pulling my eyes from my desk to find Micah standing in my doorway.

I gave her a nod to enter and swiveled my chair around to face away.

"I love you. Hurry back to me."

"I love you. And I will."

I waited for her to hang up, unable to cut the connection myself. Each day I loved Samantha even more. Something I never thought possible.

I turned my chair around and found Micah patiently waiting for me.

"Everything okay at home?" she asked. "I mean, in New Orleans."

"Yeah," I sighed. "How'd you know it was Sam?"

"The look on your face. I knew you were done the second you met that girl."

"Well, *that girl* thinks you don't like her."

"And what do you think?" Micah asked, unaffected by my comment.

"I think it would be hard for anyone *not* to love Samantha."

"You *would* think that."

"Be careful, Micah. That's my wife you're talking about."

"No disrespect meant to Mrs. Callahan."

"What's up your ass?" I was tired of playing games and I was really tired of her attitude—especially with my family's safety on the line. "Honestly, I don't know why you've been so steely to me over the past year. I'm *sorry* I'm leaving the Bureau."

She smirked and made me even angrier. "I'm *sorry* I'm not here anymore to fight with you every damn day about absolutely nothing," I continued.

"Humph" Micah snarked sending me into a shouting fit.

"I'm! Sorry!" I pounded the desk with each word.

She stared me down and I didn't waver in my eye contact. I was pissed. And she knew it.

"Jesus," she sighed, finally breaking the silence. "You're so sensitive."

"Micah." I rose and walked around the desk to sit on the corner and with each step turned up the volume of my voice. "I care about you. You've been a friend to me when others haven't. You've never taken any shit off of me, and I applaud you for that. But I love Sam. I'm excited about my new life, and I'll be damned if I'm going to let you hem and haw or make snide remarks behind my back or to my face and make me feel bad because I left you behind in D.C. So let's just air this shit out. What is your problem?"

"Hem and haw?" she asked quietly, taking my over-the-top tone down a notch. "I love it when you talk ... *Southern.*"

"Please, Micah."

"I'm glad you're back in D.C. Even if it's just for a few days," she said as she stood and walked to the door.

"Micah," I said with regret. "I'm sorry I yelled."

"It's fine. I'm used to it."

"Why all the hostility? We've always been at each other's throats. But not like this. I mean," I paused. "I thought you'd always have my back. Now I'm waiting for you to stab me in the back."

"Whatever, Mac," she uttered calmly as she turned to leave.

"Stop being a dick. I need you. Do you understand me?"

She stopped in the doorway but refused to turn and face me. "Yes."

22

MAC

I t was day three at the Bureau and the longer I stayed in Washington, D.C. it became evident to me that as much as I'd promised myself I needed to hand over the case completely, I couldn't leave behind the idea of catching Hector personally. I wanted his balls on a plate and I intended to do the castration myself. As my phone rang, I wondered how I'd break the news to Samantha that I wasn't coming back right away.

"Hello?"

"Mac, it's King."

I panicked. "What's wrong? Is it my mother?"

"She's stable," he said calmly.

"What happened?" I panicked.

"Mac, I need you to calm down and listen carefully. You're under a lot of stress right now, but I need you to keep a level head. Are you with me?"

"Yes." I was aware of my erratic behavior. I was on edge and I knew it.

"Nancy's had a heart attack, but she's stable."

"What does *stable* mean?" I tried to match his tone but

was failing miserably. "I mean I *know* what it means, but I need you to give it to me straight."

"A nurse found her short of breath and holding her arm earlier today. She was awake and responsive, but she's had a heart attack."

I met his explanation with silence, unaware of what to do or say. I was in shock.

"She's stable, Mac. There was no need to use a stent. The cardiologist gave her a thrombolytic medication that dissolved the small clot."

"Thank God." I sank into my chair. My very world was falling apart around me.

"There's more," King continued. "We had to cath her to see what was going on. This isn't the only blockage she has, Mac. Her proximal left anterior descending coronary artery is ninety percent occluded. But she has multiple blockages."

"What do we do about that?"

"That's up to you. She could do fine with the surgery, and then again she might not."

"What kind of surgery?"

"Bypass."

I dropped my head into my hand and fought off all the emotions that flooded my mind.

"The anesthesia from the invasive procedure will likely increase her Alzheimer's and dementia exponentially," King explained.

"You can't just put a stent in?"

"No, Mac," said King. "Now, it's up to you to decide if the risk is worth the reward."

"The reward of what?" I asked as my voice trembled. "What you're telling me is my mother has a bad heart, and if I try to fix it she'll be mentally gone forever."

"I'm sorry. Look, Mac, your mother has an advance directive, but she didn't have a DNR."

"I'm lost," I sighed, still trying to take in the weight of everything King was saying.

"An advance directive means she's made provisions with us – her health care team – of her wishes under certain circumstances. She didn't want to be kept alive on any type of life support, but she doesn't have a DNR or "do not resuscitate" order. Meaning, she wanted to be kept alive if she had quality of life. Do you understand?"

"Yes," I paused. "I don't know what to do."

"You don't have to make any decisions today. But you should know, if she has another heart attack she might not survive."

"And if I opt for her to have the surgery?"

"There are no guarantees for anything at this age, Mac."

"I'll be there as soon as I can," I mumbled.

"Again, she's stable, Mac. We're keeping a close eye on her. She's been moved out of her room and into the cardiac care center."

"Where are her guards?" I asked.

"Unfortunately they can't be as close to her. She's in a ward right now with other cardiac patients, but she'll be back in her own room tomorrow."

"King, I can't take any chances."

"Don't worry. Your agents are swarming the place," he mumbled. "And much to the dislike of most of the other patients."

"Thank you, King. I appreciate everything you've done. For my mother and the rest of the family."

"You're welcome."

"I'll be there as soon as I can."

I hung up the phone and walked to shut my door. I

dialed Sam and tried to hold it together.

"Hello, sweetheart," her sweet voice sang on the other end. "I miss you."

It was my breaking point. I took a deep breath, hoping I could get through it without crumbling.

"Mac? Hello?"

"Hi, baby," I managed to say.

"What's wrong? Mac, are you okay?"

"No."

"Mac, are you hurt?"

"It's my mother."

"Oh God, no. What happened?" she gasped.

"She's had a heart attack. King just called."

"What?"

"He said she's stable, but she's got a blockage and I have to make a decision to either have them operate, with no guarantee that she'd survive, or just wait it out."

"But she's stable now?" Her voice shook.

I knew if she started to cry, I would be helpless to hold in all the emotions I'd been harboring for the last week.

"King says she's stable – for now. But I need to get to Shadeland."

"I'll meet you there," Sam offered. "We'll do this together."

"That would be great, Sam. But for right now, I need you to stay put. There's a lot going on and I need to know you're safe."

"I'm not staying here while you deal with this alone."

"Listen, Sam. I love you so much, but right now I'm just trying to keep all the women in my life alive. What I really need is for you to do as I say."

"You can't do this alone. I don't want you to do this alone."

"It'll be fine."

"I can hear it in your voice, Mac. You're not *fine*."

"You're right," I confessed as my voice finally cracked.

There was a drawn out and quiet moment. I didn't know what else to say, or if there were even words to describe how helpless I was feeling. I heard Sam catch her breath and sniffle. I waited.

"Tell me what you want me to do."

"You're doing it."

"I wish I was there to hold you. You know as long as we have each other, everything will be okay."

"I wish you were here too, baby. I just feel like everything is such a shit-storm."

"That's because it is," she agreed.

"Those are your words of comfort?" I laughed through my anxiousness.

"What's the saying? If you're going through hell, keep going."

"Winston Churchill," I replied.

"We've got to keep going, Mac. There are too many people who need us."

I sat up in the chair. Samantha was right. I needed to stay strong. I took a deep breath and nodded at her words.

"Mac?"

"I'm nodding."

"Okay," she whispered.

"I can hear the smile on your face," I confessed. "I just wish I was there to see it."

"We'll be together soon."

"Not soon enough. And by the way, it's *my* job to comfort *you*. Make you feel safe."

"It's both of our jobs. In good times and in bad – remember?"

"How could I forget? It was just last week. I guess I just assumed the two weeks that were supposed to be our honeymoon wouldn't be…"

"What?"

"This catastrophe," I sighed.

"This *catastrophe* is life. It's *our* life. And we will make the best of it. Is it more exciting than the normal family trials? Yes. But I knew what I was getting into the day I met you. And I wouldn't have it any other way."

I managed a smile. "I thank God every day for you, Samantha."

"Ditto."

"As much as I want you with me, I still think it's best for you to stay in New Orleans with Z for the time being."

"I'll do whatever you want me to."

"When I get to Shadeland, I'll assess the situation and give you a call if you need to come."

"Okay," she whispered. "When are you leaving Washington?"

"I don't know. I'll call you later. Okay? Where is Z?"

"Out with Polly."

"What are they doing?"

"Courting?"

"What?"

"That's what Mimi said you were doing when we first met. She told me you were courting me."

"That was different. He's supposed to be on a case," I snapped.

"Yes," she droned. "And as I recall you were also supposed to be on a case when we met, and you swept me off my feet with flowers and gazebos and Chinese food –"

"And lovemaking on the boardroom table?"

"Oh Lord," Sam gasped. "Do you think they're – you

know."

"Z has quite the reputation."

"So did you."

"It's not the same," I corrected.

"How is it not the same?"

"Baby, I loved you the moment I laid eyes on you. It was like being hit by a truck. I thank God every day that I've never recovered from it.'

"I love you, you smooth talking Southern boy."

"God, I love you, Samantha," I sighed, feeling like a completely different man from the one who'd called her with the news of my mother.

"Get home," Samantha sighed. "And call me."

"What did I ever do to deserve you?"

"I feel that way about you. Every day," she cooed.

23

POLLY

"Two days in a row." I sighed as I sat across the table from Leo in the courtyard of Café Amélie in the heart of the French Quarter.

"Can't a gentleman just enjoy lunch with a beautiful lady twice in one week?" he asked with a devilish grin. Every time Leo Xanthis smiled, I felt like he was undressing me with his eyes. It was the most platonic, overt sexual act I'd ever witnessed, let alone been the target of.

I told myself as I watched him sip his freshly squeezed lemonade that my feelings could be one-sided, but easily pushed that thought from my mind. Leo was sending off vibes. And they weren't just Southern gentlemanly vibes. This man had an invisible ignition switch. I didn't know if his pheromones or my libido was in overdrive. What I did know was I liked him. I liked him a lot.

"Are you going to answer my question?" he asked as the soothing sound of the fountain beside us and the darkness of his eyes lulled me into a quiet trance.

"I'm sorry," I stumbled. "What was the question?"

"I said," he repeated soft and low, "can't I just enjoy the

company of a beautiful lady two days in a row?"

"And the answer to that questions is yes. Of course," I quipped as if I'd not made myself clear the first time. "I'm just not used to this kind of attention."

"I find that hard to believe."

His eye contact was unwavering but in the past two days I had discovered something about him. When he was nervous, or maybe even when he wasn't and was possibly just thinking, he uttered a low hum of *Mmm* as if something tasted really good. It gave him a naughty mischievousness that caused me to daydream of sounds he would make while having hot sex.

"Thank you again for the clothes yesterday. It wasn't necessary to do so much. I mean, we're not staying here for a month," I giggled.

"What a shame," he replied.

"I don't want to be rude. You've been more than accommodating – for everyone. Especially me. But I'm not the kind of girl who falls for the slick come-ons and aw shucks good ole boy Southern charm."

"I'm not sure I follow," Leo said as he took another sip of his lemonade.

"Of course you follow."

He stared at me and cocked his head to one side. It was quiet in the courtyard of the restaurant and the birds were out singing, happy that spring was arriving again in full force. I met his unyielding gaze and held my own. I'd said my peace and I wasn't going to apologize for how I felt.

"Tell me about growing up in Montana. What was that like?" he asked, ignoring my last comment.

"What?" I continued. "It was…great, I guess."

"Happy childhood?"

"Yes, doctor," I chided, wondering what he was looking

for.

He smiled and continued. "What about Princeton? How'd you meet Samantha?"

"Sam and I were matched as roommates our freshman year. The rest is history."

"Surely there's more to it than that," he smiled without moving his body an inch. He was the most stationary man I'd ever met. He didn't feel the need to use his hands or be overly histrionic when he spoke. The emphasis when he talked was definitely in the quiet stillness in which he delivered his lines. It was, for a lack of a better word, unnerving. He was smooth and unflinching. It was the kind of behavior a trained psychologist would expect of a cold, calculating sociopath. And yet I knew he wasn't. The calmness he displayed contrasted to my usual exaggerated behavior. We were opposites.

"What do you want to know that you've not already read about me in one of your files?"

He raised his eyebrows to me. "What makes you think I have a file on you?"

"C'mon, Leo. Don't insult my intelligence," I stated with a smirk.

"I would never."

"So?" I asked, quickly turning the tables on his interrogation.

"I want to get to know you. *Not* your file."

"So there *is* a file," I exclaimed. "Well, I hate to break it to you. There's a lot about me that you'll never find. Even in an FBI file."

"Tell me about Princeton," he continued, ignoring my comment.

"What's there to tell?"

"Any boyfriends?"

I hesitated as I thought back to how Sam and I became best friends, and in that moment I was discovered.

"Yes," he drawled calmly.

"What?"

"I don't always need a straightforward answer to know what's true," he replied.

I shook my head at him and scowled. "What do you think you're doing?"

"I'm getting to know you."

"Why do I feel like I'm naked – emotionally naked, that is – while you're getting to know me?"

"Do you feel emotionally naked?"

"Stop answering my questions with another question, Dr. Xanthis."

He said nothing. I studied his face for a sign of anything. There was no concern, there was no joy, he showed zero emotion. Yet I didn't waver. I met his staring contest head on until I saw the slightest muscle movement in the corner of his mouth. It was a hint of a smile, and it was all I needed. His eyes brightened and I knew. Leo Xanthis liked me.

Our lunch arrived and as he waited for me to begin eating, I made a conscious decision. What did I have to lose? I'd probably never see this man again after Mac wrapped this case. I'd already looked into applying at a few schools to go back and get my Ph.D. I was soon to be long gone.

"Fine," I stated. "What do you want to know?"

He didn't hesitate and stopped eating to give me his undivided attention. "How did you meet Samantha?"

"I was in an abusive relationship my freshman year at Princeton. He was popular, well liked, a student athlete, smart and a complete head case. It started out innocently enough. He would become jealous if I spent time with anyone, even if it was purely platonic. That moved on to hitting me in a drunken, jealous rage, lying and finally not even needing the alcohol to lay hands on me."

"How long did this go on?" he asked.

"A year." I paused. "A year too long. In my defense he wasn't always a bad guy. He could be incredibly sweet. He always apologized and said it would never happen again and then…"

"And then the pattern would repeat itself."

"Something like that," I agreed, looking to my plate and nervously wiping my mouth.

"How did it end?" Leo asked, shifting his weight in the chair. It was the first time he'd moved the entire time we sat in the courtyard of the restaurant.

"Not well," I shook my head. "After a black eye and a lot of coaxing from Samantha, I went to the police and took out a restraining order."

"But that wasn't the end. Was it?"

"No. The school wanted to cover the whole thing up. He was one of the golden boys of Princeton. A fifth generation legacy, the university wanted it all to go away. They wanted *me* to go away."

"But you didn't."

"I didn't leave Princeton. He came to me crying, apologizing, telling me he loved me and he was wrong. But I was done."

"Did you see him after that?"

"Not really. Our paths stayed pretty separate. I'm sure the board of trustees had a little something to do with that."

"How'd that make you feel?"

"Again with the touchy-feely," I snapped. "I went from sad to mad to don't care."

"How so?"

"I was sad in the beginning. I loved him. I never would've stayed with him if I didn't. I wanted him to be a better man. He just wasn't capable."

"Then you were mad."

"I was upset that right didn't prevail over wrong...again. I was pissed that money trumped truth and justice. He should've been kicked out of school. He should've been arrested. That's not the way it works when you have money."

"And then?" he asked as he nodded.

"I became a stronger person," I sighed. "I got my degree from Princeton. I have no idea what became of him. Don't care. He's someone else's problem."

Leo said nothing but nodded, keeping his unyielding eye contact.

"I have a question for *you*," I began.

"Yes?"

"How did you know the restraining order wasn't the end of the relationship? I mean, I told you I had a black eye and had gone to the police."

"Samantha forced you to go to the police."

"How do you know that? Is that in my file?" I smirked.

"You said it took a lot of coaxing from Samantha. I'm sure you were scared and upset, but you were also ashamed you'd allowed it to happen. You wanted it to be different and facing the truth validated what a piece of shit he was. Sorry for being disrespectful and using foul language."

"It's fine. He was a piece of shit."

"You thought it meant you were weak if you went to the police. In fact, it was very brave to admit to what was happening. Not an easy thing. Especially when you're nineteen."

"Wow." It was all I could say. He'd analyzed, explained

and commended me in a single breath.

"Were you a psychology major before all this happened? Or after?" he asked.

"Before. Why'd *you* choose it?" I asked as the waitress brought the check and set it on the table. She lingered and smiled at him, waiting for him to acknowledge her.

He caught her eye for a split second and then turned back to me, unaffected. "That's a conversation for another day, cher."

"That's a little unfair, don't you think?" I laughed.

"No."

"No?" I'd had enough of the give and take with all give and no take.

"I never said I was going to reciprocate when I asked about your childhood and Samantha. The rest was your doing."

"That's not true. I was merely answering your questions," I protested as he dropped a hundred dollar bill into the vinyl cash folder that contained our check for lunch.

"I didn't force you to tell me anything. You gave the information up voluntarily."

"Uh–" I snapped. He was right. I had. What had come over me?

"All you had to say was 'Leo, I'd rather not discuss that'. And I wouldn't have continued."

I stood and dropped my napkin on the table, brushing the full pale green skirt Leo had purchased for me as part of my new wardrobe free of breadcrumbs. "This is horseshit," I murmured.

Leo was on his feet as soon as I stood, quickly holding my chair. He leaned into my neck as I refused to look at him and inhaled, breathing me in. I tried to ignore the way the heat from his body and the sheer masculinity in which he held himself made me woozy.

"Your mouth is too beautiful to utter such words, cher," he whispered into my ear.

Stunned, I felt all the blood rush to my face and my ears began to ring.

"I think you're amazing," he continued, keeping his solid and tight frame so close without touching me. "Beautiful, smart and…"

"And what?" I faced him, accidentally grazing my lips on the collar of his shirt, leaving a red lipstick stain. Our bodies remained inches apart and I blushed at what I'd done to his white shirt.

"Full of sass."

The word dripped off his tongue like honey and I was at a loss for what to say next. *Thank you* seemed inappropriate, so I moved into the closeness. Our lips were a breath away from one another as I whispered what I was really thinking, "I hope screwing with my mind is a precursor to something vastly more satisfying, Dr. Xanthis."

24

SAMANTHA

I sat in the White Room where the children slept at Jackson House rocking Dax in my arms and singly softly as Katy slept in the bassinet.

I see the moon and the moon sees me. God bless the moon and God bless me. I know an angel watches over me. God bless the angels and God bless me.

I felt helpless as he looked up to me and batted his big blue eyes. I wanted to protect my little family and everyone seemed to think the best way was to sit idly by and hide while everyone looked and waited for Hector to appear.

I'd been accommodating, encouraging and as helpful as I knew how to be, but enough was enough. I wasn't the kind of girl who sat by and watched the people she loved get destroyed mentally and physically. I was weary of Hector. I might not be an FBI agent, but I'd been a single mother and I was a Southern woman. No man, not even Hector wanted a piece of that action. It was high time I stepped up.

Sure I was alone in New Orleans. Sure I was afraid. But being scared had never stopped me before. Ever.

I put Dax on the bed and covered him with the beautiful wool and silk blanket that was casually and yet perfectly lying across the bed.

After sneaking out of the room and quietly closing the door, I picked up the secure phone in the hallway and dialed for information. Once I got Pete Peterson's phone number I knew what I had to do.

"Miss Samantha," the voice bellowed on the other end. "How are you, darlin'? I'm bettin' good money that Mimi gave you a call. Didn't she?"

"Yes, sir. She did," I confirmed. "She told me that Richard had been to the courthouse to check on the deed and legal description of her house or something. Is that so?"

"That is the long and the short of it."

"What is he looking for? I mean, my name's on the deed with Mimi's."

"Yes, that's correct. And I have a copy of Mimi's sealed last will and testament here in my office."

"My understanding is the house is mine after Mimi's death."

"It is. But I think what he wants to know is how far down the line he is for anything from your Mimi."

"And?" I asked.

"Well…" He began to waver. "Only Mimi can show you her will while she's alive. I can only read it to you after she's passed."

"That means Richard can't have a copy either, correct?"

"That's correct. But know this – I think your cousin Richard could slide down a hundred-foot locust tree with a wildcat under each arm and never get a scratch."

"And in English that means what, Pete?"

He laughed at me, but I wasn't kidding.

"I don't know how," Pete began. "But he always seems to come out ahead in all matters of business."

"This isn't business. This is family."

"I hate to break it to you, honey, but if I had a dollar for every time a family thought that everyone was gonna play nice when the wealthy matriarch died, I'd be a very rich man today. Tears turn into gettin' while the gettin's good."

"I'm not waiting until Mimi's gone to fight with Richard. I need you to give it to me straight. What's my exposure?"

"The deed to her estate is in her name and your name. When she passes on, the estate is yours free and clear."

"So I have nothing to worry about," I sighed.

"Not until *you* pass away. I know you are married again. You need to update your will."

He spoke on, but my body went numb and the loud buzzing in my ears was too hard to overcome. Could Richard the Dick be so cold hearted that he wanted me dead?

"Pete," I interrupted. "What would happen to the property if something happened to me *and* my heirs?"

"You mean if *everyone* is dead?"

"Yes," I replied softly, the thought now rolling through my head. "If my family is dead, then what happens?"

"If your will doesn't specifically name someone, it would go into probate."

"And then?"

"Potentially to the surviving relatives of the family."

"Thank you, Pete. I'll be in touch soon."

I hung up the phone and called Mimi. After several rings I knew she was out of her room. I called Mac.

"Dan Kelley's office."

I recognized Micah's rasp at once. I took a deep breath and answered.

"Hello, Micah. It's Samantha Peterson…ah, I mean

Samantha Callahan."

"I knew who you meant," she grunted. "Mac's not in the office. He's in a briefing. Do you want me to call him out? Is this an emergency?"

"No emergency. I didn't want to call his cell in case he *was* in a meeting."

Micah had a way of always making me feel like I was intruding on Mac's life.

"I'll let him know you called when he returns," she offered.

"No need," I quipped. "I'll text him."

"Feel free to text him if Agent Xanthis has given you a new phone. Otherwise, you'd be best served to wait until *I* tell him you called."

"And you will," I stated.

"Will what?" she coughed.

"You will tell him I called," I repeated.

"That's what they pay me to do, *Mrs. Callahan.*"

The snide remark would've normally made me laugh. I didn't care how tough Micah claimed to be, she had no idea who she was dealing with. I would be cordial until the situation dictated otherwise, but she was teetering on the otherwise. Teeing me off was a place I was certain Micah didn't want to go with me.

"Bless your heart, Micah," I sang sweetly and in my best drawl. "Now don't go sailin' out farther than you can row back. Please, call me Sam."

My passive-aggressive nature was met with silence.

"You'll tell him I called?"

"Yes," she muttered.

"Thank you. I really appreciate all you do for Mac."

"Sure," she sighed. It was obvious she'd had her fill of me and wanted off the phone.

"Thank you. And Micah?"

"Yeah?"

"Have a nice day."

"Mommy?"

Dax walked into the hallway rubbing his eyes. His naps were becoming few and far between. "What's up, sweetheart?"

"I wanna go home."

"Me too," I agreed as I pulled him in for a tight hug. "But for now we need to stay here."

"Honeymoons are loooong," he sang out as he stomped his feet and threw his head back in frustration.

"Sometimes they are," I agreed, thinking of my nonexistent honeymoon. "What would you like to do while Katy is asleep? We could take a walk in the garden."

He rolled his eyes and took my hand. "Adelay and I do that every day, Mommy."

"We could draw," I suggested.

His eyes lit up and I knew I'd struck a chord with him. Dax loved his crayons and paper.

"Where's your backpack with your paper and crayons?"

"I'll get it."

Walking back into the children's room, I looked out onto the beautiful grounds and then into the bassinet that held Katy. I had everything to be thankful for. I was living a life I never thought I'd have. I wasn't going to let Hector steal my joy.

"Here it is, Mommy!" Dax shouted excitedly.

"Shhh…" I smiled. "Don't wake your sister."

I pointed into my room and Dax followed, tiptoeing and giggling as I joined him.

We sat on the old hardwood floor and he began to take out his things deliberately and one at a time.

"These are my crayons...this is my paper..."

He sang each item, gliding up the scale as if he were asking a question. He was the ray of sunshine I needed today.

"Here are some of my pit-tures, Mommy," he said, proudly handing me a stack of artwork from the days past.

I shuffled through them, smiling at the pictures he'd drawn of the wedding, of Katy, and even Mimi and Nancy at King's house. There were pictures of Mac and Dax together, Polly and now Adelay and even Leo.

"Dax, these are so wonderful. You're such a talented artist."

"What's that?" he asked.

"You are very good at drawing pictures."

"I'm a good drawl-ler," he nodded.

"Tell me who all of these people are."

"This is you," he said, pointing to the stick figure with long dark hair. "This is Polly," he continued as he showed me Polly's long ponytail.

"Is this Katy?" I asked, pointing to the baby wrapped and lying in the grass.

"Yes," he smiled. "That's baby Katy and this is Adelay."

"These are just amazing. Is this Mac? I mean Daddy?"

"Yes. That's Daddy," he explained as he sifted through the stack of construction paper. "And that's Mr. Leo, Mimi, Miss Celia and Coco."

I looked to the paper wondering if *Coco* was somehow Mac's mother and had to laugh at Leo's hair. "Dax, Mr. Leo's ponytail is as long as Polly's."

"I know," he smiled. "I like Mr. Leo."

"Me too."

"Now," I began as I looked through the pictures. "Who is Coco? Do you mean Miss Nancy? Daddy's mommy?"

I looked to him as he began drawing another picture. He began with a sun in the sky and green grass at the bottom of the white paper.

"Daddy's mommy?" he asked again.

"Grandmother Callahan," I said as I pushed his hair back and away from his eyes. "I don't want you to be afraid of her just because she doesn't talk very often. She has a hard time remembering people and things."

"I know. Miss Celia says she thinks up here like me," he said as he tapped his head. "But she can't say it here," he continued as he put a single precious finger to his mouth.

"That's a very good way of understanding your grandmother. But she loves you very much."

"I know. She told me," he said flatly.

"She did? When?"

"In her room. Coco was there."

"Dax," I stopped and began to look through his pictures again. "Who are you talking about? Dr. King's housekeeper? You know the nice lady who made breakfast in the big house on the lake?"

"Yeah," he answered without looking up from drawing.

"So that's who Coco is?"

"No."

I was becoming frustrated with his answers. "Dax, stop drawing and show me who you're talking about."

Dax put down his green crayon and began to calmly sift through the stack of drawings. Pulling out a dog-eared piece of paper he smoothed it out and pointed.

"There. That's Coco."

My heart sank as I looked at a drawing of Dax, clearly at Lone Oak under the old tree with the house in the background. Beside him was another person with dark hair covering his face.

"Who is Coco with at Lone Oak?"

"Me. We play. He calls me Diego," Dax laughed.

I took Dax by both hands and made him look at me. "Dax, I need you to tell me who this is. Is he someone who works at Daddy's house? At Lone Oak?"

Dax shrugged, unaffected by my questions.

"When was the last time you saw Coco? Before the wedding?"

"No," Dax drawled. "He was at the water."

"What water?"

"C'mon, Mommy." He held his hands out in exasperation. "The water. Where all the you-in-alls were."

"What?"

He leaned into me and whispered. "You know…where you can pee but not in the toilet."

"Urinals?"

"Yeah," he confirmed as he went back to drawing. "Daddy explained it to me."

"Dax, I need you to think very clearly. Tell me everywhere you've seen Coco."

"I dunno. Lots of places. He's always around," he said as he made a big circle with his arms. "But no one knows," he whispered. "It's a secret."

I began to look carefully at each of the pictures Dax had drawn. There was the dark figure with Dax at Lone Oak, at Mimi's house, King's at the lake and now Leo's in New Orleans.

I felt as if I was going to vomit as I stared at the crayon drawings.

"Dax," I mumbled, unable to catch my breath. "Have you seen him since we've been at Mr. Leo's house?"

"He was in the flowers this morning."

Dax stood and walked to the open french doors that overlooked the gardens. He pointed down and nodded. "Down there."

"Hey!" Polly exclaimed as she breezed into my room and tossed her purse onto the bed. "What's going on in here? Looks like fun. Can I color too?"

"Polly," I uttered. "Where's Leo?"

25

MAC

"**M**icah!" I shouted into the hallway.

"Jesus, Mac. What?" she cried with exasperation. "You know I missed your sorry ass around here, but now I'm starting to remember why you used to piss me off so much."

"Get me Agent Moss at Sam's house. I want to know what Richard is up to."

"He just called."

"Moss?" I asked as I saw Micah nod. "Can you get him back?" I huffed.

I was in no mood today. I needed to get as much information on Hector as I could before I left to go to Shadeland to be with Mom. Nothing was happening fast enough and no one was working hard enough for me. I needed answers, I needed information and I needed it now.

The phone rang as Micah shouted into my door. "Pick up the phone, Mac. It's Agent Moss."

"Agent Moss, this is Mac. I need an update," I said, foregoing any formal hello.

"It's pretty quiet here, sir. Mr. Peterson has set up an

office and brought in three employees."

"We've tagged his phone," I said. "But I want a bug set up wherever he's working and anywhere else in the house he spends time."

"Yes, sir."

"Have there been any visitors? I mean other than his employees?"

"No, sir."

"Has he gone out?"

"He's in and out all day, sir."

"I want a tail on him. I want to know his every move. Do you understand?"

"Is there a reason we're treating him like a suspect, sir?"

"He is."

"Mac," Micah said as she walked into the room. "We need to talk."

I gestured to the chair in front of the desk and continued looking through the intel I'd just received from Shadeland.

"First off, your new wife has a bug up her ass where I'm concerned."

"What?" I snarled.

"Your wife," she said distinctly and with sarcasm. "Have you forgotten about her already?"

"I have not forgotten about her, nor *will* I forget about her, Micah. What's your point?"

"She doesn't like me very much."

"Funny," I scoffed. "She says the same thing about you."

"About me?"

"Jesus, Micah. Think about what you just said to me. I can see why she thinks you don't care for her."

"Whatever…" she droned.

I missed Sam terribly and my grumpy demeanor was going to rear its ugly head if Micah continued down this slippery slope.

"Ya know what," I ground out as I slammed a file on my desk. "Let's just clear the air. Because I plan on knowing you for the rest of my life and I plan on being married to Sam for the rest of my life. So," I paused.

"So what?" she smirked.

"So what the fuck, Micah?"

She stood and paced the office like a caged animal. Micah was tough as nails, but you didn't want to get her dander up. She'd come at you like a rabid dog.

"What do you want me to say, Mac? That I'm glad you're gone? That I'm happy you got married and left me here in D.C. with all the other assholes? I'm not," she shouted as she threw her arms in the air. "Is that what you wanted to hear?"

"What did you expect me to do, Micah? Stay here with you and Dan while everything I ever wanted was waiting for me in Shadeland? You know me better than that," I shouted back.

"I thought I did."

"What's that supposed to mean?"

"The Mac Callahan I knew was a badass motherfucker. Tough, unafraid, had a taste for life and wanted to live it. Now you're a shell of who you once were. You're not an FBI agent. You're a *family* man."

"I *am* still an FBI agent, dammit, Micah. I'm a husband. I'm a father. I'm exactly what I was supposed to be."

"What? A small town guy in a tiny-ass town? The most action you're ever going to see is at a Friday night poker game at the country club."

"I don't need to chase criminals to feel alive, Micah. I'm alive because I have the love of a wonderful woman and two beautiful children to call my own."

"What. Has. Happened?" she asked pausing between words. "I don't even know you."

"Maybe you never knew me. Because if you did, you'd understand how happy I am. You'd be happy *for* me."

"I don't know you. *I* don't know *you?* I know everything about you, you shithead. I'm the one person who knows about all the women – and I mean *all* the women."

I sat back in my chair. She *did* know all the women. And there were plenty. But I'd long put that life behind me. I never loved any of the one-night stands. And more than that, each of the women knew exactly what they were getting themselves into with me. Not only did I have the reputation of never settling down, I told each of them before we ever went to bed that I wasn't the serious relationship type.

"You know," she began as she sat back down in the chair. "I never thought of you as the asshole the women you were screwing over said you were. I thought you were a good and decent man. But now I *agree* with most of the women in Washington, D.C. You are a huge dick."

I took a deep breath. "Micah, do you remember what you told me once about scorned women?"

She sat silently and shook her head.

"You said, and I quote, *women who hang on when it's over are jealous little bitches –jealous of the next girl who'll come along and hold your attention.* Do you remember that?"

The glare she shot me confirmed that she remembered.

How could she not? It was her mantra where my love life was concerned.

"What do you want me to say?"

"I just want you to be happy for me. That's all."

She paused and stared at me. "I'm happy for you," she lied.

I raised my eyebrow and gave her a wicked smile.

"See?" she continued. "I really want to hate your fucking guts and then you do something like that."

"Like what?" I protested. "I just smiled."

She nodded and for the first time since I'd known her she dropped her shoulders and began to cry.

"What's this all about Micah?" I asked as I walked around my desk to be near her. "We don't do this with each other. Our deal is we shoot each other straight. Right?"

She nodded and continued to look down as she wiped her tears and runny nose with the grace of a truck driver.

"What?" I asked again.

"It's just…I miss you and I love you."

"I know," I agreed. "I love and miss you too."

"No. I *love you*, love you," she confessed.

"What?" I stood up and moved away from her as if she'd told me she was contagious.

"I can't help it, goddammit," she sniffed. "I do. And I never thought I felt that way about you, ya know? For years you slept with all those women. But I was the constant in your life. I was always the one you talked to. I was the consoler, the goof. I made you laugh. *I* was the woman in your life," she bellowed as she tapped her clenched fist into her chest.

"Why didn't you ever say anything?" I mumbled as I sat back down in my chair.

"I didn't know I had to. I guess I thought it was pretty

obvious. I guess men, including you, are as stupid as I've been led to believe."

I laughed at her comment.

"Don't laugh. You're only making it worse, dammit."

"I'm not laughing at you –"

"You are –and with good reason. I turned into one of the stupid, stupid girls that had you and can't let you go."

"I guess I'm still confused. It's not like we ever had a physical relationship, Micah. I mean, you're one of the best friends I've ever had. And I don't have friends who are girls."

"Women are funny that way. We get attached. Even when the relationship is platonic."

I shook my head in bewilderment. For the first time in my life, I thought of Micah as a woman and not my trusty sidekick and right hand man. It was more than I wanted to know. It was more than I wanted to wrap my head around – especially today.

"What do you want me to say?" I sighed. I wanted to be mindful of her feelings, and yet at the same time I was a very happily married man who was supposed to be on his honeymoon.

"I don't want you to say anything. I shouldn't have told you. Now there's gonna be this awkward as fuck *thing* between us."

There was the Micah I knew.

I chuckled softly.

"I said don't laugh, you son of a bitch," she ordered.

"I'm not laughing," I smiled and pointed to her. "It's just *that* is the woman I treasure."

She stood and looked away. "I need a smoke."

"You need to quit," I joked. "No man likes to french kiss an ashtray."

"You're such a bastard," she smiled.

"Indeed," I agreed. "But I still need you to do something for me."

"What?"

"Be kind to my wife. She has no idea what we've been through together, but she respects our relationship. She knows how much you mean to me. I just want you to understand how much she means to me too."

"Don't you know I want you to be happy? I just didn't know I was going to feel this way. And I guess until you got married, it still wasn't real to me."

"Even though we just had a baby? You can't get more real than that, Micah."

"Believe me," she sighed. "I know."

"Are we good?" I asked as I hugged her and kissed the top of her head for the first time in as many years as I'd known her.

"We're good," she agreed. "I'm fine."

I nodded and walked away. "I'm leaving to go back to Shadeland this afternoon. My mom's not doing well."

"I know. I'm sorry. Speaking of," Micah scowled. "I should've told you, but we got all tangled up in my feelings and shit."

"What?"

"Sam called. She wants you to call her back."

"Is everything okay?"

"Yeah, she said it wasn't important. I mean an emergency."

"*Everything's* important right now."

26

MAC

"Callahan," I answered as my phone buzzed in my pocket.

"It's Z. We've got a problem. Hector's been following your family."

"What?"

"Dax has drawn pictures of him. He called him Coco. I might be Greek, but I'm pretty damn sure Dax means El Cucuy."

"What?"

"It's Spanish — it means the —"

"Boogeyman," I finished, "Is Dax okay?"

"He's only been talking to him, but Mac, Hector has followed Samantha from Alabama to Pontchartrain and New Orleans."

"How? And how did he get past the agents?"

"Beats the hell out of me. I've pulled up the surveillance tapes of Jackson House to ID him. Dax says he saw him this morning in the gardens."

"Why has Dax been playing anywhere by himself?"

"He hasn't, Mac. He's been with Sam, Polly, or Adelay

the entire time."

"What about Adelay?"

"She's clean, Mac. I can promise you. Everyone in my house is clean."

"But my family's not safe!" I shouted. "They're not safe anywhere."

"Mac, if Hector wanted to hurt Dax, he would've done it by now."

"Where's Samantha?" I barked.

"She's right here. Hang on."

"Mac." Her voice trembled. I knew she was scared.

"Are you okay, sweetheart?" I asked as I paced the room and ran my hands through my hair in nervous desperation.

"He's been everywhere we've been, Mac – Lone Oak, King's house and now Leo's. We're not safe."

"He wants to scare us. He wants us to be afraid of him," I muttered as I thought about Hector's face, twisted with rage right before he pulled the trigger to shoot me a year ago.

"He's doing a good job," Sam sobbed. "He's been talking to Dax. He's been inside, outside. I don't understand. How is this happening? We have FBI agents everywhere and this guy is talking to our son?"

"I don't know, honey."

"I can't do this, Mac. It's too much. Before it was just us, but now he's involved the children. I don't know what I'd do if I lost a child."

"Calm down, sweetheart. We're not losing anyone. I'm going to hang up and send the plane for you. I'll meet you in Shadeland."

"Leo's already a step ahead of you. A plane is waiting for us now. He's coming with us to Shadeland."

I exhaled, thankful that Z was taking care of business. "I love you, sweetheart. Try to stay strong. We'll be together soon," I promised.

"There's more, Mac. I called today, but Micah wouldn't let me talk to you,"

"Yeah, well, that's a whole other story…"

"What?" she asked.

"I'll explain later. What else?" I asked as I frantically began to pull my papers together to get the hell out of D.C. as soon as possible.

"It's Richard," she said. "I called the family attorney today and I think maybe he's up to something."

"Like what?" I stopped shuffling papers.

"He's pulled the deed on Mimi's house and property and has asked about her will."

"Okay…" I paused.

"I get the house and property when Mimi passes away. But if something happens to me…"

She didn't need to say anything more. It hit me like a ton of bricks.

"Sam," I pleaded. "Do not leave Z's side. Do not leave the children alone. All of you stay together and with Z. I'll be right behind you."

"Mac," she sobbed. "You're scaring me even more. Do you think Richard wants me…" She paused and I could hear her hiccup through her tears. "Dead?"

"I don't know, sweetheart," I lied. "But promise me you'll stay with Z and the other agents. Nothing by yourself."

"Okay," she sniffed.

"Say 'I promise, Mac'."

"I promise," Samantha choked out.

"I love you very much, baby, and I'll see you at Lone

Oak."

"I love you too."

"Remember, stay with Z. Now let me talk with him before you hang up."

I sat down and held my head in my hand and tried to hold in what was left of my sanity. I was trained for a hellfire shit-storm. It was different when it was my own family.

"Yeah," Z's voice boomed on the line.

"Are you on the move?"

"Affirmative. We're trying to get a twenty on Hector."

"The safety of my family is in your hands."

"I understand."

"I'll meet you at Shadeland. If he's tailing us, he'll show up soon enough. Hector wants a party and I'm gonna kick down the front door to bring it to him."

"Agreed," Z answered.

I hung up and immediately called Moss at Mimi's home.

"Sir," he barked.

"I want a twenty on Richard Peterson."

"Be advised he's on the premises."

"I want him kept there. I don't give a good goddamn what you have to do to make it happen. Don't let him leave," I ground out.

"Yes, sir."

"I'm on my way to Shadeland. If you have any trouble out of him, you can let him know I'll personally put a boot up his ass."

"Yes, sir."

"Who's covering my mother and Mrs. Peterson at Autumn Valley?"

"I just got word. Your mother is out of the cardiac unit and back in her room. They each have an agent at her door and the state police are watching the grounds closely."

"I'm on my way."

I hung up without saying another word and shouted for Micah.

"Yes?"

"Call the pilot. I want to be wheels up in an hour."

"Where to?"

"Home."

The jet didn't arrive fast enough for me and the flight path was too long. I was anxious to get to my family and everything seemed to be in slow motion.

I looked through the evidence we had on Hector and now Richard. There was no doubt in my mind they were working together.

My phone rang as I began to come to grips with that reality.

"It's Micah," she began. "We got the trace on the call in to Richard Peterson."

"And?"

"Pretty sure it's Hector. They've traced the originating calls from Shadeland, New Orleans and..." she paused. "Slidell?"

"Lake Pontchartrain," I muttered. "It's him."

"There's more."

"What?"

"They're tracking the phone right now via GPS, Mac. It's in Shadeland, Alabama."

"He's there already. Where?"

"Last report was the town square. What's that close to?"

"Autumn Valley."

We landed and the black sedan that met me knew I was going to the nursing home. I'd put out an APB on Hector, but we had nothing.

I pulled the phone from my pocket as we drove and dialed Z.

"What's the word?" he answered.

"I'm on the ground and on my way to Autumn Valley. We had a lock on Hector's phone. He's here in town. I've got agents out looking, but he's pulled the battery or tossed the phone and we've lost him."

"Our ETA is nineteen hundred hours," Z reported. "We'll head straight to Lone Oak. I've called ahead. It's secure."

"I've got Moss watching over Peterson," I replied. "He's on lockdown until I can get to his ass."

"I'll let you know when we're back at base."

"Thank you, Z."

"You'd do it for me."

"You know I would."

As we drove up the lane to Autumn Valley, I took a deep breath and prayed Mom was safe.

It was past six o'clock and visiting hours were over as I stopped at security and flashed my badge.

"Plenty of y'all around tonight," the guard replied.

I nodded, thinking that was a good thing – the more agents the better.

I walked the familiar hallway, wishing so many things were different. As I wandered the C wing and approached the door to Momma's suite, I spotted King behind the nurses' station.

Giving him a nod, he held up a finger and quickly hung up.

"Mac, wait. Come with me," he said as he quickly ushered me into a small room beside the nurses' lounge, closing the door behind us.

"What's up? I asked. "I'm anxious to see my mother."

"Mac," he hesitated. His face was ashen and his eyes lifeless. I knew the words that were coming next. I didn't want to hear them. I looked away and back to his face again hoping he'd give me a different expression, but his pale and quiet tone said everything he didn't want to. "I'm sorry."

My ears began to ring as I sat in one of the fading leather chairs in the small room. I glanced over and saw a single box of tissues on the end table and realized *this is the room where you hear the news.*

"She's gone, Mac," said King.

My mother was dead. The room began to spin. I could see his mouth moving, I knew he was talking to me, but the buzz in my head was deafening and everything seemed in slow motion and on mute.

"She had another heart attack. We did everything we could, but we were afraid this could happen. We couldn't revive her, Mac."

I felt the cold leather under my hands as I shook my head. I wasn't getting what he was saying. I knew what the words meant, but it was as if he wasn't talking to me. It wasn't real. He wasn't talking to *me.*

"Mac?" he said again, trying to get my attention.

"I don't understand," I stumbled.

"There was nothing we could do."

"What?" I asked again.

"I think you're going into shock, Mac."

"No. I don't understand."

King grabbed my shoulders. It was as if I was watching everything that was happening but no longer a part of it.

"Mac, your mother has passed away. Now, I've not let your agents in the room. I wanted to talk with you first."

The words sank in. *Your mother has passed away.* My mother was gone. My mother was gone and I didn't get to say goodbye. "I can see her?" I asked.

"Yes. I'll take you to her, but I need to know you're understanding what I'm saying."

"My mother is dead."

King nodded and stood. "Do you want to see her now or do you need a minute?"

"Now."

We walked into her suite as the cardiac equipment was pushed from the room. The nurses cast their eyes to the floor as I passed them.

King silently stopped the agents before they made it to me, and I heard one of them say the word *sorry*.

The room was growing darker as the sun had almost set outside and one small light above her bed illuminated her frail body.

I walked to the bedside and King placed a chair behind me.

"Stay as long as you'd like. No one will bother you," King assured me. "Would you like for me to call Samantha?"

I shook my head. "She's on a plane with the kids. She'll be here in an hour."

I felt the weight of his hand on my shoulder before he turned, leaving me alone with what was left of my beautiful mother.

I touched her frail hand, now resting on her chest outside a blanket and dropped my head. With one breath I began to sob.

She was empty and somehow no longer even looked like herself. The once vibrant woman with the beautiful smile and contagious laugh was gone. And just like Dad, I'd missed saying goodbye.

27

SAMANTHA

The wheels screeched as the plane landed in the small airport outside of Montgomery. We were still thirty minutes from home and the children were already asleep.

Polly kept a close eye on them as I asked Leo question after question. I wanted to know the plan. I wanted to know everything. Where had Hector been? Where was he going? Was he still following us? Had Mac landed and where was he?

Leo did his best to comfort me, but he divulged little and by the time we hit the runway, I just wanted to get to Lone Oak and get the children into their beds. We'd been on the run for a week – a week too long.

Timms met us at the airport along with two FBI sedans. We had an escort all the way home.

As Leo's phone rang, he looked to me and said one word, "Mac."

My heart jumped.

"What?" Leo said softly into the phone as he turned away from me. "Of course. She's right here. I'm so sorry,

Mac."

Leo handed me the phone over the front seat and gave me a solemn look.

"What?" I asked in a whisper as I took the phone from Leo.

"Mac?"

"Sweetheart." His voice cracked with emotion. "It's so good to hear your voice."

"Mac, what is it?"

"It's my mother, Sam." He paused as I heard him gasp for air. "She's dead."

I put my hand over my mouth and closed my eyes. Trying to concentrate solely on the sound of his voice drowning everything else out.

"When?"

"Just before I got here. She had a fatal heart attack. I didn't get to say goodbye."

"I'm so sorry, sweetheart."

He was quiet on the other end of the line. I knew from past experience there was nothing to be said in this moment. No words were consoling enough to take away the pain. He was numb. And I understood.

"Will you come to the nursing home? Z needs to stay with the children," he whispered, doing his best to hold in his emotions.

"I'll have them drop me there first. We'll be there as soon as we can," I promised.

We sat in silence and I listened to him breathe on the phone line. Neither of us had anything to say. There was nothing *to* say.

"I'll stay on the phone with you until I arrive."

I heard him take a deep breath and sigh through his tears.

"No."

"Are you sure?"

"Just knowing you're on the way makes me feel better."

"I'm on the way," I whispered.

"I love you, baby."

"I love you," I whimpered into the phone. I tried to be strong for Mac, but I'd lost the ability to hold in my tears.

I handed the phone to Leo. "Thank you."

"I'm so sorry, Samantha," Polly added.

I leaned into Timms as he drove and stroked his arm. "Timms, I have some bad news."

"Miss Nancy has passed," he replied, not taking his eyes from the road.

"Yes."

"I'm sure Mr. Edward was waiting for her," he nodded. "It's as it should be."

"I guess," I replied.

"I *don't* guess," he continued. "Heaven gained an angel tonight, Miss Samantha. I'm sure of it."

Leo made sure an agent met me at the doors of Autumn Valley and I rushed through the entrance trying to make my way to Mac as quickly as possible. I turned onto the C wing and spotted King in the hallway. He opened his arms to me and pulled me in for a hug.

"Where is –"

Before I could finish my sentence, King nodded to Nancy's room.

"He's been in there alone. I told him to take as much time as he needs."

"Thank you," I whispered as King gave my hand a reassuring squeeze.

"She made all her own arrangements, Sam, so let Mac know there's nothing he needs to do except meet with the counselor. Everything can be handled from there."

I nodded and slowly opened the door.

Mac looked up to me as I walked to Nancy's bedside. It was as quiet as anyone might expect. Death was funny that way. And even though I knew he'd gone through this with his father and I with Daniel, nothing prepares you for the finality of it.

He stood and I rushed into his arms. We held each other tightly without saying a word. I rocked him back and forth and felt him begin to sob on my shoulder.

I knew I had to be strong. It was my turn.

I finally took his face in my hands and kissed his tear-stained cheeks. "We'll get through this," I promised him. "We'll get through this together."

He nodded and kissed me.

"Z's with the children?"

"Yes," I confirmed. "And Polly. They should be home by now. Sweetheart, I told Timms."

"He loved her so much. Took such good care of her."

I nodded and choked back the emotion flooding my body.

"Tell me what you need," I said as we sat down on the couch in Nancy's suite. "King said we could stay here as long as we want. Everything is already planned. We just need to meet with a counselor before we leave for some instructions."

He nodded and dropped his head into my lap. "I didn't get to say goodbye, Sam. I didn't get to tell her goodbye."

I stroked his hair. "I remember when we left King's

house you held her hands and told her you loved her. You even asked if she understood and she nodded. Do you remember what she said to you?"

"Be good."

"Be good," I agreed as I continued to stroke his back.

"I don't want to leave her."

"I know, sweetheart. You don't have to," I cried, unable to hold my tears in any longer. "You know, Timms said something tonight. He said it was as it should be. Your mom was never *really* happy after your father died. He said Mr. Edward was waiting for her to arrive."

"It's true. They never spent more than a couple of days apart the entire time they were married. They couldn't bear to be away from one another."

"Kinda like us," I smiled through my tears.

"Exactly like us," he agreed.

I nodded and took his hand in mine. "Sorry our honeymoon has been such a disaster."

"*I'm* sorry it's been such a disaster."

I nodded. "Couldn't be helped."

Mac sniffed as he sat up to look at me. "Timms is right. She's not confused or afraid anymore. Most of all, she's with my dad."

I nodded and wiped my tears on the sleeve of my sweater.

"Sorry, baby," Mac said as he stood to search his back pocket for a linen handkerchief. "I didn't bring a handkerchief today."

"It's okay," I smiled as I walked to Nancy's bathroom in search of a Kleenex. I flipped on the light and looked across the marble vanity for the box I knew was there. Pulling a tissue, I blew my nose and looked into the mirror expecting to be horrified by the mascara running down my cheeks.

I blotted my eyes and turned on the faucet to splash water on my face. I opened my eyes and stumbled backwards and out of the bathroom with a gasp.

"Mac," I whimpered.

"Yes?" he asked as she stood over his mother's body shaking his head.

"He's been here."

I backed away from the bathroom and put my hand to my mouth. Mac walked toward me and I pointed my shaking finger to the mirror where a single kiss mark in red lipstick was smudged in the center. Two words were written underneath. *Remember me?*

"Mimi!" I shouted.

I rushed past the agent and walked into her room, startling her at once.

"Who's there?" she asked.

"It's Sam."

"Samantha?" Mimi's voice cracked.

I walked toward her bed as she turned on the lamp by her bedside. "Thank God, Mimi."

"What's wrong?"

I paused to catch my breath now that I knew she was safe. "Why would you think something's wrong?" I sobbed, breaking down and dropping my head into my hands.

"Darlin'," she consoled as she reached out to me.

I fell into Mimi and cried uncontrollably. For the first time I let out every emotion I'd had over the past two weeks. I was mad, heartbroken, afraid, frustrated and confused. It all poured out of me at once as if the leaky dam had burst into a cataclysmic wave.

I laid my head in her lap. She didn't say a word, but continued to stroke my hair from front to back.

"Life's hard."

"I guess if it was easy, we'd call it something else," she said softly. "Do you want to tell me what's wrong?"

I lifted my head and wiped the tears from my face with the sleeve of my sweater yet again. "Nancy died tonight."

Mimi took a full and deep breath and I watched as her tiny body expanded and contracted with her sigh. She was so frail these days, her body starting to revolt from the ninety-nine years it had protected her.

"She was a beautiful lady inside and out," Mimi sighed. "I shall miss my friend. Mac's taking it hard, I'm sure."

"It's worse, Mimi. Hector was in her room. He's been here. He's followed me everywhere and I don't want to worry you – I think Richard may have something to do with all of this. I was worried that you –"

"Now stop." Mimi pursed her lips. It had taken me years to know when she was really angry. This was it. She took another deep breath and looked me in the eye, "I gave up worrying years ago. Worrying is for amateurs, people who think they have some sort of divine control over their destiny. If you live to be as old as I am, you've seen just about everything."

"Mimi, I'm talking about our safety. Hector wants me dead. And now I'm pretty sure Richard wants the same for both of us. Aren't you afraid?" I asked as I hiccupped through my tears and stood to pace the room. "If Hector can get to Nancy, he could get to you and I'm done with people dying. I've had enough of it!"

"Afraid?" Mimi asked. "Afraid of Hector? Hell no. If he thinks he can end me then tell him to bring it on. I'm about twenty years past my expiration date already."

"And Richard? I called Pete Peterson. Richard's pulled the title and deed to your house. He wants it."

"You think he's gonna kill you and me to get that house and property?"

"No. He'll have Hector do it for him."

Mimi shook her head and motioned me to her. "Come here, sweetheart. You're worrying about things you needn't worry about."

She took my hand and kissed it, giving it a loving squeeze. "You take care of your husband. He needs you right now. Be strong for him."

"I'm tired of being strong," I whined.

"Samantha, it takes balls to be a woman. And you've got 'em. I should know. You got 'em from me," she smiled. "Now find your husband and take care of him."

"What about you? I couldn't bear it if something happened to you. If Hector…"

"I know, I know," she nodded. "But I have a big strong FBI agent outside my door with a firearm on his side. I think I'll be just fine. That is as long as he can shoot straight. God forbid he hit an oxygen tank in here and blow us all to hell."

I gave her a single laugh through the tears still streaming down my face.

"That's my girl," she sang. "Now, get your balls out of your purse and go find your husband. You're a Peterson. Act like it."

I said the only two words she wanted to hear from me. "Yes, ma'am."

"King?" I asked as he walked down the hallway. "Do you think Hector could've caused the heart attack? I mean, do you think he scared her and then it happened?"

"There wasn't anyone in the room when we got to her for the cardiac code. She was still on telemetry from her last episode a couple of days ago. I guess anything's possible. I just don't know how anyone would've gotten past the agent at the door."

Mac wandered the hallway. I looked into his eyes as he walked past me toward the room as if I wasn't there.

"Mac," I spoke up. "I'm right here, sweetheart."

He turned and the distant gaze of his empty face left me worried. He was a broken man and it showed.

"Tell me what can I do for you."

"Nothing," he said, looking back into his mother's suite. Nancy's once beautiful room had been transformed into a crime scene in the blink of an eye.

"Do you want to go home and get some rest? We can check in on all of this tomorrow."

"I'm not leaving," he said without making eye contact. "But you should go home."

"I'm not going anywhere without you, Mac. If you stay, then I stay."

"Whatever," he said as he walked away.

Suddenly my husband was absent. He was absent from himself and I was more worried for him than I was for my own safety.

28

MAC

I sat in Dad's old study and looked around the room. On my desk were photos of the lipstick on the mirror from my wedding day and now Momma's room.

I sipped on Maker's Mark as I looked at all the portraits that hung there. Over the fireplace were my parents. Young and vibrant, they held onto each other in love. The other portraits, my grandparents and their families before them. I was the only Callahan left. A long line of fine men and women and what was left? Me. Piece of shit me.

I looked into the painted eyes of my father and whispered, "I'm sorry." I didn't know what else there was to say. I was an FBI agent and I couldn't even keep my own family safe.

I thought I'd finally made it past the guilt and feelings of inadequacy when I met Sam and had a child of my own. And yet, here I sat, alone in my pity. My father would be so disappointed in me for not keeping my mother safe.

I took the last gulp of bourbon and poured myself another. The numbness was beginning to overtake me, and everything was slipping away, including my will to care.

I heard a knock at the door and Sam's voice calling to me.

"Mac, open the door."

"I just want to be alone right now," I shouted. "Please," I begged.

"I'm worried about you."

"I'm fine," I mumbled.

"I can't hear you, Mac. Please open the door."

"I said," I shouted as I dropped my head back in a drunken surrender. "I'm fine!"

"Mac," Samantha insisted as she banged on the door causing a rattle. "Open this door. Now."

I said nothing as I stared at the photographs on the desk. I could feel my eyelids drooping with each deliberate blink.

"Mac, open this door or I'm taking someone's gun and shooting the lock off. I'm coming in one way or another. Now," she continued with gusto. "If you want me to ruin this two hundred year old mahogany door, I will. Or you can just open it!"

I pushed myself away from the desk and stumbled to the door. With one turn of the wrist I unlocked it with the skeleton key and walked away.

Samantha burst through the door just as I took a seat.

She looked at me with wild eyes. I just wanted to be left alone. Was that too much to ask? I couldn't look at her. It was too hard. I couldn't look at her and not think about everything that had happened in the last week.

She walked straight to me and dropped to her knees in front of me. I looked away as she took my hand and kissed it. I was drunk, pissed off and had never felt so overcome with emotion before. I wasn't strong. I was weak. So weak that I'd allowed a man to come between my family and me.

I'd allowed a man to get the best of me, professionally and personally. I wallowed in it and I sank into the couch further, pulling my hand from her as I tried my best to disconnect and simply feel the bourbon.

"What are you going to do, Mac?" she asked as she walked away from me. "Sit in here and pretend what's happening isn't happening? There are armed men standing outside our children's bedrooms right now. A crazy man is on the loose – talking to our son and looking for *me*. And yet you're in here getting drunk?" she ranted as she picked up the wax-sealed bottle and gave it a strong shake before slamming it on the desk.

I looked up at her through my blurred vision. "I'm sorry," I whimpered, my voice cracking.

"I'm sorry," she repeated as she took a seat next to me on the couch. "Mac, I want to be your rock, but shutting me out when all we have is each other isn't going to work."

I nodded. "I couldn't save her, Sam. I let her down. I let my father down."

"Is that what this is about?" she asked. "You think because your mother had a heart attack, which King told you was inevitable, you've somehow failed as a son?"

I couldn't even respond.

"Your mother had a beautiful heart that stopped working."

"I let it happen."

"All you've done is try to take care of everyone. Hector is evil and I'm scared to death of him." She took my chin and turned my face to meet hers. "But I *believe* in you."

I blinked in an alcohol-fueled slow motion.

"Now, I love you. But I'm not above kicking your ass right now. It's time to buck up *and* sober up."

I nodded.

"All the arrangements have been made for your mother. The funeral is day after tomorrow. She had everything planned down to the last detail."

"I suppose she knew I wouldn't handle this well."

Sam nodded and gave my hand a squeeze. "Let's get you in the shower and I'll have Celia make you some coffee."

"Oh God," I gasped. "Miss Celia. Did you –?"

"Her father told her, sweetheart. Everyone is more worried about you."

"I'm worried about *you*," I slurred as I took her face in my hands. Abruptly I stood and walked to the desk and picked up the photos again. "He's not finished, Sam."

Sam snatched the papers without looking. "He may not have anything to lose, but I've got *everything* to lose. And I'll be damned to hell if I'm going to let Hector take it."

I awoke on the couch in Dad's study, covered in a blanket. My head ached and my mouth was dry. As I sat up, Miss Celia walked into the room and gave me a glare.

"Well look who's decided to join the living."

I rubbed my hands through my hair and realized I still had on a shirt and tie from last night. "Celia," I began. "I don't know what to say."

"Baby, you know I'd do anything for you. I love you like you are my own child."

I nodded, knowing I was in for a lecture when all I really wanted to do was hug her.

"But your momma would be upset with you if she knew you were acting this way. You're a Callahan."

"I know," I groaned. "And she'd say it just like that I'm

sure."

"You've got a mess of people running around this house who are counting on you. And I don't think I need to remind you that there are two little people who are counting on their daddy to take care of them."

I nodded. "Celia, I wasn't there. I couldn't stop him from scaring her, and now..."

"And now she's gone," she said. "Baby, if I know Miss Nancy, and believe me I do, she wouldn't give Hector the satisfaction of scaring her to death. Miss Nancy's stronger than any old lowlife."

I nodded again.

"Now the question is," she paused. "Are you?"

I didn't answer her but instead asked a question. "Where's Sam?"

"She's upstairs with the children. Your FBI friends wanted me to wake you, but I told them anyone who woke you up would have to deal with me."

I gave Celia a half-hearted smile.

"It's a new day, McKay Waverly Callahan. Get in the shower. Go to your bride. I'll get you some coffee."

I stood and stretched as my head pounded with each beat of my heart.

"Miss Celia?" I asked, dropping my arms to my sides. "Can I get a hug?"

"Everything's gonna be okay, baby," she sighed as she hugged me tightly. "Your momma and daddy knew this day would come. All they ever wanted was for you to be happy and have a family of your own. They're together again, and I know they're lookin' down on you and smilin' at you and those two beautiful babies."

"You're right. I know," I managed.

"Now get yourself in the shower. You smell like sweat

and drunk hippies."

I raised an eyebrow at her.

"Don't give me that look. I lived through the seventies and I know what no-good smells like."

I shook my head at her and walked to the phone. Calling Agent Moss, I waited for him to answer.

"Yes, sir."

"Meet me at Lone Oak in forty-five minutes. How's Richard handling being on lockdown?"

"He's not, sir. I think I've been called everything in the book and he's had his attorney contact us."

I scoffed. "Good. He's gonna need him. Forty-five minutes."

"Yes, sir."

My room was empty and the bed hadn't been touched. I wondered where Sam had slept last night. I quickly showered and shaved and walked the long hallway to the nursery hoping to find her.

As I opened the door, the hinges gave a creak and she looked up to me watching her rock Katy while Dax sat at a small table and played.

I said nothing but went to her and dropped to my knees. I kissed Katy on the head. It was the first time I'd seen her in days. A flood of emotions overcame me, but I choked them down as I swallowed hard to speak.

"I'm sorry." It was all I could say.

"Apology accepted."

"You're too good for me. You know that?"

She shook her head. "How are you feeling?"

"I've had some Advil and Celia's got coffee waiting for me downstairs."

She nodded and kissed Katy on the head as I walked over to Dax and picked him up from the drawing table, wrapping his arms around my neck myself.

"How's my big boy today?"

"Good."

"Mommy says you've been drawing. Can you show me?" I asked as I sat him back down in his chair.

"You mean Coco?" he asked as if he was in trouble.

"Yes."

"Mr. Leo has them," he said, looking down at his hands.

"Dax," I began. "You're not in trouble for talking to him."

"Who?" Dax asked. "Coco?"

"Is that what he told you his name was?"

"He said I could call him that."

I nodded. "Where did you meet him? I mean the very first time. Where did you see him first?"

"Here."

"Here, where? Lone Oak?"

Dax nodded. "He was in the garden."

"Doing what?"

"Flowers."

"He was hiding in the flowers?"

Dax shook his head. "He was planting the flowers."

I looked to Samantha wide-eyed and stunned.

"Where did you see him after that?"

"Dr. King's house."

"Dax drew a picture of El Cucuy by the lake," said Samantha.

"You did?"

"Yeah," he mumbled.

"Where did you see him again?" I asked.

"With Adelay. He was in the garden."

"At Mr. Leo's house?"

"Yeah, the big house with all the flowers."

"What was he doing there, Dax? Do you remember?"

"Planting flowers."

"Did he work for Mr. Leo? Did Adelay know him by name?"

Dax shook his head. "She didn't talk to him. Only me. He says only I can see him."

I looked to Samantha. I could see the fear in her eyes as she tried to remain calm.

"We're not talking to strangers ever again. Are we, Dax?"

"He's not a stranger. He's my friend."

"He's not a friend, Dax," I explained as I sat him down and looked him in the eye. "Sometimes bad people want us to think they are our friends, but what they really want is to get close enough so you'll trust them. They want you to be comfortable."

"I'm not allowed to talk to him anymore," Dax said as he looked into the crayon box for another color.

"It's best if you stay inside and play for a few days. Besides I think it's going to rain today and probably tomorrow too," I explained.

Dax said nothing but looked up to me with the big blue eyes that matched his mother's and blinked. "You've not done anything wrong, Dax. In fact, you're being a huge help to me and the other agents."

"Promise me you won't hurt him, Daddy."

"What?" I asked.

"I said, promise me you won't hurt him. He's my friend."

"Dax," I said.

"Mac–" Sam interrupted. "May I speak with you in the other room?"

I nodded as she put Katy in her crib.

"Stay here, Dax, I'll be right back," Sam promised.

We walked the hallway without saying a word to each other and I closed the door to my bedroom behind us.

"I can't promise Dax that I won't hurt Hector. I *want* to hurt Hector," I said as I paced the old creaky floor of the room.

"He doesn't see the bad in anyone, Mac. He's an innocent child."

I grunted as I pulled on a suit jacket and adjusted its collar. "I need you to stay in the house today, understand?"

"I'm going to see Mimi a little later."

"What? No." I ordered.

"Don't tell me what I can and can't do, Mac. I'm going to Autumn Valley to see Mimi today and that's final. You can send a agent with me, but I'm going."

"And who's going to stay here with the kids?"

"You are."

"What?" I asked. "I've got Agent Moss on his way here so we can go over everything. Hector's somewhere close. I can feel it"

"You just *think* he's close. You don't know. He could've moved on by now. Especially if he realized that Nancy…"

"What? You think when he realized he killed my mother last night that he'd go into hiding somewhere? Wake up, Sam!" I shouted. "He wants you dead. Do you understand? Dead."

"I've never seen you like this, Mac."

"What? On the verge of losing everyone I love?"

"You've got to calm down," Samantha insisted. "You're

of no use to us if you're out of your mind."

"I'm sorry, Samantha. I have a wife and two kids I'm trying to keep safe, a dead mother I have to bury tomorrow and a crazed psychopath hot on the trail of the people I love. Oh, and let's not forget the psycho's been playing with our son! Not to mention your crazy-ass cousin who's up to God knows what."

"Are you finished?" she asked calmly.

"I don't know," I said sarcastically. "Did I miss anything?"

"I really don't like you right now."

"You don't have to like me. What you have to do is listen and follow orders. You are *not* leaving this house today."

"Watch me," she said as she walked out of the room and slammed the door.

29

SAMANTHA

"Polly," I shouted up the stairs. "Polly?"

I saw her make her way to the top of the banister sporting a guilty look.

"Yeah, Sam. I'm right here," she shouted over the side of the staircase. "Sam?" she asked again, still not seeing me at the bottom.

"Oh for goodness sake," I sighed. "Wait there. I'm coming up."

With each step I took toward Polly, I became weaker and more emotional. The past week was supposed to be the happiest of my life, and instead it'd been the most stressful days I'd had since Daniel died.

"Are you okay?" Polly asked as Leo joined her in the hallway.

I'd almost forgotten that Leo was even in the house. Between the agents scrambling around while I consoled Mac, I was clueless as to who was really even staying my home.

"Hey, Leo." I tried to smile at both of them, but the feeling was escaping me.

"How's Mac doing?" Leo asked as he rubbed his dark two-day beard. I could tell he was sincerely worried. Leo felt bad about Hector breaking the security at Jackson House.

"Not too good. I need you both to watch the children today. I'm going into town to see Mimi at Autumn Valley and tie up some loose ends in Nancy's room."

Neither of them said a word, but both nodded and I knew from the look on Polly's face she was with me.

"I'm going to shower and shave and I need to meet with Mac and Agent Moss, but I'll keep an extra eye on Dax today. He'll need to stay inside," said Leo.

"He'll understand," I agreed.

Leo gave me a nod and walked away, but not without giving Polly a glance.

She watched him all the way down the hall and I stood dumbfounded as he shut the door to a guest room behind him.

"What?" Polly said as she met my questioning face.

"What's going on with you and Leo?"

"Nothing," she sang as she began to walk away. I wasn't letting her off the hook that easily and followed.

"*Nothing* isn't going to cut it with me, Polly."

I followed her into Dax's room where he still sat at his table drawing.

"What do you want me to say?" she asked with a silly grin on her face.

"I guess I want to know if you're..." I paused and moved closer. "Sleeping with Leo."

"No," she chided. "Why would you say that?"

"Maybe the looks you're giving each other? Anyway, I can't handle anyone's life but my own today," I sighed. "Never mind."

"Is Mac that bad off?"

I looked to the floor and held in my tears. "He's a mess. He's trying his best to cope by going full force after Hector."

"Any leads?"

"I don't know. I'm just trying to keep my head above water at this point."

She nodded and pulled me in for a hug.

"When are you leaving to see Mimi?"

"Now," I replied as I took a deep breath and walked to Dax for a kiss.

"Dax, be a good boy and listen to everything Daddy and Mr. Leo tell you today. Okay?"

"Okay," he relented. "Daddy says I can't go outside today."

"There's lots of fun things we can do inside, Dax," Polly added. "I know Miss Celia was planning on making cookies today and I'd just bet she'd love to have an extra set of hands in the kitchen."

"Cookies?" he asked as his face lit up. "What kind?"

"I don't know, but if you'll come with me we can ask her," said Polly as she held her hand out to him.

I hugged them both and walked into the bedroom for my purse. I gave myself a glance in the bathroom mirror and thought about the words that had once been there.

Remember me? What did Hector want me to remember? That he still wanted me dead. Did he want to tell me he was never going away? I shook my head and opened the vanity drawer to find some lipstick. I didn't want to look too haggard if I was going to see Mimi. She worried about me so much. The stress of the last couple of weeks had taken its toll and I couldn't imagine what it had done to my ninety-nine year old grandmother.

Pulling the drawer halfway open I looked into my

makeup and thought again about Hector. *Remember me?* How could I forget him? He'd been everywhere and yet nowhere at all. Maybe he really was the boogeyman he'd proclaimed himself to be to Dax.

My makeup had been arranged ever-so-carefully by the organizing team when the movers brought my things to Lone Oak. The lipsticks, organized by shade from darkest to lightest were each in their own little compartment in the clear acrylic holder. I ran my hands over them, deciding on a nude to match the tan sundress I'd already donned for the day. I pulled the drawer out fully to look for spare mascara.

The second group of lipsticks came into view. The dark pinks to the reds. And there it was – an empty spot that should've held my favorite Chanel red lipstick.

A pit landed in my stomach and I wondered if Hector had taken it from its spot in the drawer. I grabbed my purse from the bed and emptied it looking for Chanel Red 98. Sifting through the remnants of last week I found a pacifier, a blue crayon, gum, my wallet and finally my red lipstick. I sat on the bed and sighed.

I decided to forgo the mascara. I'd probably only cry it off when I saw Mimi. I whisked myself through the house and out the back door without telling Mac goodbye. I'd already told him where I was going.

I grabbed the keys to Pussy Galore, his father's 1963 Aston Martin DB5 convertible. Mac and his father loved this car. It always seemed to give him a little pick me up when he drove it, so I decided it might do the same for me.

As I roared out of the driveway with the top down I realized I'd not told an agent to come with me. Before I could even dig my phone out of my purse it was ringing.

"What do you think you're doing?"

I could tell by the tone of Mac's voice that he was on

the verge of completely losing it. "I'm on my way to see Mimi. I hope you don't mind that I took the convertible."

"I don't care about the car. What I *do* care about is my wife. Why did you leave without an agent?"

"I'm sorry. I guess I wasn't thinking."

I was being honest. My mind was all abuzz to get to Mimi and then to Nancy's room to collect her things. I didn't think to ask one of the agents to come with me.

"I've got Agent Davis on your tail now. He'll follow you to the nursing home and stick with you. Okay?"

"Okay," I agreed as I looked into my rearview mirror and saw the black sedan.

"Sam, I'm trusting you to go to Autumn Valley to see Mimi and come straight back. I don't have time to worry about you today."

"I promise," I agreed, not divulging the fact that I'd be cleaning out and boxing up Nancy's suite.

"I love you, Mac."

I could hear his heavy sigh on the other end. "I love you too." The crack in his voice reminded me how fresh the wounds of his mother's death were even though he acted as if catching Hector was really on his mind. It was more of a distraction than anything. The funeral tomorrow would be brutal.

"I'll come straight back. Don't worry about me. I'll stay with my agent."

"Mimi?" I called to her as I pushed open the big door that lead to her suite.

"Come in," she chimed.

Mimi was sitting by the window dressed in a yellow sweater set and khakis. She looked good considering I'd woken her up in the middle of the night.

"How are you today?" I asked.

"How am I? How are *you*?" she asked with the best smile she could muster.

I nodded, fearful if I opened my mouth the tears would begin to flow.

"I'm not buying what you're selling, sweetheart. Come here and let me give you a hug."

I walked to her and knelt on the floor, burying my head in her lap. "I just want it to stop. I want it to stop and all end."

"What, sweetheart?"

"Everything. All I wanted was a beautiful wedding, two happy and healthy children and a husband who loves me. What I have is Hector, who's trying to kill me and a cousin I think might be trying to help him. Not to mention my mother-in-law just died and I'm pretty sure my husband's ex-assistant is in love with him."

She stroked my hair and smiled. "I'm only going to say this once, Samantha. Get down off the cross."

"What?"

"You heard me."

She brushed the flyaway hair that surrounded my face after the windy ride to Autumn Valley. "Get down off the cross, Sam. Someone else needs the wood."

I gave her a tearful smirk. "Can't I just wallow for a few minutes?"

"Do *you* think you have time to wallow?"

"No."

"Well, then," she said with a twinkle in her eye. "Then it's time to get on with it. Isn't it?"

"You're a tough old broad, aren't you?" I deadpanned.

"I've said it once and I'll say it again—you can't live as long as I have and not have seen a few things."

I nodded.

"C'mon, Samantha. Listen to what you're saying. You *did* have a beautiful wedding and you *have* two happy, healthy children. I know Mac loves you and for goodness sake, he's hotter that hell – women are always going to make eyes at your husband. Wear it as a badge of honor. You know he's yours. So does he. And as far as Hector and The Dick, well, there's just evil in the world."

"And what am I supposed to do about that?" I asked. "Mac is falling apart after Nancy's death and I don't know what to do for him."

"Sure you do," she said, taking my hands. "Be yourself. Love him."

"What if it's not enough? I'm continually bending beyond what I think I can take. But in my own defense, I don't break."

"Of course not. You're a wife and mother. You're a Southern woman. Anyone knows that's a combination you don't fuck with."

"Mimi," I gasped. "I knew where you were going. You didn't have to drop the F bomb."

"It takes balls to be a woman."

"Yes, I know. You've said this to me before."

"If you know, then it's time to let 'em swing."

"Mimi," I scolded.

"Hell yes. Let them swing so big that everyone can see them."

"I don't even know where to begin or what to do. I'm overwhelmed."

She shook her head and used her walker to stand.

"Where are you going?" I asked.

"It's where *we're* going."

"Mimi, you need to rest. I've had you on a wild ride since the wedding day."

"Ha!" she laughed. "It's been a wild ride for a while now, sweetheart. Come with me."

She motioned for me to join her as she opened the door to her suite. As the light shone from the fluorescent blubs casting a pale green light into her room, I was reminded that she *was* living in a nursing home, no matter how much they disguised it with upscale furnishings. People came here to live out their last days—including Mimi and Nancy.

"Come with me, handsome," Mimi smiled at the agent guarding her door. "We've got some work to do."

Mimi sat on the couch of the now empty suite. We'd been packing Nancy's things and sorting through items for the last two hours. She'd been at Autumn Valley for five years – a little longer than Mimi, and in those five years she'd amassed quite a few knickknacks. There were books – I knew Mimi read to her often, postcards and letters from Mac telling her about his adventures and a drawer full of cards from the florist –no doubt that accompanied many birthday and Mother's Day arrangements Mac had sent to her.

Her beautiful clothes were perfectly aligned in her closet and color matched from darkest to lightest. Even in her Alzheimer's she loved order.

I stared at the safe in the wall that separated her closet from the bathroom. Most patients at Autumn Valley were wealthy and brought valuables with them to the home to live. Nancy was no different.

She'd cleaned out the safe and given Mac the key six months ago, afraid that in a confused state she might give away something she would later regret. For the most part, she'd removed most of her valuable jewelry with the exception of her pearls. He knew she wore them almost every day and in fact died in the grand style of a great Southern lady – wearing her lipstick and pearls.

I pulled the key from my pocket, and as the lock clicked I didn't really know what to expect. There were several jewelry boxes, some papers, a small letterbox and a book.

I took them out in one motion, using the large envelope that sat below everything as a tray.

Placing it all on her empty bed, I began to sort through what Nancy thought valuable enough to place in her safe. The jewelry boxes contained a beautiful strand of black Tahitian pearls, a gold ring with the Callahan crest – something I thought only the Callahan men wore, and assorted jeweled earrings.

The final velvet box was large, as if it contained an elaborate necklace of some sort. As I opened it, I smiled and began to cry. Threaded together on a long piece of red yarn, she'd kept a necklace made entirely of macaroni noodles. There was no doubt in my mind that Mac had made it for her when he was probably no older than Dax. She'd kept it among her most prized possessions, locked safely with the baubles and pearls she couldn't live without. It was touching, and yet as a mother I understood completely.

I wiped away the tears as I moved on to the papers. There was her certificate of baptism, copies of her marriage certificate, her will, the funeral plans and three sealed letters. One was addressed to Mac, one to Timms and one simply marked: To the future Mrs. Callahan.

"Mimi." I sat, putting my hand over my mouth, overcome by emotion.

"What is it?" she asked as she stopped sorting and tossing old magazines from the corner of Nancy's reading nook.

I held up the envelope as if she could read it from where she sat.

"Honey, you must think I'm still twenty-twenty, but that's really only the case when I have a pistol in my hand. You'll have to read it to me."

"It's a handwritten letter. There are three of them," I began. "One to Mac, one to Timms and this one. It's addressed to the future Mrs. Callahan."

Mimi grinned and nodded. "Atta girl, Nancy."

"Do you think she meant it for me?"

"You're the only Mrs. Callahan left, my dear. I'm positive it's for you."

I didn't know what to do with the letter. I was afraid to open it, and yet I was so honored she wanted to know me and in turn, wanted *me* to know her.

"You don't have to read it now, sweetheart," Mimi offered. "It's obviously meant as something special for the two of you to share."

"But how would she know?"

"Know what? That Mac would eventually get married? Believe me, when she was really herself she worried a lot about Mac. She wanted him to get married, but she knew he was fighting with himself and his past."

"But Mac is the most traditional man I've ever known."

"He is now," she said. "I'm not telling you anything you didn't already know about your husband."

"I know," I sighed. "I mean, I *don't* know. I've heard."

"Do you want to read it?" Mimi asked.

I shook my head in uncertainty.

"I've made you buck up and do a lot of things you didn't want to today. I'm not going to push this on you too. Although," she sighed, "cleaning out this room will make it so much easier for Mac to close out this chapter of his momma's life."

"I agree."

"Save it for later if you want. But don't hang on to it too long," Mimi advised.

Wiping the tears from my cheeks, I carefully opened the top of the white envelope and looked to Mimi as if I needed permission. She nodded and I slowly unfolded the letter.

As I looked down at the white linen paper, what struck me first was how lovely Nancy's handwriting was. It was almost a work of art. No one wrote letters anymore —real letters – and I could already tell this would be a moment I'd remember always.

I took a deep breath and read it to myself.

To the future Mrs. Callahan,

I write this not knowing if it will ever be opened, as my lovely son McKay has told me he has no plans to ever marry. However, if by some chance, he meets the girl of his dreams and I am no longer living, I wanted to have a moment with you. With the way my memory works these days, I'm sure I will have long forgotten about this letter if I do happen to meet you. Regardless, I want to welcome you into our family. You are the new Mrs. Callahan. Use the moniker with pride, my dear. We are a small group.

I decided long ago when my husband Edward wrote our will, that there were more important things than where the money, the property, or my jewelry ends up after our demise.

The one thing I cannot will to anyone is McKay himself. If you're reading this, he's done that for me.

Mrs. Callahan, I know beyond a shadow of a doubt that you are beautiful, smart and kind — Mac would never agree to spend his life with anyone less. I want to welcome you into our family. It's one filled with a rich history of Callahan men, and the women who've loved them come hell or high water — and there's been plenty of both in our history, I assure you.

Mothers-in-law always feel the need to give advice without getting in the way, and I would be lying to tell you I'm different. So here's my two cents:

Love each other fully and without judgment. Never let the sun set on your disagreements and always put each other first. I know you and Mac may never have children of your own, but I urge you to adopt as our family isn't made of flesh and blood, but love, sacrifice, faith and fortitude. When you make that decision it will be scary — starting a family always is. Just try to remember that even though my grandchildren may live a life of privilege, the best gift you can give them is to love each other.

Take care of my precious Mac and demand that he do the same. And although I don't know you, or perhaps I do and I've long forgotten as my brain doesn't seem to cooperate as well these days, know that you have my blessing, that I love you and I'm proud to call you my daughter. Edward and I always wanted a daughter to call our own, and now Mac has provided that for us.

Try to live for all the small moments that don't seem to matter very much at the time. As you age, you'll discover these are the ones that are the sweetest to revisit in your old age.

Finally, thank you for loving my son. He isn't perfect,

as I'm sure you've discovered, but loving each other openly and with all your heart makes all our faults fade into the background. Remember to give each other hope in the darkness, and you'll always find your way back to the light of your love.

Sincerely,
Your mother-in-law, Nancy

I dropped the letter into my lap as a single tear hit the page and ran the ink from the fountain pen she'd used long ago. I took a deep breath and leaned into Mimi as she gave me a tight hug.

"Everything okay?" she asked. She gave my back a gentle pat as if I were still a baby.

I nodded as she held me close and I smelled her perfume – Jean Patou's *Joy*. She'd worn it ever since I could remember and it immediately brought me back to her every time.

Mimi held me at arm's length and gave me a long look. "Are we finished for the day?"

"No," I sighed, remembering Nancy's words. "I need to get everything boxed up before tomorrow. Mac can go through her things later when he's up to it. I'll have a moving service pick all of this up and bring it to Lone Oak."

"I think that's a fine idea," Mimi agreed. "Why don't you head home? You've got two babies and a husband that need you right now. We've sorted through the important stuff."

Mimi struggled to her feet using her walker as a crutch. It worried me to see her getting so frail and the last thing I wanted to think about was cleaning out her room at Autumn Valley.

I helped her to the door and as we walked down the

hallway, Nancy's letters and precious items from the safe were cradled in my arms. I needed to get to Mac. I needed to take care of him. Most of all I needed to give him his own letter.

30

MAC

I sank into the chair, still numb with grief and anxiety. I looked around the study at the faces I knew all too well from the Bureau. Everyone, with the exception of the young agent who'd asked to be transferred before I could get rid of him myself for allowing Hector to slip into my mother's room, was accounted for.

"Let's hear it," I demanded. I wanted a quick and up to date report on everything from Hector to Richard and back again.

"Don't start without me."

I knew the raspy voice and I dropped my shoulders, knowing exactly why she'd come to Alabama.

"Micah," Z drawled with a smile. "How's it hanging, cher?"

"Fuck off, Z," she chimed, giving him a smile as if it were a compliment.

I stood and she gave me a hug without reservation. Awkward at first, I felt my body release as she hugged me tightly.

"Do you want to postpone, Mac?" Z asked sincerely.

"We can give you a couple of minutes."

I pulled away from Micah and gave her a wink. "No, I'm fine," I blurted.

I sat down again as I watched Micah pull a chair into the small circle of agents. "Moss, talk to me."

"All the surveillance tapes from Autumn Valley, Lone Oak and Jackson House have been pulled. Hector's been using different identities to slip past us. We think he was dressed as an orderly at Autumn Valley when he went into Nancy's room. He was credentialed, so I'm sure the agent who let him pass thought he was legit. We think he posed as catering staff here on the wedding day, and possibly grounds at Jackson House."

"Dax always draws him in green in his pictures," Z offered. "When I questioned him about it, he said that Cucuy worked in the flowers."

"Someone wanna fill me in on who the hell Cucuy is?" Moss asked.

"El Cucuy," Z continued. "That's the name he gave himself to Dax, Samantha's son."

"*My* son," I said. "He drew pictures of him."

"The boogeyman," Micah interjected.

"Yes," said Z. "I've put copies of Dax's pictures with the report on your desk. I've had the security tapes pulled from my house where he posed as a gardener. He had a passkey to get onto my property. It's required of all the workers. They each have their own passcode to come and go from the property. It's how I know who's been there to work."

"And there wasn't anything out of the ordinary?" I asked.

"No. And all the employees have been questioned."

"That's hard to believe," I ground out.

"Hector has been inside *your* house," said Z. "How the hell did that happen?"

"He followed us to the King Giles home too," added Moss.

"He's a crafty asshole, that's for sure," said Micah.

"He's got an inside track, but he's messed up this time," said Moss. "We've got his DNA from the lips on the mirror. If we can bring him in, we've got the evidence to put him away."

"And Richard?" I asked.

"He says we can't keep him in the house."

"He's right. Did he leave?"

"Not yet, but when he does, he'll have a tail," Moss assured me.

"Speaking of Richard," Micah added. "We've got the info back on the phone call. It traced to a burner phone."

"The burner phone that we lost in town last night?"

"Same."

"If Peterson is working with Hector, I want to question him immediately," said Moss.

"Not yet," I added. "I'm perfectly fine with Richard thinking he's off the radar. In fact, why not let him roam around a little? You never know who he might hook up with."

When the meeting wrapped, the agents quickly dispersed – except for Micah. I knew she wanted to talk. I knew she felt like we had unfinished business. Maybe we did.

"Surprised to see me?" she asked as the last agent left the study.

"Not really."

Walking past her, I shut the door. If she wanted to finish our conversation from D.C., the last thing I wanted was for the fifteen agents roaming the hallways of Lone Oak to be privy to it.

"I just..." she began.

"Look Micah. About the other day—"

"No, I want to apologize, Mac. I had no right to say those things to you – especially in the middle of this fiasco. I just wanted to tell you I'm sorry and it won't happen again."

"Micah, I'm glad that you care about me. You were the only woman who really did, other than my mother for a long time. But you have to know how happy I am with Samantha. We're meant to be together. It's like nothing I've ever experienced in my life. She *is* my life."

"I understand," Micah nodded as she rose from her chair to meet me. "I was just worried about you and with your mother dying, I guess I just wanted to be close to you. I wanted you to know you had my support – as a friend."

"Thank you."

She sighed as she put her arms around my neck and hugged me tightly. "How am I ever going to survive without you? You've always been the most important G-man in my life."

I pulled away from her and nodded. "You've always been my Betty."

The floorboard behind me creaked and I turned quickly to find Samantha standing in the door.

"I didn't mean to interrupt," she whispered as she stared past Micah and through me.

"You aren't," I said as Micah and I quickly dropped our embrace. "We were just finishing up a meeting."

"Mac, I'll follow up on the... ah —" Micah stuttered as

she breezed past Samantha on her way out the door. "Good to see you, Samantha. Sorry for your loss."

She shut the door behind her as I walked to Sam to give her a hug and kiss. I wanted to explain immediately what she'd just witnessed. "Hi, baby."

"Hi," she managed.

"How was Mimi?"

"Um," she hesitated as she walked away. "She's fine."

"Did you hear from the church? They're worried there won't be enough space for the crowd we're expecting. I don't know what to do about that," I sighed. "I want Momma's funeral to be small and low key. I don't know how to accomplish that in a small town where she and my father were so loved."

"Is there something between you and Micah that I should know about?"

"No." It was true. I paused, momentarily wondering if I should tell her the entire story, and thought better of it.

"It seems like maybe there is."

"Samantha, I have a killer stalking you and the children, a dead mother and a funeral tomorrow. Can we not do this?"

"Of course," she agreed as she wiped tears forming in her eyes.

"Wait," I sighed grabbing her arm and circling her around to pull her flush with my body. I kissed her on the neck. "Please don't be mad at me." I worked my way to her lips, speaking in short gasps. "I'm trying my best to keep everyone safe and happy."

She nodded and reluctantly kissed me back.

"You," I said, taking her face in my hands and looking her squarely in the eye, "are the most important thing in the world to me. Nothing and no one is ever going to change that. Not Hector, not funerals, nothing. Do you understand?"

Taking my hands away, she put my palms together in a praying position and gave them a shake. I knew she was too choked up to utter a word and I felt like a complete heel.

"I have something for you. Wait here."

I sat behind my dad's desk and looked through all of the evidence. It was a distraction from what I'd be doing tomorrow – burying my mother.

"Here," Samantha said as she handed me a white envelope that had one word written on the front. *Mac.*

"Where'd you get this?" I asked, knowing the handwriting belonged to my mother.

"I cleaned out Nancy's suite today at Autumn Valley. I packed everything up and arranged for a service to deliver the boxes here in a couple of days. There were some items in her safe. This was one of them."

I sank in my chair, clutching the envelope in my hands. "I don't understand."

She walked to my side and lovingly squeezed my shoulders. "She left three letters in her safe. One for you, one for me and one for Timms."

I was speechless.

"That was why I came in here and," she hesitated. "Interrupted your time with Micah."

I looked at her and ran my hands through my hair. "I don't know if I can read this right now."

"You don't have to. You can wait a few days. You can wait longer. Just read it – eventually. I think she has some things she wanted to make sure you knew."

"Did you read yours?"

"Just take your time with it, Mac. You'll know when you should read it. Okay?"

"Yeah," I replied. "Yeah, okay."

"I'm sorry about the whole Micah thing. I promise you. There's nothing going on."

"I know," she replied as she shut the door behind her.

I placed the envelope on the old desk and turned on the lamp. The thick white linen stationery stood out among the sea of clutter that was the evidence on Hector Quintes. Momma's letter was a calm in the middle of the storm.

I laughed out loud at how fitting it was that her message should come to me this way—she always did have a way of calming me down.

Miss Celia had left sweet tea for me in its usual place on the silver tray in the corner. I poured the tea and as I sipped took a long hard look at the portrait of my parents that hung over the fireplace.

The first night I brought Samantha to Lone Oak, she commented on it. I told her, it was how I liked remembering them both. It was even truer today.

"Here I am, folks. Right here where you thought I'd eventually end up," I said to the portrait. "You knew, didn't you?" I asked, pointing to their images in the oil painting.

Staring into my father's eyes, I watched him watching me. I'd always felt as if he was right over my shoulder whenever I worked in his study.

I walked the circular room and noticed all the photos, knickknacks from his trips and scraps of paper containing words he wanted to remember. This one room really signified the world my parents built together. It was here all the important decisions in my life were made, and now I used the room for the exact same purpose.

I knew this day would come. The day when everything that the other Callahans had passed on became mine. The responsibility was now mine – not that it hadn't been since

Momma moved into the nursing home, but the finality of death brought it all to light. I'd grown up. I was the one with the wife and children. I was the one with the responsibility.

I was still running on adrenaline from the past week. I'd barely slept, hadn't spent any time with the children or even Samantha. I was a short rope that was unraveling quickly. How would I get through tomorrow?

Maybe I should read the letter from Momma. Maybe I should get some sleep. *I'll get Moss and we'll drive around town and look for Hector.* My mind was racing and I felt my chest thump loudly with anxiety.

I took a deep breath and eyed the bourbon on the bar table. I needed a drink. I *wanted* a drink. I wanted anything that would take my mind from where it was heading.

"Mac?"

"Come in," I shouted.

"Baby," Miss Celia smiled. "I know it's been a long day, but you need to eat. Now, don't tell me no, cause you know I'm not taking no for an answer."

I gave her a half-hearted smile. "What's for dinner anyway?"

"Whatever you want, baby. Whatever you want."

"Why are you so good to me, Celia?" I asked as I took a long drink of my sweet tea and loosened my tie.

"Because you're my baby, baby."

"I thought Dax and Katy were your babies now."

"You're all my babies."

I sighed.

"I worry about you," Celia said.

"It's nice to have so many people worrying about me."

"Your sweet wife worries something awful about you."

"Yeah, I know."

"And that girl — the one from your office?"

"Micah."

"Miss Samantha heard her on the phone trying to make a hotel reservation and insisted that she stay here."

"Really?" I asked. "Well, I'm not surprised by the grace and hospitality of my amazing wife."

"She *is* amazing, McKay Waverly Callahan. I knew it from the moment I met her. Don't go forgetting that."

I knew I was being warned. "I don't know what you're thinking, Celia…"

Her loving expression changed on a dime. "I don't *think*. I *know*. A married man ought not to be huggin' on another woman callin' her his *Betty*."

"First off, how did you hear that and secondly, do you even know what that means?"

"These walls have ears. And you know it. I don't care what it means. A married man needs to keep his hands to himself. Never give your horse more attention than your wife unless you like sleepin' in the barn."

"Can I explain?"

"No need. Fried chicken's for dinner," she announced as she opened the door to leave.

"I thought it was whatever *I* wanted?" I yelled after her.

"Sometimes you don't get what you think you need," she shouted back.

31

SAMANTHA

"Sam?"

"In here," I called from Mac's bedroom.

"The children are ready. How are you doing?" Polly asked as she joined me at the mirror.

Our eyes met in the reflection and yet we didn't say anything. "We did this a few days ago. With the tears and everything," Polly said.

"You told me it was a new beginning," I sighed. "I guess today's an ending."

"Every ending is a new beginning, right?"

"Is a funeral a new beginning?"

"For the people left behind. Life and death – the beginning, the ending – it's all really one big song that just goes on and on," Polly added. "Circle of life."

"What are you talking about?" I asked.

"*Lion King.*"

"*It's the circle of life,*" she sang at the top of her lungs. "Blah, blah, blah, you get the picture," she smirked.

"How do you do it?" I asked Polly.

"What?"

"Make me laugh when I should be crying?"

"It's a gift. Like knowing when to stroke the balls while giving a spectacular blow job or taking steaks off the grill at medium rare."

I laughed. I laughed hard and it felt good. It felt good to feel normal. Polly had always been there to make me feel this way.

"I've got to make it through today, Polly. I have to."

"You will. I promise."

"Have you seen Mac?"

"No, why?"

"I'm worried about him. He's doing part of the eulogy and I don't know if that's such a good idea."

"It'll be fine, Sam."

"It has to be."

My feet ached from standing in one spot for so long. I was tired of being gracious. Many of the same people we'd just seen at our own wedding were now shaking my hand again, offering their condolences. I tried to be strong for Mac, hiding my tears whenever he was near. The blank look on his face told me everything I needed to know. Mac had been stretched beyond his limit.

The children made an appearance, but left with Polly and Leo one hour into visitation. It was too much for Dax to understand and I was too weary to explain something I couldn't comprehend myself.

When the funeral was about to begin, we gathered together in the church vestibule where the minister, who'd married us days ago with a cheerful smile, now had a solemn timbre to his voice.

I looked around the church, filled with FBI agents, some here to pay their respects and others here to keep Hector away from yet another family event. I'd overheard Tom Moss tell an agent that everyone from the funeral home and church had to be double checked by one of the owners and a church secretary to come in or out of the back of the house. The rest was just a free for all and it needed to be over soon.

We took our seats at the front of the church. The closed casket was below the pulpit and a beautiful oil painting of Nancy sat on an easel close by. She was probably forty or so in the painting. I glanced down at the emerald ring on my right hand and looked to the portrait, finding it on Nancy's hand that casually held the back of the chair she stood next to.

The sanctuary was filled not with flowers, but flowering magnolia trees and bushes. How they'd managed to move them all into the church was beyond me, but it was simply beautiful, just like Nancy.

Mac held my hand without looking at me until it was his time to speak. Before leaving the church pew, he gave it a squeeze as he stood to walk to the front of the church.

I had no idea what he was about to say and I didn't know how much longer I could remain strong. Since Daniel's death I'd hated funerals, I hated the smell of the flowers, and I hated everything about them. Funerals were barbaric to me. They were a way for *other* people to say goodbye and mourn. I knew from experience the real mourning would come later. Much later.

I watched my husband take the pulpit and begin with a deep breath. Pulling a tissue from my purse I dabbed my eyes.

"My mother's abiding love for my father and me was what sustained us," he began as I heard a sniff from the back of the church. "She was a hopeless romantic, believing that love happened all the time, every day. And why wouldn't she? She was married to my father. Together they set the bar very high. So high I never thought it possible to reach—that was until I met the love of my own life, Samantha. Once again, my mother was right. Nancy Waverly Callahan was never pessimistic, never ironic, and never cynical. How she managed to have a son who was all of those things, we'll never know. Because of how she lived her life, I have an example of how I should live mine. Maybe how we all should live.

She was the quintessential Southern lady, a true flower of Dixie, a sweet smelling magnolia on a spring afternoon. Better yet, a steel magnolia, ready for war at a moment's notice. I was proud to call her my mother. She was gracious, humble, loving – she always made everyone feel at ease. She was always beautiful, no matter what the occasion, and you could count on three things—she'd be wearing pearls, lipstick and a smile. She was considerate, helpful and probably holds the record for most handwritten notes in a lifetime. She was quite simply a lady in every aspect. She was an angel on earth. I know that's what my father believed, and as I grew older I came to know exactly what he meant. My one consolation is I know they are together now. I know she's no longer suffering. And my mother left this world knowing she was loved. She will be missed, especially by her grandchildren who won't have the privilege of her presence in their lives, but they will know her by the amazing good deeds she did in her lifetime."

I watched as Mac paused, trying to hold back the tears coming to the surface.

I looked away and held my breath, hoping not to break.

"I will see to it," he whispered as his voice gave into his emotions.

Mac took a long pause and deep breath. I knew he wouldn't be able to go on much longer. He was a tough man, but he loved deeply and it showed today.

He stepped closer to the microphone and looked to the ceiling as he held in his tears. "Mark Twain once said, 'My mother had a great deal of trouble with me, but I think she enjoyed it.'"

There was a muffled laugh in the sanctuary and it was a welcomed relief. I took a deep breath for him and prayed he made it to the end without losing it.

"My mother never said goodbye to me. Ever. Instead, I would ask if she loved me. And she would say, 'You know I do.' I thank God every day she did."

He folded his paper and walked back to the pew to sit with me. I gave him a quick kiss on the cheek – so proud of him.

The minister said a quick prayer, and we rose to leave the church as the pianist began to play, *I'll Be Seeing You.*

Giving Mac's hand a squeeze, I looked into his face hoping to see his relief. He was almost finished with the required ceremonies. Soon we could mourn on our own without the entire town of Shadeland and an army of FBI agents around every corner. I'd hoped to find relief in his face. Instead I saw emptiness.

As we left for the cemetery, Celia and Timms stopped to hug him. He was distant, disconnected and I knew where he'd gone. It was a headspace I never wished upon anyone, but I knew it well from my own experience.

"Mac, sweetheart," I said as we rode to the graveside. "Your mother would've loved what you said."

He stared ahead and gave a small nod to let me know he'd heard me.

"Are you okay?"

Another nod.

"We're almost finished. Then we can go home."

He was silent and I knew to leave him be. He needed to process what was happening. He'd been trained to kill and track the criminally deviant, but nothing prepared him for being alone and apart from his parents completely. It was going to take some time for him to accept what had happened in the last three days. I knew I needed to be patient, supportive and loving. And I would be – forever.

There must've been a hundred people or more at Lone Oak for the repast. A buffet line was set up as well as a bar and a dessert table. I was always amazed at how the burial of someone ended up with carved roast beef and an open bar, but Nancy didn't want it any other way.

Polly and Leo had the children tucked away upstairs in a private section of the house. Mac had given specific instructions. No one was to go in or out of the room and Leo was armed inside the nursery. It was all so stressful, and yet I put on my lipstick and gave the crowd a reluctant smile. I wanted Nancy to be as proud of me for entertaining as she was of Mac's eulogy.

"Celia," I said as I finally found her in the sea of people.

"Miss Samantha," she smiled as she hugged me tightly around the neck. "How are you holdin' up, sweetie?"

"I should be asking you that. Did you make all these arrangements for this?" I asked as I looked around the room at the party that seemed to be going on.

"Miss Nancy had it all planned out. I just had to follow her instructions. It was fine."

"Nancy did all of this before she died? She planned *this*?"

Celia nodded and grinned. "Miss Nancy said she always threw the best parties in Shadeland, and she wasn't going to have her final one be a bust because Mac didn't know what to do."

"Smart lady."

"Very."

"Can I get you anything, Sam?" she asked.

"No, I'm fine. Again, I should be asking you that."

"No."

"Have you seen Mac? I went upstairs to check on Dax and Katy and I lost him."

"No, darlin'. I've not seen him. I did notice the door to the study was shut."

"Thanks."

Standing on my toes, I continued to look for Mac. Everyone seemed so tall and the rooms were completely full. I really wanted to ask people to leave, but I knew that proper etiquette required me to be a good hostess in my own home.

I walked to the study and turned the knob only to find it was locked. I wasn't surprised.

"Samantha?"

"Richard?" I was shocked and let my feelings be known by gasping at the sight of him.

"That's not happy to see me," he rasped.

"Just surprised," I replied.

"Can we talk?"

"Now? What could you need to talk about right now,

Richard?"

"Frankly, I'm a little tired of agents climbing up in my business every little whipstitch if you get my meaning."

"I don't believe that I do," I stated calmly as I looked over his shoulder to see Agent Moss carefully watching every move Richard made.

"I need to conduct my transactions in a businesslike fashion and they're always around. Frankly, it makes me look bad."

"No one is forcing you to stay at my house."

"Well, that's another thing, Sam. Let's talk about the house for a second."

"Richard?" I ground through my teeth. "I just buried my mother-in-law today. Now unless you want to be buried in the next couple of days, I suggest you back off."

"C'mon now, Samantha," he drawled. "We're family. Now I'm startin' to feel like a banjo, cause y'all are always pickin' on me."

"What?" Richard was making me angry, but I didn't want to cause a scene.

"You heard me. Now, darlin'," be began again. "We need to work something out over Mimi's house."

"Richard." I said his name deliberately and was filled with so much disdain I truly wanted to call him *The Dick*. "Mimi thinks you're as crooked as a dog's hind leg and twice as dirty and I'm starting to agree with her. For the record, that house is mine. Do you understand me? Mine. And no one, including you, is going take it away from me."

"I just think in light of the past few weeks you need to think about what would happen to our family's finest property if something should happen to you."

"Well, I've got news for you, *Dick*. You can use any trick you want—bring it on, you piece of trash. That house will never be yours."

"I didn't mean to upset you, Sam." Richard whispered as he watched Tom Moss close in on our conversation.

"I'm not upset, Richard. It's just that I've seen Mimi's will, and guess what? You're S-O-L," I spelled out with deliberate contempt. "Now back off, you chubby, self-righteous, gold-digging bastard. Stay away from me and my family or you and me and my gun," I pointed into his fat chest, "are going to get real cozy, real quick. I'll give the FBI something to *really* investigate."

"Are you threatening to shoot me, Sam?" he asked loudly so Agent Moss could hear.

I dropped my head back in laughter. "If I wanted you dead, you'd be gone by now. Death is too good for you."

"So you *are* threatening me with a gun," he bellowed.

"You're not worth a bullet through the heart," I replied. "I'd aim low. I'm a pretty good shot too. Even if the target is as tiny as your dick…Richard."

"Why you little bit-".

"Watch it, Dick," I spat. "I'll change you from a rooster to a hen with one squeeze of the trigger and never give it another thought."

I didn't wait for his reply, but instead turned on my heels and walked away to hide in the kitchen where I found Celia.

"What are you doing back here, Miss Samantha?" she asked.

"I don't know," I sighed. "What are *you* doing back here?"

"I'm hiding out."

"Me too. I still can't find Mac. The study was locked, which worries me. The past couple of days have really taken a toll on him."

"They've taken a toll on all of us – you included," said Celia. "The curse of being a momma is always holding up when everyone else is letting down."

"Does that ever get better as you get older?"

"No, baby. It doesn't."

She held her arms out to me and I went to her. As she encompassed me I could feel the kindness radiating through her body, wrapping me in tenderness. This was what Mac loved so much about Celia. She was love incarnate disguised as a fifty-something year old woman. I knew Dax and Katy would always feel this kind of devotion from her and I let go of the idea of losing Polly.

As she rubbed my back I wondered where Mac could be. If Celia and I were hiding in the kitchen, where would he hide?

"Do you think Mac could be in the garage or something?"

"Baby, he's probably in the wall."

"The wall?" I laughed. "What wall?"

"He's never shown you the wall?"

"I have absolutely no idea what you're talking about."

"Miss Samantha, there are secret passages all throughout Lone Oak. Mac never showed them to you?"

"No," I muttered, amazed that there was something I didn't know about him or the house. "Why?"

"Honey, this house is old. I mean old," she emphasized. "They're passages in and out of the house and in between some of the rooms. It was a place for the Callahans to hide folks during the Civil War."

"What?" I asked, still stunned from what I was hearing.

"I can't believe he never show them to you. Then again, he was never one to use them much when he was a boy. They can be a little scary if you don't know where the lights are."

"Celia, are you telling me there are secret passages throughout this house that I don't know about?"

"Yes, ma'am. That's what I'm telling you. It was used for a time to keep slaves who were heading north safe for the night. I suppose the passages have been used for many a thing in the past two hundred years," she sighed.

"Do you think that's where he is?"

"He's probably up in his room waiting for everyone to leave. That's why I'm in here. I just wish they'd all go home. They've paid their respects. It's time to get."

"I agree," I yawned.

"See? Even the lady of the house is getting tired. They need to go."

"Well, I think I chased one of them out anyway. I threatened to shoot my cousin Richard a few minutes ago," I said matter of factly.

"What did you just say?"

"I said," changing my answer, "I think maybe you're right. It *is* time for these people to leave."

She nodded and gave me a strange look.

"I'm going to look for Mac."

"Miss Samantha?"

"Yes?"

"Stay away from the firearms tonight," she smiled.

"Don't worry. I will."

I pushed open the doors from the kitchen into the butler's pantry and past the catering staff. As I made my way through the dining room and into the entrance hall I was happy to notice that the crowd had thinned considerably. There were still the agents standing idly by in nearly every corner of the house, and as the sun began to set on the day we buried Nancy, her friends, old and young began to say their goodbyes.

I made excuses for Mac, acting as if he was somewhere

else in the house. I told countless people that I'd be sure to let him know how sorry they were. As the last few herded themselves out the door, I knew I had to find Mac.

"Tom," I shouted down the hall.

"Yes, ma'am?"

"I'm looking for Mac. Have you seen him?"

"No, ma'am."

I climbed the staircase and began my search in Dax and Katy's rooms. I knocked and Leo quickly shouted, "Yes?"

"Leo, it's Sam. Open up."

Polly opened the door and I saw Leo sitting with Dax as Katy slept in her crib. "Have you seen Mac?"

Silently she shook her head no, trying not to wake the baby.

"Leo?" I whispered, looking past her and into the room.

"No, Sam. He came in a few hours ago, but I've not seen him since."

"Thanks," I said as I began to turn.

"Mommy?" Dax asked.

"Yes, sweetheart?"

"Can we come out now?"

"Sure. I think most everyone is gone."

"I'll radio down to Moss to get the go-ahead," said Leo.

I hurried down the hallway and into our bedroom. The luggage from our honeymoon and Mac's trip to Washington was still on the floor, but the room was empty.

I knocked on the door to the study. There was no answer. "Mac? Please let me in, sweetheart. Everyone is gone. Leo's bringing the kids downstairs."

I listened as best I could through the thick door and heard silence.

"Don't you want to hold Katy?" I asked as if he could hear me. "Rock her for a bit and say goodnight?"

Nothing.

"Mac?"

Celia walked into the front hallway and I motioned for her to come to me. "Celia, is there a key to this lock?" I asked as I pointed to the old keyhole.

She nodded.

I ran my hand along the grain of the old mahogany door, longing to touch my husband. I wanted to tell him that everything was going to be okay.

"Here, honey," she said as she handed me a large skeleton key.

"Seriously?" I asked. "How old is this thing?"

"About two hundred years."

I raised my brow in disbelief and shoved the old key into the lock. With one full turn, I heard the lock release and I opened the door.

"Mac?" I called into the darkened room.

I nodded to Celia to let her know I was fine to take it from here. If Mac was upset, I didn't want to embarrass him.

Closing the door behind me, I called to him softly. "Mac?" The day was ending; the grey clouds had given way to a dark purple sky as the sun dipped into the horizon. It cast a dark shadow on the room, save for the one light that shone brightly coming from Mac's desk.

I flipped on the switch that lit the overhead crystal chandelier. "Mac?" I called again as I walked to the desk, expecting him to be behind the tall leather chair sitting with its back to the door.

"C'mon sweetheart, I know you're in here somewhere. Who else would've locked the door?"

As I walked around the desk, my heart began to pound. I had an uneasy feeling. I spun the chair around and called his name again, "Mac?"

It was empty.

32

MAC

I looked around the bar. It was a dive at best and a drug deal waiting to happen at worst. Blacked out windows with tables and chairs that had seen their fair share of brawls, the joint looked on the outside the way I felt on the inside.

"Want another?" the waiter asked as I slouched in the broken vinyl booth in the darkest corner of the place. I was near the putrid smelling bathroom and an old jukebox no one had bothered to update in years. I listened to Hank Williams wailing, *I'm so lonesome I could cry*, and nursed my feelings of inadequacy.

"Dude?" the waiter asked, anxious for a quick answer.

"Yes. Please."

"Whatcha drinkin'?"

"Maker's," I mumbled.

"Maker's Mark?"

"Did I stutter?" I snapped with sarcasm.

"Geez, dude. Don't be a dick."

"Just bring me the goddamn bourbon," I insisted.

He stared me down, and I gave it right back to him, but

then broke. "Sorry, man. Just bring me the drink, okay? I'm a good tipper."

He walked away without giving me another care. I ran my hands through my hair and sank deeper into the grungy old booth. The whole place smelled of stale beer and despair. I fit in perfectly.

I ran a silver dollar over and over through my fingers, flipping it endlessly as I stared at the white envelope with my name on it. I'd carried it with me everywhere in my coat pocket since Sam had given it to me yesterday. And now, here we were – grief, my mom and me.

I'd sunk pretty damn low in the last seventy-two hours and I was man enough to admit it. What I wasn't man enough to do was read the letter.

I'd snuck out of the house through the first floor passage between the study and the garden leaving Sam and Celia to deal with the friends and neighbors. I honestly couldn't stand to hear one more story about my mother. I knew they meant well, but I wasn't ready for her to die, and I sure as hell wasn't ready to hear stories of how wonderful she was. No one knew her like Dad and I did. And now no one would know her again.

I smiled to myself as I thought about the day I showed Dax the secret passages inside Lone Oak. I gave him the tour exactly the way my dad had given it to me. It was a rite of passage for Callahan men to know all the secrets of Lone Oak. Her passageways and exits were just the beginning. He now knew where they were and how to show or usher others out in case of an emergency.

"Here ya go," the waiter gruffed as he clumsily sat the glass on the sticky table.

"Thanks," I murmured.

The longer I sat in the booth, the slower everything

seemed to happen. I knew I was buzzed and I didn't care. My mind raced as I thought about my mother's last few moments. How horrible it must've been for her to see him in her room when she couldn't remember anyone or anything. It was a perfect storm – her bad heart, the Alzheimer's and Hector's wily nature. I'd promised her I'd never let anything happen to her, yet I wasn't there to protect her.

Hector…Hector…you piece of shit. Before I'm dead, I'll see the heel of my boot at your neck. If it's the last thing I do.

The old jukebox changed songs again and Johnny Cash began to wail. I stood and sauntered into the men's room. As I stood at the urinal, I caught a glimpse of myself in the cracked mirror in front of me. I couldn't tell if it was split in more than one place, or if I was getting wasted and there were two of me peeing.

I flushed with my elbow and shuffled to the sink to wash my hands. I pushed the soap dispenser to no avail. "Ha!" I laughed aloud. "Why would there be soap in this godforsaken place?"

I gave my two faces in the mirror a shrug and pushed open the door, nearly tripping and sliding back into my crappy booth.

"Waiter?" I motioned.

"Yeah, man?"

"I need a check, young man."

"Do you need a cab?"

"I need the balls to open this letter," I mumbled. "What do you think about that?"

"I just work here. I don't think."

"Well, how's this? I think you should bring me a check before I call the Alcohol Beverage Control Board and have them bust your ass for the group of underage drinkers playing pool in the corner."

"Whatever," he muttered as he walked away.

I took another look at the sealed envelope. "What do you need to tell me?" I mumbled as I brushed my fingers over my name.

"Here," the waiter said as he put the paper check under my empty glass.

I gave him a nod but said nothing. I shoved the envelope in my coat pocket and checked my watch. Surely everyone had bugged out by now. Sam would be angry with me, but I had a feeling today of all days I would get a pass.

I took a deep breath and watched the boys drinking beer and playing pool in the other room and thought back to when it was good to be young and stupid. Too young to know anything bad could happen, and too ignorant to ever think we didn't know what we were doing.

The front door swung open, briefly shining the street light into the dark and smoky room. Another pitiful soul had come here to drown in the alcohol. He looked around, not giving the corners of the room much attention and walked to the bar and bellied up.

I searched through the stack of cash from my pocket and tossed a hundred dollar bill on the table. I'd promised to be a good tipper, and I was, if anything, a man of my word.

I rested my elbows on the table and hung my head in my hands, rubbing my head. I knew I needed to go home, but my legs didn't want to go anywhere, and I didn't need get behind the wheel of the farm pickup I'd driven here just yet. Surely if he saw the money, he'd leave me be in this shitty little booth to sober up at my leisure.

"Dos Equis," I heard him order.

I sunk deeper into the booth and heard the old vinyl wretch under my weight. I watched the man drink, deciding

I'd wait until he'd had at least five beers or forty-five minutes, whichever came first before leaving. I just needed to make it fifteen miles down the road to Lone Oak – just fifteen miles.

My heavy eyelids drooped with each blink, and I tried to concentrate on how many beers he'd had. I was pretty sure it was Dos Equis number two, but I was already thirty minutes into the deal I'd made with myself.

When he made it to beer number three, I knew I was minutes from my deadline. I was tired, but not as buzzed as I'd been.

"Do you need anything else?" the waiter asked one last time as he took his money.

"Nope," I sighed. "Keep the change."

"Really?" he asked.

"Sure."

As I mustered up the energy to walk with dignity out of the hellhole I'd wandered into, I saw his face come into the light of a neon Bud Light sign. I blinked hard and moved back into the safety of my dark corner.

He turned again as the door swung open and a strong breeze blew through the stale tavern. It was Hector. I knew it in an instant. I didn't need to be completely sober to know the man. I'd studied him for an entire year. A flashback overcame me and I thought of Hector's gun in my face at the rock quarry where he tried to kill Samantha.

I felt my pocket for my cell phone and found nothing. I tried to think clearly where my phone was. As I looked under the table nonchalantly, I remembered I'd left it on my desk.

I sat, waiting for Hector to do something. Anything. Now that I had him, I wasn't letting him go. I would follow him to the ends of the earth until one of us lay dead.

I checked my watch again, making sure I was deep in the corner. I knew he'd recognize me if he had the opportunity to see me head on and as I sat crouched in my booth I prayed. Not to sober up or for backup – I prayed that Hector had a big bladder and wouldn't need to walk past me on his way to the men's room.

The waiter came back again to check on me. "You sure you don't want anything?"

"Actually," I rasped with quiet anxiety. "May I have a cup of coffee?"

He gave me a smile and nodded. "Good choice."

Hector stood without saying anything to anybody and tossed cash on the bar top. I waited for his next move.

He walked my way and it seemed as if he was looking right at me, and yet as he neared the men's room he didn't seem to notice me at all.

As soon as the door closed I was up and on the move. I'd wait him out in the truck. I blew out the door and began to write down the license plate of every car parked in front of the bar on a cocktail napkin.

Hector didn't know it yet, but his time was running out. I was a ticking time bomb, and he was my victim.

I sat in the truck with no phone and sobered up as I watched the front door waiting for him and holding the letter from Momma in my hand. I waited. And then I waited longer. I became sleepy as the alcohol began to wear off and the taxing day of burying my mother began taking its toll.

And then it happened. He walked out and I sat up in my truck across the street and took notice. After climbing in an old green Chevy Nova, Hector drove away. I waited before following him. It was late, but not so late that he'd be expecting to be on the road alone.

I tailed him and my mind scrambled with rage. It was all I could do to keep my distance and not run him off the road and into a tree. I was fueled by madness, alcohol and grief. I wanted Hector dead.

He continued to drive into the night. I didn't know how far he was going, but I only had a half of a tank of gas and my plan would need to be modified if he was running.

Twenty miles outside of Shadeland, he pulled into a roadside mom and pop motel. I drove past and circled around, watching him slip into room number six. As he shut the door the number slipped upside down into a nine.

I parked on the side of the building and waited momentarily before I decided to go into the lobby and call for backup. I opened the door to the pickup and leaned against the building. I didn't have my badge and I didn't have a gun.

I rounded the corner and heard the door and quickly leaned into the side of the building again. Hector left room six and jumped into the Nova and sped off. He took nothing with him and as I watched him speed into the night I cursed myself for being such a drunken shit.

I walked the concrete sidewalk that connected the ground floor motor lodge and looked into the window of room six. It was dark, but I could see a duffle bag on the table by the window.

I searched my pockets. I didn't even have a pocketknife on me. All I had was my wallet and my letter.

Pulling out a credit card, I swiped through the crack on the doorway, hoping the motel was old enough to be easily broken into.

I shook the doorknob as I shoved the American Express card into the narrow opening and gave it a second push.

In one wrench of the door, it opened and I was in. I shut the door behind me and looked around the room. I was breaking and entering, I hadn't called for backup and I didn't give a shit. I was as rogue as rogue could get.

I looked through his duffel bag. There were a couple changes of clothes, shoes and a couple of small bundles of heroin. I walked further into the stale room and toward the bathroom. On the open hanging rack were uniforms. A cop uniform, green gardening shirt and pants, checkered chef's pants and a white double-breasted chef's coat. Above the rack on a shelf there were hats and wigs. Hector had been busy. I turned on the light in the dark bathroom and found his razor, shaving cream, a toothbrush and a tube of red lipstick. I knew without looking to whom they belonged. I touched nothing.

I turned to get the hell out of there and call Z and Agent Moss for backup when I saw it. It was only the corner of the paper, but I'd seen it before.

Rage filled my body and I found it hard to breathe. I bit down on my lip as I pulled the crayon drawing out from under the hats on the shelf above the coat rack.

It was one of Dax's drawings. In the garden by the gazebo at Lone Oak, he'd drawn himself and Samantha holding Katy. In the background there was a hooded man and next to it was a lipstick stain.

Hector had found himself in the picture and loved it so much he kissed it. I had no way of knowing if Dax gave him the drawing or if Hector had taken it from our home. It didn't matter.

"Damn you!" I screamed. "Damn you! Take a piece of *me*, you fucking coward. Leave my wife and children alone and come get some of me, you piece of shit!"

I tore through his clothes and ransacked his every belonging. As I turned around and around in the room looking for more, everything began to spin and I could no longer think. I looked at the room, knowing I'd wrecked any evidence with my own fingerprints, but I was beyond it now.

A yellow legal pad lay in the floor – a casualty of emptying the drawers in the room. On top of it was a black sharpie pen.

I grabbed it from the floor and walked to the mirror. I wanted to him to know. I wanted him to know it was me.

"The tables have turned motherfucker," I hissed as I wrote furiously on the mirror with the black marker.

I finished and stepped back to admire my work and closed the cap on the pen and slid it into the top inside pocket of my suit coat.

They will remember me. The man who ripped you apart with his bare hands. I'm the shadow you can't see. I haven't forgotten. I'm waiting.

I walked out the door, leaving the lights on and the door open. I pulled the pickup around to do just as I'd promised. Wait.

At seven in the morning, Hector pulled back into the motel parking lot. I watched as he hesitantly looked into his room, pulling a gun from the back of his pants. He searched the room and within a minute, he emerged with his duffle bag stuffed with the things I'd turned out into the floor.

Throwing the car in reverse, he tore out of the gravel lot, spitting rocks as he roared onto the two-lane highway.

I followed, not caring if I had enough gas, knowing I had no backup. It didn't matter. This was between Hector and me and I was settling it once and for all.

33

SAMANTHA

"No," I said as Tom Moss questioned me. "I didn't see him before he left. Have you heard from him?"

"No, but then again, we found his phone in the study. He left everything behind when he went. Samantha, did he say anything out of the ordinary?" he asked putting a finger to his embedded earpiece, straining to listen.

"You mean like, 'I'm losing my mind because my mother is dead and a man who's been stalking my wife and children for a year is on the loose'?"

"Mrs. Callahan," Moss continued. "We just got confirmation from the phone tap that Richard Peterson is soliciting a contract killing."

"On me?" I gasped. "He's hired Hector?"

"He's already looking for a more reliable source than Hector."

"Samantha," Leo chimed in. "I know this is hard, but we need you to calm down."

I nodded, wanting to cry and then quickly recovered as I remembered Nancy's words to me. I needed to be strong for both Mac and me. "I threatened Richard yesterday after the funeral."

"What did you say?"

"I told him I was going to shoot his balls off."

"What?" Leo asked, trying to conceal a smile.

"Agent Moss heard me," I said as I pointed to him across the room.

"What did I hear?" Moss asked.

"You heard me threaten Richard."

"I didn't. I saw you talking to him."

"Are you serious? I was shouting at him."

"Someone pick up Richard Peterson and get his ass over here. And I mean now," Leo shouted.

Finally someone besides me wanted to see more action and less conversation.

"I'll send a team over to pick him up, but we've got the rest of the agents on the road looking for Mac. I won't have backup in from Birmingham for another hour," Moss explained.

"Go," Leo shouted. "I'm telling you to go. I'm here and if Mac shows up, you'll be the first to know."

Tom pulled his team together and moved them out of the house and for the first time since before the wedding, Lone Oak fell silent.

"Where's Polly?" I asked Leo.

"She's in the kitchen with Celia and the children."

"Leo, nothing can happen to Mac. Do you understand me? Nothing. I need him back here safe and sound."

"I know you do," Leo consoled me. "It's gonna be okay. Is there anything I can do for you?"

"You're going to think I'm crazy, but I really want my grandmother. She's the one person who can calm me down."

"Mimi?" he asked.

"Yes."

"I'll have someone pick her up."

I hit the speed dial on my iPhone and Mimi answered on the first ring. "What's wrong?"

"Mac's missing. He snuck out of the house yesterday afternoon after the funeral and no one has seen him. Will you please come to Lone Oak? I really need you."

"I'd be there in a flash, but you know these bastards won't let me drive anymore."

"No, Agent Xanthis has called your guard there at Autumn Valley. He can bring you to me."

"I'm on my way."

She hung up without saying goodbye and I watched Leo nod his head to me to confirm Mimi would soon be here.

Dax ran into the study and fell into my lap. "Mommy, do you want cornflakes for breakfast?"

"I'm not very hungry, sweetheart."

"Why are you so sad?" he asked as touched my face.

"Daddy stayed out really late last night and I'm just worried. That's all."

"Where'd he go?"

"I don't know exactly."

"Probably somewhere secret."

"Do you think Daddy has secrets?" I smiled.

Dax said nothing, but shook his head with as much animation as he could.

"What aren't you telling me, Dax?"

"Nothing."

"Dax?"

"The Callahan men have secrets," he proclaimed as Celia followed him into the study.

"There you are," she smiled. "Now c'mon, baby. Let's

get you some breakfast."

"What secrets do Callahan men have, Dax?"

"What are you goin' on about?" Celia asked him.

"Nothing."

"Dax, do you know about the secret walls that lead in and out of the house?"

"How do *you* know about them?" he asked.

"I just do. Can you show me? Is there one in here?"

He nodded and Celia smiled.

"Dax, meet me in the kitchen," she asked him.

Without a word, Dax jumped from my lap and ran off.

Leo's phone rang and I jumped to his side as he answered.

"Talk to me," he announced. "Well, tell him that's too bad. Get his ass here. And I mean now."

As Leo hung up, he answered before I could ask. "Richard's is giving them some trouble about coming here to answer questions."

I nodded and turned to find Celia gone.

Polly walked into the room looking fresh and rested. It was a sharp contrast to my sweatpants, t-shirt and floppy robe. Her cheeks were rosy and her blonde hair was pulled back tightly in a sleek ponytail.

I caught my reflection in a mirror in the corner of the study and dropped my shoulders. The dark circles under my eyes were taking over my once fresh face and as I stared at Polly, I knew she was what I wanted to look like – young, happy and in love.

"Good morning all," she said as she eyed Leo.

I turned to him and caught the tail end of a wink.

"What?" I asked in confusion as Leo's phone rang yet again.

"Yeah," he shouted. "Yeah. Okay. No, bring him here.

Right. No, keep me posted. I'm staying put until the next detail arrives. Because I'm *it*. Call me back!" he shouted.

"They've found Mac. He's heading south coming into town. Someone spotted the truck. They're tailing him."

"Hector," I whispered.

"What?" Polly asked.

"Nothing," I replied. "I'm gonna run upstairs and change quickly. I'll be right back."

I climbed the stairs two by two, racing into the bedroom and to the nightstand. As I opened the drawer, I pulled the gun from its holster and locked the magazine into place. Dropping it into the pocket of my robe I walked down the stairs ready to give some orders of my own.

"Polly, will you please take Katy back upstairs and find Dax and Celia in the kitchen. Tell Dax he can eat his breakfast in his room, okay?"

"What's up with you, Sam?" she asked.

"Just do it!" I shouted.

The room was silent for a moment and I quickly apologized. "I'm sorry, Polly. It's just that Richard's on his way here and I threatened him yesterday. I don't want Dax to hear anything that might...you know...come out of my mouth that he shouldn't."

"Alright, then," she cheered me on. "Go Sam." She gave me a fist pump and shot Leo a smile before kissing Katy on the head and turning for the door.

"Why don't you stay with them, Leo?"

"What?"

"Really, Leo. I'd feel better if you were with the kids personally. At least until the backup gets here."

"I'll get them settled upstairs. But then I'll be back down."

I nodded. "That's a great idea."

I heard him shout as he gathered Celia and Dax from the kitchen and escorted them to the second floor.

I pulled the gun from my pocket and steadied my shaking hand as I held the weight of it in my palm.

I looked out the window and could see dust fly as a car rolled down the lane and to the rear of the house.

I looked out the window, barely moving the curtain from its rightful place and watched as a young agent held the door open and helped Mimi from the front seat to the safe handlebars of her walker.

I took a deep breath, thankful it was only her, and then quickly realized I'd invited her to an impending firestorm.

I walked to the front of the house and watched out the window as another car came roaring down the lane, quickly followed by the pickup truck I knew so well from the garage behind Lone Oak. It was Mac, and if I was right, Hector was coming to pay me a visit.

I heard Leo rush down the stairs and into the foyer, cocking his gun.

"Get out of here, Sam," he shouted to me.

I walked away as I saw even more cars make their way up to the house. All black, I knew immediately that every agent who'd been in Shadeland was now at Lone Oak.

I snuck my way into the kitchen and shouted for the agent and Mimi to get inside.

Tucking Mimi in a powder room off of the hallway, I told her to lock the door and hurried past the young agent who'd joined Leo in the front hallway.

"I told you to get out of here, Sam!" Leo shouted again.

I began to walk away as Mac burst through the front door. I ran to him and threw my arms around his neck as he pulled himself away from me. He smelled of sweat and liquor. His suit was rumpled and his shirt was dirty.

"Mac?" I trembled.

"He's gone around back!" Mac shouted to the other agents. "Get to the study, Sam!" he shouted as I backed away and walked calmly to the study, shutting the door. The skeleton key I needed to lock it from the inside was gone.

I crouched behind the bar table and shook in fear. I wrapped my arms around my knees and began to rock, trying to hold myself together. I began to pray.

I could see my reflection in the old floor to ceiling mirror. I was watching myself fall apart in the room where I fell in love.

I could hear shouting throughout the house and again I staved off the fierce emotion that coursed through my body.

I heard a click and jumped, feeling the gun in my pocket to make sure it was still there. I looked up and saw Micah standing in the doorway of the study. Before I could say anything, she held a single finger to her lips and I watched her quietly move behind Mac's desk, getting low.

I waited for Mac to come in next. Surely he wanted to protect me. He wanted to be by my side. Lone Oak was swarming in agents by now. I wanted my husband with *me*.

I looked to Micah and shook my head. *What now?*

I sank back into the floor and looked back to my reflection. I did a double take as I saw the mirrored wall swing forward and into the room.

I scrambled on all fours across the floor and hid behind a couch. Peeking around a corner, I saw him. Hector slipped into the room through a secret door.

Not knowing if Micah saw him, I moved to catch her attention and caused the ancient floorboards to creak.

I felt the pain as Hector pulled me from the floor by my hair.

He had me.

"No!" I screamed.

"Shut up," he hissed. "Don't open your mouth again or I'll shut it for good."

It was too late.

Mac and Leo burst through the door with guns pulled.

"Let her go," Leo shouted.

"Why?" Hector asked in an eerily calm voice.

"Don't make this worse than it already is," Leo continued.

Mac stood straight – eyes wide open, intently watching every move Hector made. He jerked my head again and I shouted in pain.

"We can talk this out, Hector," Leo offered. "Let's make a deal. You let her go and we'll talk about the drug cartel's plans. If you help us, we can help you."

He calmly shook his head and said nothing as he grabbed me around the waist and pulled me close to him, holding onto my hair tightly.

I looked down to my pocket and knew the gun was still there.

As he slowly reached behind his back to pull the gun from his waist, I slipped my hand into the pocket.

"Mommy?"

I froze and looked to the mirrored wall as Dax stood in his pajamas.

"Coco, what are you doing?"

"Diego, you shouldn't be here," Hector yelled.

"What are you doing?" he shuddered. "Why are you hurting my mommy?"

Mac dropped his gun slowly and held his hands open to Hector as he spoke to Dax.

"Hey, Chief. I need you to go back the way you came. I need you to check on your sister," Mac said, his voice trembling with each syllable.

Dax looked to the ground and nodded. "I'm sorry."

"I'm sorry, Diego," Hector whimpered.

"Coco, don't hurt my mommy," Dax begged.

I watched Micah slowly moved from behind the desk to get an angle on Hector.

"Daddy?"

"Yeah, Chief?"

"Don't hurt my friend."

Dax disappeared into the wall just as he'd entered and I felt Hector hesitate as Mac dropped his shoulders in relief.

In a fluid motion, I elbowed Hector in the ribs, doubling him over as I fell to the floor and his gun fired one round into the air.

I looked up to him as he pointed the gun in my face. This was it. I knew I couldn't escape death twice. Hector was going to kill me, and I dropped my shoulders in surrender. If I was going to die, I wanted to be at peace with it.

"Go ahead, Hector," I whispered. "Do it."

I heard the thirty-eight-caliber pistol cock as I slowly shut my eyes. I didn't want the last thing I ever saw to be Hector.

BAM!

The body fell to the ground with a thud as a rush of air swept past my tear-stained face. I sat up and moved away. I was alive. Hector was dead.

As Mac rushed to my side and pulled me into his body, I screamed aloud, the emotion finally taking its toll. He cradled me in his arms.

"It's over. It's over," he repeated as he held me tightly and rocked me back and forth.

"How long have you been hiding behind that desk,

Micah?" Leo sighed.

"Long enough," she replied.

"You're a crafty little bitch, aren't you?"

"Suck it, Z."

"Get me out of here," I shouted. "I don't want to look at him. I don't want to see."

Mac picked me up and carried me in his arms out of the study and into a parlor room. He brushed the hair from my face and put his forehead to mine, breathing in and out. I didn't know who was more shaken, Mac or me.

"It's over," he said again.

I dropped my shoulders in relief.

"Stay away from me, you old bitch!"

The shouting came from inside the house and Mac pulled away from me in a flash.

"Hey!" I heard Mimi shout from the kitchen. "Where in the hell do you think you're goin'?"

BAM!

I jumped at the sound of another gun and screamed to Mac, "Where are the children?"

"Wait here," he shouted as he rushed up the stairs, running the length of the hallway as he shouted for Polly.

"Well, I winged him," I heard Mimi bellow as she slowly rolled into the front hall, inching every step of the way with her walker.

"Did you hear where the shot came from?" I shouted frantically.

"Hear it? Hell, I fired it," she shouted back to me.

"Mac!" I called up the stairs as he rushed down and past me.

"The children are with Polly. Everyone is safe."

"Mimi?" I asked again.

"Well, shit. He was trying to get away. I couldn't let that

happen. And the agent just left me. And *you* shoved me in a bathroom," she smirked as she pointed. "What'd you think I was gonna do, roll over and play dead?"

Leo rushed into the foyer. "Who fired the shot?"

"For the love of God," Mimi spat. "I did. I'm getting too old for this shit. Do you want to cuff me or something?"

"Who did you shoot?" I asked frantically.

"Who the hell did you think I shot? The *dick*."

"What?" I asked.

"He was trying to get away. Now listen," she began with a calm demeanor. "I know two wrongs don't make a right, but they sure as hell even things up a bit. He's out there rolling around on the back lawn, probably getting blood everywhere."

Leo shouted out the front door to the agents who were beginning to pile in. "Call an ambulance. We've got a suspect down. And call the meat wagon."

I sat in a heap, trying to process everything. I took a deep breath and looked up. "Mimi, where did you get the gun?"

"Well..." she hesitated. "Miss Nancy kept pearls and letters in her safe."

"Yeah?" I asked, shaking my head in confusion.

"I kept Smith and Wesson."

34

SAMANTHA

The last of the agents began to file out of Lone Oak, one by one – each giving their condolences and their accolades to the ladies of the house.

Mac's study had been taped off and would remain a crime scene for a few days longer. But I knew I could handle anything now that Hector was gone for good.

"Micah," I smiled as she stopped at the front door to give Mac a hug goodbye. "What would we have done without you today?"

She shrugged her shoulders and glanced back to Mac. "I was just protecting the people I care about."

I nodded, knowing that she would always love Mac. And for now, I was okay with it.

"Micah," Mac sighed as she took his hand before she walked out the door.

"You don't have to say anything, Mac. You'd have done it for me."

They gave each other a forced smile before she walked down the sidewalk to the black sedan. Micah was on her way back to D.C. to find a new agent to assist. I secretly hoped she'd someday be an agent herself.

Leo had asked to stick around for a few days. I decided he had more than wrapping the Hector Quintes case on his mind.

Richard would be prosecuted for aiding a known fugitive and Mimi would forever be known as Deadeye Dick. She smiled when Leo gave her the nickname, and I knew she liked it.

We shut the front door to Lone Oak and I sat in an ornate chair in the front hall, exhausted.

"Is it over, Mommy?" Dax asked as he crawled into my lap.

"Yes."

"And is Coco okay?"

"I'm afraid you won't see him anymore."

Dax nodded. "He was a nice man, Mommy."

I held my tongue knowing there was no way to explain how sick Hector really was.

"You'll have to have friends over to play instead, okay?"

"And I can play with Daddy in the walls."

I nodded and turned to Mac who sat motionless at the bottom of the stairs. Still in his rumpled suit and dirty shirt, he was far away from Lone Oak and his family.

"Dax, why don't you find Miss Celia or Polly? I need to talk with Daddy."

I watched Dax shuffle past Mac, giving him a confused look. The always put-together and handsome Mac Callahan now looked like he'd been on a three-day bender. "How are you doing?"

"I should be asking you that," he replied, refusing to take his blank stare from the wall.

"I'm okay."

Mac dropped his shoulders and looked to the floor

before standing abruptly. He startled me as he went from defeated warrior to disgruntled man. Without acknowledging me, he shook his head and walked away.

"Where are you going?"

"I need a shower," he replied.

"I'm glad you think so," I teased, hoping to bring a smile to his face. "I was starting to worry that you thought this was acceptable for a proper gentleman."

"No," he replied.

The lack of expression made me worry. I knew the feelings of grief that were plaguing his mind. Now that Hector had been caught, Mac had a chance to think about losing Nancy. I didn't want him to get to the point where it hurt so horribly…he didn't feel anything at all. I knew it could happen. I'd been there myself.

I shut the door to Katy's nursery and let out a heavy sigh. Lone Oak was quiet. There were still agents on the grounds, but everyone was out of the house including Polly, who'd had run off somewhere with Leo. Celia had gone home, exhausted from the past week and Mac was nowhere to be found. As I walked through the house, each creak of the old floorboards reminded me I was finally by myself.

I whispered his name as I entered each part of the house, thinking I would find him sitting quietly, drinking a sweet tea with a smile on his face. But at every turn, I only found dark rooms.

Finally I walked out onto the veranda. The strong breeze blew through me, catching my dress in its whirlwind. The tents from the wedding and reception were now down and the backside of Lone Oak was hushed. Just like the house.

I wandered out through the garden and saw a tiny flicker of light in the gazebo and was drawn to it like a moth to a flame. I knew Mac was there.

A single candle lit the small table and chair where he sat in the middle of the white wooden dome. The vines and flowers from the wedding were still intertwined – the only evidence left of our big day.

"Mac?" I called to him.

He sat, papers in his hand, blank stare across his face.

"What are you doing out here, sweetheart?"

He pulled his gaze to look at me. The look on his face told me everything I needed to know. He'd read the letter from his mother.

"Are you okay?"

He wasn't emotionless. He just wasn't there. I dropped to my knees and buried my head in his lap. "I love you."

I looked up and into his eyes glistening with the emotion he'd been holding in for days and waited for him to tell me he loved me too.

"Why did you agree to marry me?"

"What?" I asked, pulling away from him. "Why did I *marry* you?"

"Why did you ever think I could provide a safe and loving environment for you and the children?"

"Because I know you."

"So you bought my whole line of shit when I promised I could protect you?" he scoffed.

"I guess I didn't think it was shit." I replied. "Why are you doing this?"

"What if Hector isn't the only asshole out there that wants to hurt me or our family? I've put some dangerous people away, Sam."

"Then we'll deal with it."

"Really? Because I'm pretty sure you didn't sign up for this when you agreed to be my wife."

"I agreed to be your wife because I love you. I agreed to spend the rest of my life with you because I not only believed you when you promised to protect me and the children, I believed *in* you." I took his hands and brought them to my face, begging for his attention.

"My mother told me not to lose sight of the important moments in my life," he revealed as he touched the handwriting on the thick linen paper. "Said I'd know them when they happened."

"And you think you've missed them?"

"No," he admitted. "I understand what she meant. I don't want to miss the important moments because my head is somewhere else. I need to remember not to define my life by what I do, but by who I love."

"*I* love you," I whispered. "I love you more than you'll ever know."

"I want to be your everything, Samantha."

"You are."

He shook his head and looked at me.

"What if in order to protect you, I need to stay away from you?"

"I'd find you."

"I can't stand to lose another person in my life. I wouldn't survive losing you or one of the kids. I'm a different man than the one you met a year ago."

"And I'm a different woman," I whispered as I stood and pushed my body into his. Parting his knees, he cradled his head on my chest and for the first time in days I felt him let down. "I'm not letting you go. Ever."

Mac stood and pulled me close. I nuzzled my face in his neck and began to rock back and forth.

"Darling you…" I sang softly as we swayed. "Send me. I know you…send me. Darling you…send me. Honest you do, honest you do, honest you do…"

"You… thrill me," Mac sang with a rasp. "I know you, you, you, thrill me. Darling you, thrill me. Honest you do."

I pulled away from him and took his hands in mine. "No matter what you say. No matter where you go. I'm going to be right beside you. No matter what."

"Until death do us part," he nodded.

"Until death do us part."

"You know we're the Callahans now – me and you, Dax and Katy."

I nodded.

"I think my parents would be proud."

"They *are* proud."

"My Dad's saying, *Son, take that woman inside, pack her bags and take her to Paris for a proper honeymoon.*"

"I'd settle for you taking me to *bed* for a proper honey-moon."

I watched the light come back into Mac's face as he nodded and nuzzled my neck.

"I have a surprise for you," he murmured into my ear.

"What?"

"I was saving it to give to you when we got home from Paris, but…"

"But what?"

"I have an idea."

Mac grabbed my hand and walked me down the stairs of the gazebo and began to make his way back to the house.

"What are you up to?" I giggled.

"No questions."

As we made the turn for the house, Mac stopped short at the second garage and keyed in a code. I'd never been in there, but I knew it was where the vintage Bentley Timms drove Nancy around in had been stored.

Before opening the door, he turned and gave me a kiss. It was a real kiss, something he'd not done in days and I felt him coming back to me.

"This is for you. Just for you," he said as he ushered me into the dark garage before hitting the lights.

Sitting in the dark garage next to Nancy's car was a black convertible. It almost sparkled under the spotlight aimed at the hood and was covered in an enormous red bow.

"What is this?" I gasped.

"This is a Bentley Continental GT V8 S. Complete with a back seat for little people."

"What?"

"My mother had a Bentley," he explained. "And even though you drive and she didn't, I wanted you to have one too. This is your new car."

"I don't know what to say," I uttered in shock.

"C'mon. Let's take her for a drive," Mac whispered into my neck as he hugged my waist from behind.

"Okay," I squealed.

He laughed at my excitement and I could tell he loved that he'd surprised me.

35

MAC

Samantha roared down the small lane and I turned to see Lone Oak lit up in the distance. Her ponytail was flying in the breeze as I lowered the top and turned on some music.

"What would you like to hear for your first drive in the new car?" I asked.

"I just like the roar of the engine," she smiled as she picked up speed.

I nodded and dropped my head on the seat. The stars were out and the heavens seemed illuminated.

"Where are you going?" I asked Sam as she turned onto the old road that led to the backside of our property.

"My favorite place," she smiled.

We pulled onto the hill and Sam shone the bright headlights into the valley below.

"It's too dark to see anything out here, sweetheart," I laughed.

"For what I'm planning on doing, you don't need to see."

I gave her a smile as she turned off the car and pulled

on the emergency brake.

She grinned wickedly. "Are you up for some adventure?"

"I'm up," I smiled, adjusting myself. "Believe me. I'm up."

We got out of the car and Samantha wagged her finger *come hither*, beckoning me to her.

I met her in between the headlights that shown brightly over the valley and Samantha went to work without saying a word. She unbuckled my pants and pushed them down around my ankles fast and furiously. I had already sprung into action.

"Oh yeah, baby," she whispered as she opened my shirt one painfully slow button at a time.

She turned me, wrapping her arms around me from behind as she ran her hands over my chest, she found her way down to my hot, swollen flesh.

Her hand was cold against my skin and I flinched at her touch. I moaned and reached back to pull her hips to meet my ass.

Grinding her hips into me, she stroked my rigid shaft until I could no longer take it. I quickly turned her around and pushed her up against the hood of the car as the lights continued to shine between our bodies.

Grabbing under her knee, I lifted her leg to meet my straining sex and pushed myself against the fabric of her dress. "I need you," I ground out.

"You do?" she purred as she kissed my mouth and ran her tongue along my bottom lip, sending me reeling.

Frantically I began to lift the layers of her full sundress to get to her delicate softness.

She leaned against the car and moaned as I found her panties and pulled them down her sexy legs and to the ground. I slid my hands up her body, taking the dress with me. Pushing myself against her again, pulsing as if we were already making love, tipping her hips and exploring her with my fingers.

I made quick work of the three buttons that held the top of her dress together, releasing her waiting breasts. Her tight nipples were hard against my chest and with each heaving breath she took, I could feel them brush against me, making me harder and fueling my need for her.

I kissed her, encompassing her mouth in mine, frantic for more of her.

Bending my knees, I pushed up and entered her in one deep thrust as I laid her beautiful body barely wrapped in what was left of her dress across the hood of her new car.

"Mac," she moaned as I began to create a rhythm between our bodies and the gracefully gliding suspension of the freshly waxed black sports car.

"Jesus, God," I groaned as I pulled her knees to my chest to reach deeper. Her gasp for air told me everything I needed to know as I buried myself deep inside her.

Slowing my pace, I looked into her eyes to watch her.

"Yes," she whispered. "Yes," she said again as she arched her back, allowing only her hips and head to touch the car.

I felt her tighten as she answered my thrusting hips. I knew we would both give into it, leaving the last week behind us.

"Yes!" she shouted as I quickened my pace, wanting to join her in that final glorious moment of rapture.

"Oh God, Samantha," I ground out through my teeth as our bodies collided in euphoria.

Convulsing in spasm, I erupted as she pulled me by the shoulders into her body, panting with satisfaction.

I moved into her over and over, unable to finish as everything I had inside came pouring out in fits of elation. The intensity made me dizzy. I was high on the white-hot eruption and my perfect union with Samantha.

I fell into her body as we lay on top of the car. I smothered her small frame beneath me. "Can you breathe?" I huffed, still out of air. "I don't want to crush you on top of your new car."

"Don't leave me," she whispered.

"Never," I promised as I kissed the top of her head and pulled away just enough to see her beautiful face.

A single tear rolled down her cheek and I kissed it, catching the salt in my mouth. "Don't cry, sweetheart. It's all over now."

"It's just beginning," she smiled. "Our whole life is just beginning."

I lifted her body, picking her up off the car by her perfect bottom and stood naked from the waist down as she wrapped her legs around my waist.

I kissed her deeply, knowing I would never be satisfied. I adjusted her in my arms, never wanting to let her go.

"We'd better get back before an agent sees the light back here and comes to investigate," I smiled. "Can we continue this in the bedroom?"

"More?" she laughed. "You want more?"

"I'll never have enough of you," I promised as I sat her on the ground and picked up her panties, tucking them in my shirt pocket before pulling my pants up.

"What are you going to do with those?" she asked as she buttoned up the front of her dress just enough for us to make the trip home.

"I'm gonna hang them from the rearview mirror of my Aston Martin," I laughed.

"You mean your dad's car? Pussy Galore?"

"I mean *my* car. *We* are the Callahans. It's time I started acting that way."

She shot me a sexy smile as I climbed behind the driver's seat to drive us home.

The engine roared to a start and I leaned in to kiss her sweet-smelling neck. "Besides, you're the only *Pussy Galore* I'm ever gonna need."

36

POLLY

I was happy that Leo had decided to hang out for a few days. Especially since I was planning on leaving Shadeland after Mimi's one-hundredth birthday party.

Sam had begged me to stay in town and offered Mimi's house as a place to live, but I knew my time with Samantha and Dax had come to a close.

I'd been looking at Ph.D. programs across the country, and it would take some time to apply and get accepted. I didn't even know where I wanted to go.

"Cher," Leo smiled as he joined me at a balloon-filled table. "What are you doing over here all alone, lost in thought?"

"I don't know," I sighed. "Thinking about my next move, I suppose."

"And?"

"Sam and Mac are leaving tomorrow for Paris. Miss Celia is now officially in charge of the children and it's time for me to be on my way."

"Why?" he asked.

"Because my work here is done. Sam is settled into her

new life–"

"And now it's time for you to have a life of your own." Leo continued.

"Something like that."

"Ever thought about profiling?"

"Profiling what? Criminals?"

I watched Leo shrug his shoulders and grin. "You're pretty good at it."

"What? And chase bad guys?" I laughed.

"It would certainly keep me from chasing *you*," he murmured.

The comment caught me off guard and I blushed and immediately waved across the lawn of Lone Oak to Mimi. "Happy birthday, Mimi!"

"Thank you, honey," she waved.

"I can't believe you're one hundred!"

"I know," she smiled. "I'm so old my friends already in heaven are gonna think I didn't make the cut."

I laughed and looked back to Leo who still sat across from me – his gaze unyielding.

"What?" I asked as it became uncomfortable.

"I don't want to leave you, cher. I'm going back to New Orleans, not Virginia. Come with me."

"What?" I asked again.

"You heard me."

"Look, Leo, I've made some bad decisions in my life concerning men. I don't know if I'm ready for a Leo Xanthis," I said as I gestured to him up and down.

"You didn't make mistakes, cher," he drawled. "You dated them."

I gave him a smile and cocked my head. I couldn't argue with his logic.

"Come to Jackson House while you sort through your

next move. It'll be fun."

"Leo," I sighed. "You don't know what you're asking to get involved with. I'm complicated. I'm not one of your Southern girls in pearls. There's a lot about me you *don't* want to deal with."

He nodded and searched his inside coat pocket. "I thought you might say that."

He casually pulled out a long, flat blue Tiffany box complete with white ribbon and held it in his hand, waiting for my reaction.

"What...is...that...?" I coughed.

"A little something for my *Midwestern* girl."

"Leo," I began. "I know I've been a bit of a tease, but it's only because no man has paid attention to me in a really long time and I just –"

"Shhhhhhh..." he whispered. "You're going to hurt this gentleman's feelings if you don't accept my gift."

I looked at the box in his hand and back to him as he gave me sly smile. He was all sex and dark-skinned mystery to me and I didn't exactly know what to do with it.

I took the box as he moved it closer to me and pulled on the white satin ribbon. Nothing stood between me and his gift except my insecurities. I knew if I unwrapped it there was no turning back.

I swallowed hard and opened the blue box. Inside was a black velvet cover for whatever preciousness lay inside.

"Come with me, Polly," he begged quietly as I lifted the hinged box.

I looked down to find the most magnificent double strand of pink pearls with a diamond clasp.

"Leo," I sighed. "I can't."

He took the pearls and stood to move behind me. Before I could utter another word they were around my neck.

He gave me a soft kiss on the cheek as he adjusted the diamond clasp to rest on my collarbone.

"Leo," I began as I stroked the pearls with my open hand. "There are things about me that I can't tell you."

"Polly," he whispered. "There are many things a gentleman doesn't want to be told. We like to discover it for ourselves."

"I–"

Leo held a finger to my lips and then leaned in for a short, soft kiss. It was perfect and I melted into my chair.

"Come. With. Me," he smiled.

"I don't know," I sighed as I looked around the party for someone to help me make a decision or to rescue me from myself.

"Cher," he said with a hint of impatience.

"But –"

"No buts," he smiled. "And no reason to get your panties in a wad. I would be honored if you and your new pearls would join me at Jackson House for a little rest and relaxation. We don't have to make any decisions. Let's just take a few days and enjoy ourselves."

"Did you just tell me *not* to get my panties in a wad?" I asked as I stood.

"Yes," he smirked as he joined me, tugging on the ribbon belt that wrapped around my sundress.

"Okay," I nodded.

"Okay?" His face lit up.

"Okay," I smiled as I pulled him in for a hug and whispered in his ear, "But I won't be getting my panties in a wad. I'm not wearing any."

Leo pulled away from my embrace, his eyes twinkling with mischief as he raised one eyebrow and gave me a crooked smile. "When can you be ready to go?"

EPILOGUE
MAC

W e stood on the back lawn of Lone Oak, trying our best to stand still. As the photographer snapped the initial pictures for our portrait painter, Samantha hummed through her smile for Katy and Dax.

The girls were dressed in white, Dax and I in khaki summer suits. Sam and the children sat casually on a couch as I stood behind them. It would be our first portrait as a family that would hang in the halls of Lone Oak.

In the past four months, I'd managed to marry the love of my life, retire from the FBI and take a honeymoon to Paris. We'd also redecorated a few rooms inside the house, including the study.

Our new portrait would signify the end of one era and the beginning of another.

"Mommy?" Dax asked. "How much longer? I wanna play."

"Hang on, Chief," I smiled. "Be glad you don't have to stand here all day for an artist to paint us. All we have to do is take a great photo."

Katy began to fuss, no doubt hot and parched like the

rest of us. The summer sunshine was unforgiving and as I watched Miss Celia walk onto the veranda with a tray of iced tea, I felt like whining too.

"Let's take a break," shouted the photographer.

"Thank the Lord," Sam sighed as turned to me and handed me Katy.

We walked to Miss Celia who opened her arms to me, wanting the baby as usual.

"It's okay, Celia," I waved her off. "I like holding Miss Katy. She's a daddy's girl," I said in my best baby talk.

"Mmm, mmm, mmm," Celia laughed, turning to Samantha. "That boy has got it bad."

"I know," Sam agreed. "I feel sorry for her first boyfriend. Mac's going to make everyone's life miserable when she's old enough to date."

"No, I won't," I protested. "She can date when she's thirty. I'll be just fine with that."

Samantha rolled her eyes at Celia and shook her head at me.

"Pass that sweet tea down here if you don't mind," I requested as I took a seat in one of the oversized chairs on the veranda with a sigh.

Katy sat on my lap as she chewed on her fist. Teething was an everyday thing now that she was almost seven months old. She was getting pretty good at the crawling and needed constant attention as her daredevil instinct had already kicked in. She seemed to enjoy pulling herself up to stand at every turn. I happily took the credit for her behavior.

She hadn't really said her first word yet, but Sam assured me it was because Dax did all the talking for her.

"I got a letter from Micah this morning," Sam said as she sipped her tea.

"What's up with Micah?"

"I guess she's got a new boyfriend."

"Let me guess," I began as I shifted Katy in my lap to face me. "He's a bartender."

"Nope."

"An electrician," I guessed again as Katy grabbed onto my nose and smiled.

"No," she laughed at me. "He's an agent."

"Who?" I asked cocking my head.

"Micah's new boyfriend. He's an agent."

"I understood *that* part—I meant who is he? What's his name?"

"She didn't say." She paused. "Do you miss it?"

"What? Being out in the field with a bunch of sweaty men and tracking criminal miscreants?"

"Yes. That," she quipped.

I shrugged my shoulders and looked into Katy's eyes, knowing the real truth.

"You'd miss Daddy if he was gone all the time," I baby-talked to Katy. "Wouldn't you?"

She giggled as I ticked her tummy and my heart melted. Every day she changed just a little bit more. It was like watching a miracle unfold.

"Da da," she cooed.

I looked to Samantha wide-eyed and amazed. "Did you hear that?"

Samantha smiled.

"Da da," I repeated to her. "Da da."

"Da da da da da da," Katy said, ending with a giggle.

"Sam!" I gasped.

"I heard," she smiled as she gave us both a kiss on the head. "You know, *Ma ma* is harder to say. That's why she's saying *Da da* first."

"We know the real truth, don't we Katy?" I asked her as she smiled and gave me another sweet gurgle. "You're Daddy's girl."

I took a sip of my sweet tea and held Katy in my arms as we walked toward a fidgeting Sam and Dax. We needed to take just one more photograph.

Before settling into the couch, I gave Samantha a long and lingering kiss. She winced in embarrassment as I slipped my tongue between her lips and cupped her beautiful bottom, still holding Katy in my arms.

"You're a wicked man," she giggled as I turned her loose and handed her the baby. We settled into the couch and posed on the lawn for the portrait just as my parents, grandparents and great grandparents had done before. As the photographer gave the countdown, I thought of my mother's words to me. *Try to live for all the small moments that don't seem to matter very much at the time. As you age, you'll discover these are the ones that are the sweetest to revisit in your old age.*

This was my moment.

Kris Calvert is a former copywriter and PR mercenary who after some coaxing, began writing romance novels. She loves alliteration, pearls and post-it notes. She's married to the man of her dreams and lives in Lexington, Kentucky. She's Momma to two kids, now in college – one at the University of Kentucky, and one at New York University – Tisch. She is also responsible for one very needy dog. When she's not writing, she's baking cupcakes.

WEBSITE
www.kriscalvert.com

EMAIL
info@kriscalvert.com

TWITTER
@_kriscalvert

FACEBOOK
www.facebook.com/kriscalvert30

BLOG
www.calvertwrites.blogspot.com

NEWSLETTER
www.kriscalvert.com/Kris_Calvert/NEWSLETTER.html

A note from the Author: If you enjoyed this book, please consider leaving a positive review or rating on the site where you purchased it. Reader reviews help my books continue to be valued by distributors/resellers and help new readers make decisions about reading them. I value each and every reader who takes the time to do this and invite you all to join me on my website, blog, Facebook, Twitter or Good-reads.com for discussions and fun. Thank you for your support. I sincerely appreciate you. ~ KC

COMING SOON

SEX, LIES & PEARLS

A Moonlight and Magnolias Novel Book 3

SEX LIES & PEARLS

Everything's hotter in the South.

KRIS CALVERT

A Moonlight and Magnolias Novel Book 3

CPSIA information can be obtained at www.ICGtesting.com
Printed in the USA
LVOW06s0224290714

396491LV00001B/1/P